D1033014

TOO LATE! TOO LATE!
THE MAIDEN CRIED

BY THE SAME AUTHOR

JOAN FLEMING

Too Late! Too Late!
The Maiden Cried

G. P. Putnam's Sons
New York

FOUNDED 1838
GPPS

FIRST AMERICAN EDITION 1975
COPYRIGHT © 1975 BY JOAN FLEMING

SBN: 399-11539-0

Library of Congress Catalog
Card Number: 75-12733

PRINTED IN THE UNITED STATES OF AMERICA

TOO LATE! TOO LATE!
THE MAIDEN CRIED

I

THE village lay but two miles from the city, up a gentle slope northward from Charing Cross over the fields, so people living in the village were neither country folk nor town dwellers. Keats, twenty years before, from the grove not a quarter of a mile below Buck's Walk, wrote: *. . . from the slope side of a suburb hill. . . ,* and Byron actually said: "look's vulgar, dowdyish and suburban."

At the turn of the century, that is the eighteenth into the nineteenth, a man known as Rum Buck achieved, as a bad debt, a shelf of land upon which was a tumbledown barn in an untidy and untended coppice. It jutted out from the land which runs from the High Street where the stopping place was of the town omnibuses to Highgate and to the Heath where the cockneys would go on high days and holidays for a frolic. When the barn was taken down and the shrubbery removed, it was clearly an excellent situation for a dwelling or dwellings.

But Rum Buck had ideas: Upon that commanding position he built five small houses, all adjoining in a row. Leaving enough land in front for carriages and coaches either to turn or to drive past and out on to the lane beyond if necessary, he made tiny gardens at the back of each one. They were small houses indeed with a large

1

and small room both above and below, with downstairs a kitchen and above it a closet. There were semicircular fanlights above the front doors, and a narrow flagged footpath ran the length of the terrace.

In 1841 the occupants were the purchasers, but when they were new in 1800, all five of the "bijoux residences" were rented. The first tenant of all had called them that; she was a French aristocrat, an escapee from the horrors of the Revolution, and she had lived in her little house for forty-one years. It was well known that she had an English lover who rented the house for her and who visited her frequently. This started a fashion, and when the century was in its teens every one of the five small houses were love nests in which Regency bucks kept their inamorata. And sly jokes were made about the name: "Buck's Walk."

The view from the windows was incomparable: down the steep grassy slope to the hamlet of South End Green and then across the still slightly sloping ground to Campden Town and the huge smoky spread of London Town stretching across over the dome of St. Paul's Cathedral to the green hills of the Kent Weald.

The houses were considered too small for middle-class family houses, yet one little family occupied Number 4; Major and Mrs. Nateby had come eleven years ago as bride and bridegroom. Their baby girl was born within the year and christened Amelia, which was a popular name of the moment.

They were a pleasant, apparently happy and self-contained family; modest in their requirements, they retained a servant who came every day from a tenement behind the High Street. Mrs. Nateby was twenty years younger than her husband, whom she adored. At thirty she was in the prime of her looks with a light step, a twenty-inch waist and a gay manner; she was much admired in the village. On the day that the first brick was removed from her edifice of happiness, she had carried a light basketwork chair out into her little garden and was sitting looking at the *Times*. Looking at, as opposed to reading it because to settle down and read it, as her husband urged her to do, was not for an early spring afternoon with the birds filling the air with delightful sound.

In a few minutes Amelia would be home from school, a private establishment for boys and girls in Downshire Hill, which she attended with other children of the neighborhood.

At the moment she was strolling up the footpath, swinging her satchel in the company of a boy about the same age as herself. He was pontificating in a clear imitation of a grown-up, probably his grandfather, upon sacred matters, and Amelia was listening but not too intently.

"But what I don't understand about God, Roderick, *is*. . . ."

He frowned, waiting for her to continue.

"Is . . . he's everywhere and how can anyone be everywhere? I mean everywhere at once. I was thinking today in class when Teacher showed us India, I thought, how does a little girl in India, saying her prayers, expect God to hear, because, as my mother says, He's *here*, listening to my prayers at night. It's such a long way, I mean, to India. Halfway round the world."

Roderick frowned dreadfully. "You're stupid, Amelia." And Amelia looked pained and distressed.

"It's a . . . it's a . . . kind of magic."

"Like the fairies?"

"No, not like the fairies."

"Like what, then?"

To Roderick's evident relief they had arrived at Buck's

3

Walk. "I'll tell you tomorrow," he said with dignity and branched off to pass the old bowling green and into Well Walk while Amelia opened her yellow front door and was back home.

If her mother were not out shopping in London Town or having tea with friends, she would always run to meet her at the front door when she heard her come in. But not today. The little hall led straight through the house and the half-glass door at the end of the hall stood wide open to the garden. Bess was cleaning the silver at the kitchen and answered Amelia's first question with a jerk of her head toward the garden.

But her mother did not raise her head from the newspaper as Amelia ran out, throwing down her satchel and making a wild grab at the next-door cat. Her mother was looking worried; she stared at the folded newspaper and shook it as though flicking away a wasp, irritably. She read over again what she had been reading and turned a bewildered face to her little girl. "I don't understand," she said, "I simply don't understand!"

It was in the personal column:

NATEBY. Will Thomas Nateby Dyce late major in a Regiment of Bombay grenadiers who left the army in December 1829 and assumed the surname of NATEBY by Royal license in January 1830 communicate with Messrs. Melbury & Sons, 14 Red Lion Square, London where he will receive information to his advantage. This is the third time of asking.

Her mother stared at Amelia as though she did not see her, then she pulled her shawl more closely about her and gave a little shiver. She said it was getting cold; it was late February and a miraculously springlike day, but they

4

must go in now. Amelia carried her chair in and her mother was before a looking glass settling her pretty afternoon cap, which sat upon her head as lightly as a nervously twitching butterfly.

There was a sound upon the front-door step and Papa entered, home early from work. His wife and daughter welcomed him: He was radiant. He beamed at them and wrapped his wife in an affectionate hug, disturbing her newly settled cap.

"Ah, you have seen the *Times*, Thomas. . . !"

"The *Times*, dear? No, I haven't seen it, but I have been having lunch with Mr. Carlyle and I have such splendid news!" He threw his gloves upon the row of pegs where they stayed behind his hat. He said it was such a marvelous day; that they should go for a stroll before the sun disappeared. "Run and get your mama's bonnet, Amelia; and Bess shall have some hot crumpets ready for us in twenty minutes."

So all three strolled up the hill and watched the sun setting behind the pond, and he told them of the good fortune that seemed to have come his way. And there was nothing said then about the personal column of the *Times* newspaper.

Mr. Carlyle had invited him to lunch with a purpose, and that was to discuss a project still only in the process of being planned and that was the initiation of a fine new library, incorporating from various sources many ancient books that were not satisfactorily housed, making them available to everybody. It was to be a subscription library and available to all types of subscribers, scholars and students, and the very learned novel readers and all, and Mr. Carlyle had asked him, Thomas Nateby, if he would be willing to serve on the committee that was forming and become an assistant librarian.

"And will you?"

"But of course, Emma dear, I shall leap at it. It is the one employment I should enjoy above all others, and I am flattered beyond measure that they had thought of me when looking round for staff. Of course, Mr. Carlyle has frequently visited the little bookshops where I enjoy working in St. Paul's Churchyard. We have had great discussions and I found him always a stimulating customer with his request for books nobody but he has ever mentioned. Without boasting I must say that he and I are good friends. You remember the time you were asked to tea one afternoon, dear? 'Be sure you bring your wife!' he said."

Emma did remember it, clearly, particularly the tiny and very vocal Mrs. Carlyle who frightened her out of her wits. A noisy little woman, she thought her, who talked far too much and quite clearly got on her husband's nerves.

Holding her own husband's arm, Emma pressed it affectionately from time to time, but she did not wholeheartedly join in the excitement. She was still shocked by what she had read, but she did not wish to bring the subject up for the first time in the presence of Amelia. Not even over the hot buttered crumpets could she say anything either.

Between tea and supper a friend called in to see them, and it was only after supper was over and washed up and Bess had said good night and departed through the door in the wall of the back garden and Amelia had kissed them both good night that she could pick up the *Times* and hold it out to him.

She stood watching him, her fingers pressed to her lips. What was she expecting, a great shout of delight? She had known all along that he had changed his name; in the ecstasy of being asked to marry this splendid soldier whom she had never dared even to hope she would ever see again after their first encounter at Sidmouth, the fact of his changing his name had mattered not a straw. He explained of course, oh yes, he had not failed to explain. His father after thirty-five years as commissioner holding authority over three million men and receiving the Companion of the Order of the Star of India had then given up and quietly, unexpectedly and quite humbly died. Thomas had resigned his commission and retired from the army.

And changed his name, or rather reverted to his mother's family name, Nateby.

It did not occur to his ecstatic nineteen-year-old bride-to-be that this last act was a non sequitur as the facts were stated to her. Thought about, they were inadequate, but she had never thought about them because it did not seem to her to matter in the least that her future husband should prefer to be known by his mother's maiden name. It was only now, as a wife for eleven years, that she should, in her maturity, wonder why he should have found it necessary.

It was such a happy marriage: eleven years? It felt like eleven months, time had flown on golden wings; they loved one another more now by far, than at the start and she had never yet had an important thought which she had not shared with her Thomas. Until now when, in the space of ten seconds, she had two thoughts which she did not share.

One was why did he change his name when he retired from the army?

And the other was: Having taken on her name, why did he seldom speak about his mother? From time to time he spoke of his father with great pleasure, his school, too; he spoke about Westminster at least as an average man does speak about his schooldays. His paternal aunt and her husband were both alive when she married Thomas, old people but hale and hearty; they lived in a pleasant house in the village and Thomas had stayed with them while he and Emma were house-hunting. It was merely because of its proximity to the heath that they had chosen this little house in Buck's Walk in which they had lived so happily for these eleven years.

The relatives were both dead now, but his aunt had passed away only last year. Her estate had been divided among her children, but she had left Emma and Thomas the splendid silver tea service that had been presented to her husband when he retired.

Thus Thomas had had plenty of background. True, he had never talked to her about his first wife who had died so tragically from cholera on the way home on leave from India, but Aunt had mentioned her from time to time, mostly as an example as one who after less than a week on board caught cholera and died within hours. She would admonish her grown-up children to be careful not to do this or that or the other thing: ". . . remember your poor Cousin Mary!"

Thomas threw aside the *Times* and looked up at Emma: "Why are you looking at me like that?"

And Emma had time to think one more thought before answering, and it was the third thought within seconds that she had not shared with her husband. It was: Thomas has already seen it! She remembered this same day last week when the notice must have appeared: Thomas had been reading in the *Times* for a long time the report of the trial of the Earl of Cardigan by his peers, charged with having shot an army officer upon Wimbledon Common on the twelfth of September last in the course of a duel. He had said aloud that it was interesting reading in that everyone seemed undecided

8

whether or not his Lordship had committed a felony, the punishment for this being deportation, and could they deport a peer?

That had been last week.

Now he said, reading her thoughts, "Well, Emma, what would you wish me to do?"

"To do, Thomas?"

"It might be a hoax."

"It *might* but unlikely, dear. Who would wish to play a hoax on you? *To your advantage*, it says. Irresistible!"

"You think so?"

"But do *you* not think so?"

"I'm not sure."

"Oh, Thomas, explain yourself more clearly, dear, I beg of you."

"We're so happy, Emma, so happy here in our little eyrie looking out over the great city. I dread it being . . . being lost to us."

"Thomas! I had no idea our happiness was so uncertain . . . to you, at least."

He got up impatiently and went to the window, drawing back the curtain with one hand and looking out at the stars. "I haven't always been happy; I treasure what I have. And today has brought even greater happiness, from Mr. Carlyle."

"Come, Thomas, let us sit down face to face, like this."

They stared at one another. "I cannot understand why you are in fact suggesting that we ignore this. . . ." She had been going to say *cri du coeur*, but it was more businesslike than a cry from the heart. She said neither. "I just do not understand."

"I think it may be something . . . about my mother." She hardly heard him, his hand covered his mouth.

"Your mother. . . !"

There was a long silence.

"Come, Thomas. It is not far-off bedtime. Let us go to bed and you can tell me, or not tell me, as you wish. I can sense this is going to hurt you and you will have at least the comfort of the dark."

II

AT breakfast in the morning he dictated a note to Emma, who wrote to the solicitors in Red Lion Square that they would call at the office on Tuesday next. "Good," he said after reading it, as he folded the letter and put it in the envelope. "That will show them that we are not breaking our necks to get there."

He was late coming home the following evening as he had an appointment to call upon a customer and put a valuate on certain books which the customer wished to dispose of. Emma went upstairs to hear Amelia's prayers and to bid her good night.

"You and Papa were talking all last night, talking away, mumble, mumble, mumble. What was wrong, Mama?"

"There was nothing wrong, Amelia."

"Was it about that advertisement in the *Times?*"

Emma concealed her surprise. "Partly," she answered, busily tucking in the bedclothes round her wide-awake child. Child?

"People often change their names."

"*Do* they?"

Emma's heart sank; this would undoubtedly be the subject of an interesting conversation with Roderick on the way home from school on the lines of: Why did your

11

papa change his name, Amelia? There were times when children of their age seemed more grown-up than grown-ups themselves. Emma sat down on the edge of the bed. "If you promise to keep it a secret and not talk about it to your friends, I will tell you what your papa told me last night. Not, Amelia, *not* because there is anything shameful or wrong in it as far as Papa is concerned, but it is a private and family topic. So will you promise never to talk about it to anyone but Papa and me?"

Amelia's brightly expectant little face glowed at her over the sheet and she nodded. She had second thoughts about the long conversation she had had on that very subject of the advertisement in the personal column on the way home from school today with Roderick, but she decided upon discretion because to tell would worry her mama. She was an observant child; she had seen both her parents almost painfully engrossed in the study of the dullest part of that newspaper. Later, of course, she investigated.

"You see, Papa did not have a happy childhood, Amelia. He had no brothers and sisters, as you have none, but you have your friends and he did not and he was not good friends with his papa and his mama. His papa lived in India and was a very busy man and never had time to talk to his little boy; he was a kind of king, kind of. And his mama was a tall, slim woman who was perfectly well and healthy here in England, but who became ill as soon as she went to India and went on being ill with shortage of breath. When they sent her up into the mountains for cool breezes she was still no better, so she had to come back home to England and she brought her little boy, who was Papa, with her because he had to go to school. First he went to a dame school here in Hampstead and she lived with him in the house of your great uncle and aunt in Frognal and then later Papa went

12

to Westminster School and then he joined the army. . . ."
She hesitated; she was about to say: his mama ran away,
but she stopped herself in time and made it more com-
monplace and less like a story, "When he was fully a
soldier his mama went away."

"Yes, and where to?"

"To America, Amelia."

"Why?"

"*Why!*" Emma repeated irritably.

She could have said: She ran away with another
gentleman who was not your grandpapa, but somehow
the sting had to be taken out of the drama. She frowned
in order not to smile at the words running through her
mind: Perhaps because she was a bolter. She managed at
last. "Well, she just went and . . . er . . . Papa never saw
her again."

"And did Papa's papa?"

"Did he what?"

"Never see her again?"

"Yes. I mean no, he never saw her again."

"Why?"

"Because he didn't," Emma said crossly, feeling she
had made a grave mistake in embarking upon this
narrative at all.

She got up from the bed and pulled the blind down
hurriedly.

"So does no person know where she *is?*"

"Papa thinks she must have died; she was an old lady."

"How does he know she was an old lady?"

"Because she was a middle-aged lady when he last saw
her and that was when he was twenty and she was thirty-
eight, because she had him when she was only eighteen,
see?"

Full of suppressed excitement, Amelia, back in bed,
hugged her knees, waiting for more.

13

"And now Papa is fifty-one, so that is thirty-one years since he last saw her, which means she is very near seventy and that is an old lady. She could be alive still, but she might have died. And this solicitor's announcement in the *Times* might be about her. We don't know yet."

"But you haven't told why he changed his name from Dyce to Nateby."

Emma wrung her hands in the candlelight. "He liked it better," she said in a last feeble effort.

"Phew!" Amelia slipped down in the bed, evidently momentarily satisfied. "Can you really have a baby at eighteen?" Her chuckle was hair-raising. "I could have a baby in seven years, then?"

Emma left her, after blowing out the candle and making quite sure not to slam the door.

If Major and Mrs. Nateby wore a heavy protection of prudence on their mission to Red Lion Square, they found their opponents equally shrouded in caution. There was such a long drawn-out exchange of trivialities with Mr. Melbury senior and Mr. Melbury junior that Emma's face began to burn to her confusion and embarrassment. Finally Mr. Melbury, who was sitting at his desk with his son protectively standing behind, a little to the right, slid open his desk drawer and brought out a flat case with worn-out lettering on the lid. He opened it and displayed a necklace of three strings of graduated pearls of superb quality with a glow on them to recall the full moon.

"Have you ever seen these before, Major . . . er?"

Thomas said no immediately, but then he bent forward and looked at them more closely. 'Yes, indeed, sir, I think so from the clasp."

Mr. Melbury senior seemed satisfied with this and pushed them back in the drawer to bring out another smaller oblong case, leather-covered and worn-looking. Slightly reminiscent of a conjurer, wearing a pleased expression, he opened the box and handed it to Thomas, then sat back and watched his face. After about ten seconds Thomas broke into a half smile and, shamingly, tears were seen to have filled his eyes as he stared down at the beautiful ornament emotionally. There was a tiny scrap of torn ribbon against the edge of the lid; he caught it between his first finger and thumbnail, pulling up a velvet inner lid which lay against the domed top. Inside was a four-inch long gold hairpin. At one end was a fragment of screw between which and the pin itself was a coil of gold wire. He took the superb jewel out of its velvet slit, found the screw hole skillfully concealed in the back and screwed the pin into the hole. Then he held up the ornament.

In the center was a large moonstone and surrounding it were eleven monster diamonds edging one another; it shuddered, sending tiny explosions of light splashing into the dimly lit office.

"A *tremblante* for a woman to wear in her built-up hair upon occasions of state. It was given to my father by the Maharaja of Inguta not long before the old man died as a token of esteem. The next time my father was on leave he gave it to my mother.

"He realized that she could wear it as it should be worn only on the rarest of occasions so he took it to a Bond Street jeweler of some repute and had a gold brooch pin fixed at the back so that she could wear it for less important occasions. She wore it as a headdress only once at a government house reception, she told me; she was too sick a woman to enjoy much gaiety in India. She often wore it as a brooch at parties when we lived in Hampstead. I . . ." he hesitated, looking with pleasure at what he held.

He was a boy again, back in the past about which he had kept silent for so long.

"Your father was a government official, Major?"

"He was commissioner to a large province for over thirty years."

Both Messrs. Melbury senior and junior looked considerably relieved. The moonstone brooch had "done the trick;" they put it back in the desk drawer. Mr. Melbury senior nudged him on. "Did your mother continue to be ill out there?"

"No. She was obliged to come home and leave my father alone; India would have been quite fatal to her; it was only there that she suffered from exceedingly bad asthma; they tried everywhere, by the sea, up in the mountains, in all the now famous places, Simla, Darjeeling, of course; it was useless. She had no people of her own, her father and her mother and two brothers all died of pthysis or similar chest complaints when she was young. So my father had no alternative but to send her home to his own relatives. He was obliged to stay in India; he was engrossed in his work and he had no wish to start any other career, nor was he trained for any other work. At least my mother had been delivered of a sturdy boy baby, but the asthma continued unabated. He sent us all three to stay with his sister in her large house in Hampstead, the ayah, whom I still remember, myself aged ten months and my mother. It ruined their married life, of course.

"I was sent in due course to Westminster School and when I was a full-blown soldier my mother vanished. To me it was not only heartbreaking but utterly mysterious. Grown man though I was, I was never let into the closely guarded secret of what happened finally between my father and my mother to cause such a drastic break. Not long before she died my aunt told me she had 'run away

16

with another man' and that my father had refused to divorce her.

"I know she went to America and I cannot help but feel, sir, that the news you referred to in your letter will be in connection with my mother."

The fog and frost in which the interview had started, melted; Emma, who had been rigid with anxiety, cleared her throat to make sure she still had a voice even if she did not wish to use it at present. Everyone stirred and breathed a sigh of relief, the testing time was successfully over.

Though Thomas had never before heard of Messrs. Melbury, they were an old established firm and had been employed by the man called Pennyform with whom his mother had lived and who, it was explained, was a well-to-do widower with a grown-up family of his own. Thomas' mother lived with this American as his wife, and it was fairly certain that nobody but the lawyers themselves knew that the couple were not legally married. Thomas' mother was a woman of means, but when they finally parted, Thomas' father legally detached himself from any hold over his wife's money that the law allowed, freeing her to do exactly what she liked with it. She made a will leaving everything she possessed to her "beloved son, Thomas Nateby Dyce" upon her death and had never altered it in any way in all the thirty years since it was written.

"But why has she never wished to see me or hear from me, all these years?"

Mr. Melbury senior said that was something at which one could but guess. One must remember that these things happened in the first years of the century, before Waterloo. "It was a changing world and I personally have found myself bewildered by the changes."

Thomas said that, of course, children were brought up

17

to be uncritical of their parents and sometimes this shibboleth was never to slough off with the passage of time. "I loved and admired my mother very much, but I could not, and still cannot forgive her for slipping away without a word . . . forever."

The cups of tea were brought, and a relief on the part of everybody turned the interview into a gathering with a faint air of a party. It was greatly to Mr. Melbury senior's credit that he did not bring up the subject of Thomas' changed name, but after the couple had left he turned to his son and told him that he did not by any means forget it, he simply left the question for another time, when they were better acquainted; the poor Major had certainly suffered an emotional shock. But let him be content, for the moment, that he had established without any doubt, his bona fides.

The next move, having found Thomas Nateby Dyce, was to write at once to their lawyer associates in America who had first communicated with them through the legalities connected with the death of the so-called widow of their client Eustace Pennyform with whom they, the business associates, Messrs. Killarney, Gritley & Co. had done a considerable amount of work over many years in connection with the buying and selling of property in New York. It was, of course, Messrs. Melbury and Son who had retained the Dyce will all these years. It was the Melburys who knew the truth about the Anglo-Indian commissioner and his wife, their thirty-year-old financial arrangements and the recent consequences.

Much respected for their acumen, discretion and sheer quality, Messrs. Melbury were considered not only by themselves but by many others, to be one of the top firms of family solicitors in London. Both legal gentlemen went to their front door in Red Lion Square with their excited clients and bowed as they left the imposing premises. Emma caught her husband's arm: Her light steps, her trim waist, fur tippet flying out in the sharp breeze, she could have been a sixteen-year-old girl, hurrying beside her father.

"Why, Papa," young Melbury said, puzzled as they returned to their office, "you have told them but half the story. What about this Pennyform by-blow, who has been thrust upon our hands?"

"Marcus!" Mr. Melbury looked sternly over the top of his half-moon spectacles at his son. "*Festina lente* or make haste slowly. One thing at a time!"

"But Papa, if you are going to write at once to tell the Pennyform lawyers that you have found your mutual client Nateby Dyce, they will be for dispatching the girl as soon as possible."

"Marcus, my boy, if you will kindly disabuse your mind of such expressions as 'by-blow' we will read again the document referring to the individual named Nokomis Pennyform and make sure that they have 'left no rubs nor botches i' the work.' It is a curious legal dodge if a person can give, or if you like, deposit, a young person under age upon another individual. Even in America!" They both bent their heads over the document referred to, which lay upon the senior's desk.

They walked all the way back to Hampstead. In the hamlet of South End Green, at the foot of the rise to Buck's Walk, Emma tugged at his arm as they passed the butcher and together they stood looking through the narrow window in which it was possible to see a sample, sometimes, of what the butcher considered the choice of the day. Today it was some fine rump steak. Emma looked laughingly up into Thomas' face. "Come, love, let us act rich and buy steak for us all to celebrate that we can afford it."

Steak purchased, they stopped for a moment on the corner of the street to allow the passage of a fine coach-and-four emerge. This happened to belong to the rich aunt of the young neighbor of next but one in Buck's Row. Thomas tucked the butcher's parcel more firmly under his arm in preparation for the uphill climb. He said, "It will 'spoil' us, this money. We shall become rich and the richer we become, the richer we shall want to be."

"But no, Thomas, we shall not become richer and richer. We shall become suddenly rich and then we shall have to think. To beware."

"Of what?"

"That we neither lose our senses, delightedly throwing money about *or* that we become close and mean in grave fear that people are trying to take our money from us."

"There is only one thing I wish to do, that springs to mind now that I can afford it. And it is to join the Far East Club, which was founded twenty years ago by the Duke of Wellington for Gentlemen Who Have Served the Sovereign in the Far East."

"Oh, Thomas! No one has served the Sovereign better in the Far East than you!"

"My father for one, my silly little Emma." He squeezed her arm affectionately against his side. "Eleven years during which I have occasionally passed through St. James's Square and seen the proud new building! I had you with me once, remember?"

"I do indeed and how I mourned that you felt you could not spend the amount of the entrance money and the subscription on something for yourself, my dearest man. But now . . . you shall have one night in the week to yourself when you will be 'at the club' and oh, Thomas! it will be pleasant for you perhaps to meet old friends from your India days, people now retired, like yourself and those home on leave . . . oh! Everybody passing to and fro on leave will call at the club."

But Thomas' face took on its sober look and they made their way up the hill in silence. "Except. . . ." Emma paused, biting her underlip nervously wishing she had not started this.

"Except what, dearest Emma?"

"Except . . . about your name. Major Dyce? Or Major Nateby?"

"I shall remain Nateby as that is the name under which I have inherited." He paused for thought: "On the other hand if I am to find myself a proposer for membership of the club I shall have to use my father's name. Oh dear, how confusing it may prove to be!"

Up and up the footpath toward Buck's Walk, Emma let go of his arm and released her feet from closeness to the hem of her skirt to make walking easier. "But of course, the fact that you have inherited from your mother . . . we shall not be able to conceal it, dear Major. Respectable-shabby is what we have been till now." She laughed gaily but sobered up when Thomas did not share her amusement. "This gown, for instance, I have even patched . . . here and here . . . soon it will be: 'Ah! there goes Mrs. Nateby in a brand new gown!' "

They walked on, silent while a small worm, nay a maggot, stirred in the brain of Emma. Could he be going to be . . . difficult? He who had lived in perfect happiness with her these near-dozen years? Could the acquisition of money be going to change him in some way? If so, please God, save them from it!

At their front door she turned, her finger to her lips and hissed: "Not a word to Amelia about this, dear," and he nodded in agreement.

A few days later Thomas, in answer to a further note

from Red Lion Square, took himself once more to the offices of Messrs. Melbury, this time leaving Emma behind but taking his birth certificate and the papers concerning his army commitments. There were documents to be signed and sent off to the American lawyers and it was only as he was leaving that the older Mr. Melbury, on his own this time, broached the awkward subject he had been wearing up his sleeve.

He started by saying that he would refer to Thomas' mother by her proper name, Eleanor Dyce, since to call her by her assumed name of Pennyform would be merely confusing. It would appear that there had been considerable troubles in the Pennyform family, which had no connection at all with Eleanor. Mr. Pennyform had a son and a daughter, the daughter had been a wild, unrestrained girl who had run away from home and lived like a gypsy with a tribe of Red Indians, one of whom assumed the role of husband, being extremely possessive. Mademoiselle Pennyform, Mr. Melbury opined with a wry smile, evidently inherited a wild streak from the Pennyforms, paying no attention to tribal law; she behaved in such a manner as to enrage her nominal husband after they had been living together for years to such an extent that he had stabbed her to death.

Thomas tried hard to look disapproving and frowned dreadfully, but Mr. Melbury's eyes shone with pleasure at the Wild West adventure that should have enlivened the sober atmosphere of his dingy room.

"What happened to him?" Thomas asked.

"He galloped off into the sunset," Mr. Melbury said unexpectedly.

"A pin to see the peepshow!" Thomas murmured, wondering what this had to do with him.

As the plot thickened Mr. Melbury leaned across his desk and hissed: "But Mademoiselle Pennyform, I cannot call her by any other name because I have not been told it; Miss Pennyform if you prefer, left a child which Mr. Pennyform, after a great deal of trouble, bought with cash back from the Red Indians. And your mother, known as Mrs. Pennyform, has cared for it in the two years or so since Pennyform's death."

"Dear God!" Thomas threw his head back like a horse bucking: "and I inherit this child along with the . . . fortune!"

Mr. Melbury allowed himself to laugh and after a moment Thomas joined in. "A he or a she?"

"A she!"

"Worse and worse."

"Yes, my dear sir, there is worse to come," Mr. Melbury said. "That is why I was anxious that your lady wife would not accompany you here today. Your mother, Major, must have been a good, kind woman. I have a document here which was written on her deathbed; she evidently died of pneumonia and had time, not to write this herself, but to summon the lawyers with whom she had been in touch—indeed, they were friends— regarding her last will and testament in your favor, a short hour or so before she died." He handed it across the desk.

It was a hard-line, legally worded statement signed by three people, Eleanor herself and two lawyers, giving the girl Nokomis into the care of Thomas Nateby Dyce until she became of age or married, which may be first. A sum in American dollars from her grandfather Pennyform's estate was set aside for her, to be released only when she came of age. In the meantime it would be apportioned out to her in monthly payments sent to the solicitors in London.

"How old is she?" Thomas croaked.

"Eighteen. But unfortunately this cannot be confirmed since no record of her birth exists. It is believed, let us say, that she is eighteen."

"Dear God!" Thomas exclaimed again. "How is it possible to give an answer before one has seen the girl? I have a daughter of my own, Amelia, rising eleven, a very vulnerable age. We have but one and a half bedrooms in our little house; to have this girl would mean moving from where we are very happily situated. They could not share one room."

"Then send her to boarding school, Major. . . ." Mr. Melbury said enthusiastically; but even as he spoke, he realized that it was a silly suggestion. Eighteen! No.

Mr. Melbury said the story had great appeal for him. One associated the name Pennyform with the great Pennyform who did so much for housing problems in England; he gathered this Pennyform was of another ilk. He had amassed a fortune for himself on some of the bare places of New York State, buying and selling land that increased rapidly in value, but he died a disappointed man for reasons that the lawyers in America had not given but that the gentleman had no longer any kin of his own to inherit, other than the half-wild girl aforementioned. Their colleagues in America were fully alert to priorities and were in the process of making assessments as to how much money would come along with the girl because the majority of it had been spent in building for charity out of his own pocket.

With a feeling of rising anger Thomas declared that it did not matter to him what amount of money might be included, he was not going to fall in with this, yes slightly, immoral proposal. He was quite sure, he said, that his wife would not concur with Mr. Melbury's suggestions.

But was he?

This was the sort of situation in which Melburys throve. Old Mr. Melbury slithered over the question of

24

Miss Nokomis Pennyform, leaving it, as it were, floating. He had ideas as comfortably as a hen lays an egg and this new idea was that Major Nateby should, by all the authentic channels in existence in England at the present time, change his name or rather *establish* his name as Nateby-Dyce, with a hyphen. People assumed the hyphen as a less humble man might assume a coronet or armorial bearings except that it was much more easily attained. And Thomas agreed at once that his idea was an excellent way out of the present impasse.

Notes were made as to proceedings and the clerk was called to instigate them forthwith. More signatures were required and more cups of tea consumed.

"Thank heaven for Mr. Samuel Cunard of Nova Scotia," Mr. Melbury said genially as he went with his client to the front door. "If we write off to America at once, it is possible that we shall have a reply in four weeks' time; we shall of course notify you at once on receipt of our first, indeed, any remittance."

Fifteen days out and thirteen days home was an astonishing reality of the new era; Cunard's steam packets had been made to pay their way; the experiment had been fully tested: Mail to and from America now took barely a month to cross the rude Atlantic twice.

Mr. Melbury and Major Nateby-Dyce were pleased with one another; in middle age Thomas' future was reopening to him. Walking back up the slope he pondered at the way things were turning out and felt some of the excitement he had felt on his first voyage to India as a young man. The new bank account, the new committee on which he would serve, the new club which he would, with luck, join. He hummed and knocked little pebbles out of his way with his stick. Tiresome thoughts with the unreal name of Nokomis left his mind for more pleasurable ones.

III

DURING the evening, with Amelia gone to bed, Emma chattered like an excited child as they sat before the dying embers of the fire with teaboard and candles. ". . . and think you, Thomas, we shall have an equipage of a kind, say one suitable for a pony and we can keep it at the stables in Willow Road? And shall we see you newly attired in costly garments in the most approved taste and not simply clothes befitting an ornamental stationer and small circulating library keeper!" She flipped her flimsy cap strings away from her face and laughed gaily.

"Do not let us count our chickens before they are hatched, Emma. I shall not allow myself to ruminate upon the riches to come. Mr. Melbury has not yet handed my Inguta *tremblante* to me, that I may have the pleasure of fastening it upon your lovely person!"

Emma sighed as she pinned the needle in her work and folded it before retiring. "There are times, Thomas, when I quite fail to understand you."

"There is no time, dearest Emma, when I fail to understand you."

"Perhaps that is nothing to boast about." She bent and kissed the top of his head.

Thomas had trained himself never to look back

beyond the shining day when he had married Emma. The child of a broken marriage, he had an inherent pessimism. The disappearance of his mother when he was twenty ought not to have been the disaster it was, but he was immature and expected things to go wrong inevitably. It was no doubt due to this that he made a hurried and ill-considered choice of a first wife who was too beautiful for safety.

Security had come with his marriage to Emma, but slowly.

Thomas had a gentle, youthful face without whiskers or mustache but with a wispy beard growing all round the perimeter so that it was a face well worth looking at and noting the changing expressions upon his sensitive mouth. He sat now before his own hearth and stared up above his chimneypiece where hung a representation of the death of Wolfe.

What were the neighbors going to think? Next door on one side there was the elderly French widow, once the girl who was first kept as a mistress by the first of the Regency bucks to rent one of the little houses. A refugee nearly fifty years ago from the Revolution in which her husband had gone to the guillotine and whose daughter had followed him the next year, together with her young husband, in the name of *Liberté, Egalité, Fraternité*; she was known as Madame Mirabelle but was in fact Madame la Comtesse de la Mirabelle; she ran a successful millinery establishment in the West End of London.

The three houses on the other side were occupied by, at Number 3, two spinster ladies of very meager means who occupied, if it may be thus called, their time with going to church and watching the comings and goings of their neighbors: the Misses Eglington.

At Number 4 was a bright young spark just down from Oxford who had bought the tiny house the year before and traveled to the city every day to work in the discount market. Mr. Daniel Ramble-Smith.

"Old scratchy paws," Amelia called Miss Blockley at Number 5. Neither she nor the Misses Eglington at Number 3 liked one another, but in a crisis of any kind they would hang together as unmarried ladies, a fraction of the two million surplus women which were said to be the population's tally. The Misses Eglington had been bewildered for a long time that no gentleman had paid any attention to either of them and they still desperately longed for it to happen while knowing secretly that it never would. It was the coming to terms with this sadness that had made gossips of them. Since nothing ever happened to them, personally, they were able to endure their lives only by enjoying the affairs of others.

Miss Blockley next door had not far to go to bring life into their living deaths, but over the years her kind intentions had gone sour; it gave her no pleasure that Miss So-and-So was now happily married; it needed malice and misfortune to bring a spring to her step and a light in her eyes.

The family were upon good terms with all these, but what were they all going to think when Emma broke out into the clothes she had been happily planning with Thomas in a totally new outfit as befitting a member of the Far East Club, not to mention a neat pony and trap and from there, no doubt, a phaeton and pair.

"Speculate with it," Mrs. Nickleby's advice, had delighted him when, two years previously, he had read in installments a story called *Nicholas Nickleby* by that new young novelist Charles Dickens. Mr. Nickleby had taken his silly little wife's advice and "four hundred nobodies were ruined."

No, there must be no speculation and no flaunting of riches but just a quiet and unobtrusive enjoyment of luxuries which he had never dreamed might come their way. They had lived in great content and happiness in Buck's Walk for nearly twelve years: Why make a change for anything better?

In fact, what gave him much greater pleasure than his inheritance was that which had come to him at the same time and it was the offer of employment regarding the new library being planned. He had not yet given notice of his intention to leave the bookshop in St. Paul's Churchyard; he would be obliged to do so as soon as the London library was seen to be coming into existence. And at that precise moment, he should emerge from his dwelling, wearing his new clothes.

Tomorrow he would go to the tailors to whom his father had always gone and order himself two new outfits, and on the way back he would call at the Far East Club, ask to see the secretary; tell him he would like to be a member, that he was, in fact, one who had served the sovereign as required, ask to see the members list and pick out from it any member who might have known him in India, who might like to propose him, and another to second him.

This last thought gave him a shiver of excitement, or, in fact, a kind of dread. With the death of his first wife he had done far more than leave the army, he had stepped out of his whole way of life and taken up entirely new status and environment. And now once again he had assumed, with his middle name, a new background.

Was it wise to pick up the threads, to reappear as Major Nateby-Dyce retd. late Regiment of Bombay Grenadiers? Wise or not, after these intervening years of happiness he felt restless; life was hurrying along; he would soon be an old man; he would prefer to taste again the army flavor, to sit with his feet upon the club fender, and yarn as he used to in the mess.

29

As it turned out it was all absurdly easy. A contemporary of Thomas Dyce, now a brigadier, had recently retired from the Indian Army and bought himself and family a house in Aldershot to which he was in the process of settling. He had been in the club, staying for two nights only this week. The secretary was most agreeable to the idea of writing to ask him to propose Thomas for a member. He showed Thomas round the establishment and in the smoking room he stopped in front of a very ancient gentleman and introduced Thomas: "General Sir Martin Gibb . . . Major Nateby-Dyce whom we hope soon to have as a full member."

The eyes of the old man drooped blood red like those of a bull mastiff as he lifed his head from his chest. "Dyce!" he croaked, "not Dyce of Scinde-Khelat?"

"My father," Thomas said. The old man gave a cry like an outraged sea gull (they are so often outraged) and made several attempts to struggle out of his chair; Thomas and the secretary both finally pulled the old man to his feet where he gave Thomas' shoulder an almost ceremonial beating, with dust from the shoulder of his old jacket filling a sunbeam. He then collapsed from a coughing fit brought on by the excess of energy. The outcome seemed to be extreme pleasure and delight at the meeting, demonstrated with an enthusiasm almost lethal to a nonagenarian.

With pleasure at the prospect of such a satisfactory new member, the secretary showed him to the imposing front door and assured Thomas that he would hear from him immediately after the next committee meeting.

This meeting was held ten days later and the ex-officer from the Bombay Grenadiers was pleased to propose Major Dyce as a member of the Club.

"Nateby-Dyce," the secretary corrected gently.

"It was Dyce in my day," the Brigadier returned gruffly. "I remember him; he was a good chap in the Mess but socially . . ."

"Yes, Brigadier?"

"This is not to cast aspersions upon the poor fellow and strictly between ourselves . . . they were a failure socially. It was the wife! We lived for a time on the same station. A thoroughly spoilt young woman I'd say. There was nobody good enough for her ladyship. *Tch tch!* An impossible woman, daughter of some nobleman or other; she made life hell for poor Dyce. He was very well liked in the mess, when he was allowed out. Mind you, she was a beautiful woman, which made it, on the whole, worse because there was by no means an excess of beautiful women about, ha ha! Beautiful as the dawn, gentlemen, but after half an hour with her, one was itching to get away. It was not too difficult to avoid her, mark you, because we were a scruffy lot and beneath her contempt."

The secretary said he had liked the man and as no women were admitted to the club, he looked round; had anyone any objections?

"Now that I recall," the Brigadier said, "they went home on leave after Dadur, and he was one of a dozen or so general officers to receive a reward pension for distinguished service. His wife died on the way back home and he sent in his papers; rather sad, was it not? Now that I come to think of it I have copies of the dispatches over that period in the late thirties. When I've put my library into good order at the new house I'll look it out and bring it; perhaps by the next meeting. But yes, certainly, secretary, I will have much pleasure in proposing him."

And later that week from his new home in Aldershot the Brigadier was able to post to the secretary the following:

31

At the latter place Captain Greenaway was in command and Major Dyce set off to support him with a detachment of troops consisting of a wing of Her Majesty's 41st, the 38th Bengal N.I. and some irregular horse. After accomplishing his march with much difficulty owing to the inundated state of the country, he found that the post and town of Dadur had been repeatedly assaulted by the Brahoes under Nasseer Khan. Major Dyce immediately resolved to attack the enemy who were about 5,000 in number and ordered his party to advance upon the Brahoes, who, after suffering severely, retreated and were pursued to their camp, from which they were speedily driven. This happened on the same 3rd of November on which Dost Mahomed surrendered and Khelat was retaken.

So Thomas Nateby-Dyce was admitted to the club and on the first evening the secretary led him round and introduced him to everyone who was there at the time, with the exception of those in the card room who were never disturbed. There was one name only that Thomas remembered and that was Albert Niton, a man of his own age who stood talking with a glass in his hand to a friend in front of the fire.

"Brigadier Niton," the secretary said and Thomas' heart felt as though it were being squeezed: his best friend. He knew him instantly and looked into his face for signs of recognition on his part anxiously. Niton behaved, however, as though it were just anybody to whom he was being introduced. But as Thomas and the secretary moved on to other introductions Niton stopped talking to his companion and stared after them:

"Could it be? Yes, he's just like him from the back, but his face. . . ."

On the way out Thomas looked back and Niton gave a great cry. "Thomas!" Everyone turned round and looked with interest at the new member to whom they had just been introduced and smiled at the enthusiastic reunion of two old comrades.

Thomas was drawn across the carpet and reintroduced: "We were at Khelat together Christmas 1828 and for months after . . ." and so it went and in the late omnibus, toiling up the steep incline to Hampstead, Thomas glowed with pride and pleasure; once again, after all these years, he was "one of us." While the great Duke of Wellington remained still very much alive, army officers stayed clean-shaven; the reason Albert Niton had not immediately recognized Thomas Dyce was the light fringe of a beard which decorated the edge of his countenance and became him so well; it transformed him admirably from a soldier to a scholar and bookman of some stature. As Thomas had walked away from him at the club he was recognized immediately.

It was seven weeks before there was any further communication from Messrs. Melbury. Emma grumbled that the time lawyers take to bring out their fruit in due season was daunting, but Thomas hardly cared. He was so happy now that he realized that whereas he thought he was happy before it was a mere passive happiness. Now it was an active delight; he was a clubman, a man of the world and not a day passed without his meeting new people and experiencing new ideas in this exciting capital city and in the midst of a great social upheaval. Thus, a summons to Mr. Melbury's office again came almost as an irritant.

However, his permission was required to deposit as an

advance the sum of fourteen hundred pounds at the bankers in Chancery Lane, Dixon, Brooks & Dixon, being the one used by Messrs. Melbury and situated nearest to their business premises. Thomas managed to conceal the dull fact that he had at present no banking account whatever. With what he hoped was a suitable flourish he wrote his signature in the required position and with his other hand accepted the blank draft handed to him and slipped it casually in his new trouser pocket in the manner of the new man he was. There were other signatures to be written upon receipts, and this done, once again Mr. Melbury walked with his client to the front door and told him that he would be only too ready to help Thomas at any time in regard to any question that might occur.

Then suddenly, having actually forgotten the other legacy that had been left him, Thomas remembered. "God bless my soul!" he turned astonished to Mr. Melbury. "The girl! Or has that turned out to be a myth?"

Mr. Melbury senior wagged his finger playfully. "Ssh! Let us make no comment beyond the surmise that she has been, shall we say, *dealt with?*"

"Have I you to thank for this, sir?"

"Only in that I wrote to our American associates when I had to appraise them of events here, a short note regarding their information about Miss Nokomis Pennyform. I assured them that it would be quite impossible for you to offer the girl accommodation in your home. Oh, mind you, I was careful not to give them the impression that you were relegating your responsibility to others, but I did imply that you, well . . ." Mr. Melbury pursed his mouth and opened his hands, denoting vagueness regarding the subject and just left it at that. Well, not quite; Thomas was already on the top step of the three steps leading to the pavement when Mr.

Melbury leaned forward and whispered saucily into Thomas' left ear: "Mother's money is one thing; Mother's paramour's daughter's bastard is quite another, don't you agree?" As Thomas burst out laughing Mr. Melbury closed his front door slowly, naughtily keeping an eye on Thomas and winking just before finally closing it.

But that was the only, the absolutely single time Thomas got one iota of fun out of it at all. First he went to Messrs. D. B. & D. at 25 Chancery Lane and obtained fifty sovereigns from them. Then, with the money in the two sovereign purses he had purchased in advance for the purpose, he walked briskly home, considerably laden with the gold, which was making shapeless the top of the splendid new trousers he was wearing. "Use it," he would say to Emma and most probably Emma would take him at his word and walk along to the butcher's at the corner of Flask Walk and buy a fat capon which they would eat for dinner when Amelia returned from school.

From a distance his front door presented an unexpected appearance. Something had been delivered and still stood upon the doorstep. As he advanced he saw it more clearly and unwillingly admitted that it was, in fact, a pile of traveling gear . . . baggage. And feeling suddenly tired, he knew to whom it belonged without the slightest doubt; Mother's paramour's daughter's bastard had arrived and it was no longer in the least bit amusing.

He stepped his way over the huge trunk, the two gladstone bags, the two carpet bags, the basket with the wide leather strap round it, the basket with the handle, the umbrella and the string bag and opened his own front door. He shuddered as he stepped into his narrow little primrose painted hall.

Emma had her own ideas about house decoration; everybody else's hall was something papered with something like shiny beetroot-colored anaglypta, which was a material like linoleum with a Turkish-inspired pattern pressed into it.

This was the correct new inspired wear for the walls of a hall, but Emma had not moved forward in her ideas. She had, indeed, moved backwards with her mind on the delicacies of taste which inspired the days of the Prince Regent. Taste had mattered then and Emma, being unable to afford pale primrose silk and aquamarine satin wall panels, had chosen a semishiny paint that gave a satin impression and for eleven years these walls had drawn exclamations of admiration from all visitors to the tiny house. Now Thomas stood in his own hall with the key of the front door still in his hand and shuddered.

It was a pleasant late April morning and he wore no coat; he was warm from his brisk walk up hill, burdened with sovereigns as he was, but now he became suddenly cold from the top of his head to his smartly clad feet. He hung up his hat on one of the ivory-headed pegs and slid the now rigid sovereign purses into the umbrella stand drawer and noticed that his hands were trembling. He was rubbing them upon the sides of his pale beige trousers when Emma called him into the drawing room.

He may or may not have heard the manner in which he was introduced, he did not take it in. Though it was fairly certain she was not introduced as, "your mother's paramour's daughter's bastard," that was, in fact, who it was, and there was no doubt that he must have taken her chilly hand and bowed over it; he felt like one in a dream.

A nightmare, in fact, because though she was probably one of the most beautiful girls he had ever seen, she filled him at the same time with a revulsion and loathing that he might have experienced upon witnessing an appalling accident. This feeling was so sudden and so unexpected that, though he was aware of it, he could not control it

36

and he stood staring at her in nothing less than horror. What made him think her beautiful?

"Thomas. . . ." Emma seemed to be gently wringing her hands. "Thomas, it is your, it is your relative, Nokomis Pennyform."

"Yes."

"I'm afraid Mr. Melbury has forgotten to tell you, has he? Tell you that she was coming, in fact, has come."

"No," Thomas said curtly, "he did not forget. . . ."

She had a rasping voice, oh yes, she had to have a rasping voice, it did not go with her looks, but it went with the way he thought about her. She said in a voice like a coarse kind of file that she had omitted to inform the solicitors of her imminent arrival because she did not see what would be the point of doing so. It was Thomas to whom she was related, and with this she threw him an affectionate look, and it was Thomas, and of course, dear Emma, with whom she had come to stay.

In her way she was perfect. Not one centimeter of hair escaped from beneath her lively and overdecorated bonnet. Perhaps she was bald? She had enormous eyes and they were wide apart, which is supposed to be a sign of beauty. The French painter Greuze gave all his clients wide-apart eyes, but this girl's eyes were so wide apart that they seemed to have lost touch with one another. Yet there was no squint any more than a hen can be said to squint even though one of its eyes cannot see the other; a tortoise does not squint, nor does a lizard. A snake does not squint, but you cannot look it straight in the face because you cannot see both eyes at once. So this strange quirk is reptilian!

Nokomis was reed-slim but bendable, prehensile; she swayed and writhed and squirmed and twisted about. She was certainly not a snake, but she was the nearest approach to a snake that a human being could get. As

37

though showing herself more fully to him, she took off her bonnet and tossed it down. She had the highest forehead that mankind could produce and yet her face was so perfect that nature's folly could not detract from the beauty of it. Nature did nothing for her face, and in an ordinary person hair could have mitigated the starkness. She showed exquisite teeth in a narrow semicircle of such perfection that Thomas could barely disguise his shudders of revulsion.

If, as they say, art is the dialogue between heart and mind, then she did not qualify as beautiful in Thomas' opinion, but extremely striking and vilely repulsive.

Nevertheless he took a firm grip upon himself and did the honors, inquiring about her state of health after the long voyage and upon what packet boat she had set sail. How long the voyage had taken and at what port she had arrived.

From time to time he glanced at Emma whose little white bewildered face was turned constantly toward him. He knew he had made a terrible mistake in not sharing the Pennyform girl news with Emma. But he had had no time.

Later he would try not to make excuses. He would abase himself completely, but even as he looked at the girl a string of excuses for his folly were racing through his head. And particularly the main truth, a feeble one but more than an excuse, it was the truth. He would always try to avoid unpleasantness of any kind, except that of fighting like a mad thing when the occasion demanded. He enjoyed fighting, that is stabbing and shooting for Queen and Country, enjoining his men to follow him and to hurl themselves upon the frantic enemy. But acting the soldier and behaving as a man of peace and tranquillity and gentleness were two separate lives. His home, his wife, his child were all precious, and, to him, inviolable . . . to be kept sacred and unprofaned.

A Red Indian's bastard in the family, and soon to be upon their doorstep, came into the category of violation and profanity, something from which they must be protected even if only by brushing under the hearth rug. That was why he rejected the information, refusing to allow himself to mention its imminence.

Trivial conversation about the girl's voyage ensued. With his first and second finger Thomas automatically felt in his waistcoat pocket for his snuffbox to give him confidence. But he had put his snuffbox in the pocket of his tail coat, changing places with the prized ornament because he did not trust the case containing the Inguta jewel, which Mr. Melbury had given him, flapping against the back of his legs as he walked home; he had slipped it in his snuffbox pocket where the bulge it made was concealed by his coat.

Was it goodwilled intent that had made his mother have the jewel her husband had given her sent back to her son upon her death? And was it goodwill which made her send the girl too? Was the jewel a bribe? A reward for having the girl? Or was it because his mother still thought about and loved her son and wanted him to have the marvelous gift his father had given her?

If the latter then it was totally absurd of him to take such a violent dislike to the girl. Absurd, hysterical and selfish. But given these three things there still remained *instinct.* A man is often wiser to follow his instinct than his reason.

They were all three still standing, an uncomfortable trio in the little drawing room, and Thomas was thoughtfully tugging his fragile fringe of beard.

It appeared that she had arrived more than an hour ago and Emma had explained to her, over a cup of tea, that their house was too small to accommodate a guest, having but one bedroom. Her daughter, she had told the girl, slept in a room so small that it was not intended for a bedroom but a gentleman's dressing room. They had one little servant who lived in the village five minutes' walk away and came at seven in the morning.

It depressed Thomas when Miss Pennyform slumped down on to a chair without being asked; it also depressed him to find that she referred to his mother as "my grandmother." So much so that he objected, saying quite pleasantly, that his mother was, of course, no relation to Miss Pennyform. He could not help it.

Her eyes blazed suddenly, but she took care and replied meekly that Thomas' mother was the only person in her life who had ever cared for her; she would be where her grandfather Pennyform had always told her she should be . . . "on the streets," were it not for her.

She said sulkily, "I always reminded him that he had better stop building the streets, if that was so. We were always rowing," she said meekly, letting the toes of her slippers peep coyly out from beneath her skirt. "He hated me."

Emma was bewildered, confused and embarrassed. She wished desperately for a few minutes alone with her husband. She was waiting, alert for a moment when she could suggest it, but Thomas had now pulled himself together enough to remember the sum of money mentioned (oh, such a long time ago) by Mr. Melbury regarding Miss Pennyform. He was mumbling and stumbling in an effort to say what he wished to say, with the right approach; it was that there was, or would shortly be, money in the care of the solicitor, which could be used to find suitable accommodation for a young girl alone in London. He said this last deliberately to show Miss Pennyform that he did not intend her to become a member of his household. This, however, did not get

40

much further because the shrill cries of children could be heard. It was, of course, Amelia and with her the boy with whom she walked up the hill from school: Roderick. Like starlings they were picking over with much comment the pile of luggage upon the front doorstep.

They burst into the drawing room in a disorderly manner, as uncontrolled and pervasive as a bewildered flock of sheep. In a few words the situation was at least superficially explained. Miss Pennyform, a young friend bereaved, sent from America to make her home in London. Amelia, by no means a child of her generation who was expected to be seen but not heard (or even to be neither seen nor heard, for preference), had an instant answer to the problem and a good one at that.

"Why! Madame Mirabelle," she shrieked. "She's been all alone since Miss Craskie fell off the ladder when she was tying up the vine."

Her parents stared at her, as they so often did, with the fascination and shock as someone confronted by a basilisk, hatched by a serpent from a cock's egg.

"The old lady next door," she kindly explained to the visitor. "She has a bonnet shop in town. You could have her room," she explained to Miss Pennyform, "Miss Craskie has broken lots of things like legs and arms, she won't be back for a long time and I heard Madame Mirabelle asking one of the Miss Eglingtons if she knew of anybody who could come to keep her company." She jerked herself from foot to foot, excited and bright-eyed.

In a despairing kind of way Emma looked across at her husband who sat, exhausted now, and he, catching her eye, nodded slightly once or twice in the manner of one signaling: let us try it, it is at least an idea!

"Papa says yes. Come on Roddy. . . . Can he come with me, Papa? Miss What, did you say?" They screamed with laughter at the name Pennyform. Amelia laughed first,

41

of course, and Roderick followed, albeit nervously. "But please call me Nokomis. . . ."

"Wait a minute, wait a minute. . . ." Emma nervously pressed her knuckles against her front teeth. "I know you and she are great friends, Amelia, but is not this impertinent, even with such a good friend as our Madame Mirabelle?"

"You see," Amelia seemed to be addressing the visitor, "she had a little girl like me, only she had her head chopped off, I mean when she was growed-up and married. Yes, that's true, is it not, Papa?"

"Alas, yes," Thomas mumbled, not looking at anybody.

IV

AMELIA evidently felt she had left their visitor un-
convinced because she tried to sound more persuasive.
"When I do not call in and see her, she says, 'Why did you
not come in and see me as you always do on Sunday
morning, *ma chère petite Amélie?*' And sometimes she says
it in French."

"But if the house is the same as this, and I think it is,
there is no bedroom to spare," Nokomis put in in-
telligently. But Thomas came in quickly: "We should pay
well for your accommodation, my dear, out of your fund
with the solicitor."

"Oh, if you're going to pay, of course poor Madame
Mirabelle will be pleased, she is very, *very* poor!"

"How old is that child?" Miss Nokomis Pennyform
coldly asked, as Amelia rushed excitedly out of the room.

There was much to talk about that evening at Number
2 Buck's Walk, but it was postponed. They stayed
downstairs in the drawing room and spoke in whispers
when it was certain that their Amelia was asleep. They
spoke in amazement about the way their only child was
turning out.

"She's like my mother, asthmatic though she was,
when she was free of her complaint there was no more, I

43

have to use the word, *forceful* (though it is not quite the word I need) woman. She did not give offense by her managing qualities, but she arranged things in such a way that it took the burden from the shoulders of lesser people. She saved feebler mortals from having to think for themselves," Thomas mused.

He remembered to apologize humbly for not telling his wife weeks ago about the imminence of Miss Pennyform. He said he did not feel that Mr. Melbury fully believed in the threat of her arrival even though he had mentioned being sent money for her keep. He also said that Mr. Melbury had given instructions to the American solicitors to send her after embarkation straight to Red Lion Square; he had thus assumed that the solicitor would have the responsibility of her for the first few days, at least. What they would have done in the absence of Amelia and her astonishing behavior, he could not think. And how satisfactory it had been, coming, as it did, from Amelia who could "say anything" to her old friend Madame Mirabelle. It seemed that Amelia had also made friends with the young man next door but one on the other side, an Oxford graduate upon whom Amelia had the impertinence to dump nine pieces of baggage with the exception of an overnight bag.

"Mark you, Miss Amelia," this young gentleman had said as at her request he cheerfully started to lug in the baggage and pile it against his immaculate hall wall, "this cannot remain here for long, a week at the outside and I shall throw them back." But from the way he looked at Miss Pennyform, he would convince nobody that he meant it, least of all Miss Pennyform.

"Do you like her?" Thomas whispered.

"She has nice manners," Emma returned, "the hour that I was alone with her before you mercifully returned, she sought to . . . well . . . shall I say, make a good

44

impression upon me. But, completely unprepared as I was I am afraid I failed to be impressed. In the light of my daughter's insouciance I must have appeared a very inadequate person."

"We are both inadequate people!" Thomas said.

"I cannot see myself with her all day long; what shall I do? Show her the sights of London, take her shopping, introduce her and take her out to tea with all my friends, have tea parties for her? Oh, Thomas!" she moaned, "when shall I do my cooking, mend our clothes, prune the roses and above all when shall I *read*? She is not even my generation. And her voice and the way she speaks will soon drive me out of my mind. *Her voice!*"

Thomas carefully took the pinch of snuff which was now available and under its influence he said that her responsibility was to find for the girl a man whom she could marry. Nay, a boy would do. How about the young man next door but one? "But seriously, Emma, I do not think she should see too much of Amelia."

"Why not, pray? Though I agree, I would like to know your thoughts on the question."

"Because she is a sophisticated girl, the American I mean. And our Amelia, as we have been shown today, is growing up much too fast."

"Is there anything wrong in that?"

"Not wrong, exactly but. . . ." He had difficulty in finding the reason for deploring what he had just said. "Well, is it your wish that she should grow up fast?"

"No, Thomas. I would like her to grow up at just the right pace."

"There you are, you see. The Pennyform's manner is that of a woman of the world and I do not wish my daughter to emulate her. For instance, we were greatly relieved by Amelia's helpfulness this afternoon, but we did not find it charming, you agree?"

45

Emma tapped her front teeth with her knuckles. She wondered.

Later, lying sleepless in the dark, she allowed tears to pour down her cheeks without seeking to dry them. The event of today seemed to her to be a pollution of her home, nothing less. She did not blame Thomas for not having warned her that this might happen, for even if they had discussed what they would do with the Pennyform, they would be no nearer a conclusion than they were now.

Tomorrow, perhaps, she and Thomas should go together to the solicitor and tell him their difficulties, make it clear that they did not want the American girl living with them. That it was wholly unsuitable in a house of the size of theirs and with a girl of Amelia's age. They could not allow her to wander about a strange city by herself, and the problem of having her was insoluble. What she suggested was that a suitable "finishing school" for young ladies should be sought for her and each one closely investigated.

She slept finally but woke early and nudged Thomas awake to discuss her thoughts with him before Amelia woke. Having heard them, Thomas said he had already said as much to Mr. Melbury but had not mentioned a "finishing school." He agreed with her but said they would have to send a note to Mr. Melbury asking for an appointment because he was a very busy and sought-after man.

As it turned out, that was a Saturday, a day on which Amelia rose from her bed and started immediately upon the homework she had been set. This was because Saturdays held treats, and if her homework was not done the treat was postponed until it was. So she worked for an hour, getting it finished and slipped back into the satchel before breakfast, thus clearing the day for action, pleasurable always.

It also released Madame Mirabelle from leaving the house at half-past eight to be in her workroom in Oxford Street at nine to take a rapid and wordless roll call upon her staff. Thus, instead of stepping into her fly as usual, she took the opportunity before her guest had risen to hobble into her neighbors' and to discuss her.

"Of course I am willing to keep her so long as Craskie is away. I shall see she makes herself useful in the house; I have showed her how to get breakfast already. But what, my dear people, is she going to do all day until I am back home?"

Thomas said that was exactly what they had been pondering and Emma said that they had in mind a "finishing school" for young ladies where there would be boarders and did Madame Mirabelle know, perhaps, of a French establishment of the kind where the young ladies were polished, that is, taught needlework and a foreign language (French in this case, of course) and all the basic rules of how to behave in society, because it was clear that nothing of that sort had come Nokomis Pennyform's way so far.

"She has an unfortunate mouth, poor girl," Madame observed. "She should be taught to control it; she is all mouth; she opens it wide, wide. You can see her uvula. Her uvula," she repeated and left it at that so that both Thomas and Emma thought it was a French word. "It is the laugh of a fishwife; they laugh when there is nothing to laugh at."

There was a thoughtful pause before Madame said that she was a striking girl; though ugly, she was, in her way, beautiful: ". . . *jolie laide* we call it in France; I would like her about my showroom from the point of view of

47

seeing her there, but would I be able to tolerate her behavior? Since I have not yet sampled this, I cannot answer my own question. I could but try it out?" She looked from Emma to Thomas and back to Emma; she was wearing an elaborate and becoming bonnet, her bodice was edged with Valenciennes lace of exquisite delicacy, and her working apron was embroidered in gay colors. From her small, deeply wrinkled face, two very bright eyes looked. She sharply observed the reactions to what she had to say.

"*Exactement* . . . who is she?"

"A stepdaughter of my mother who lived in America," Thomas said after a few moments of reflection. "My mother died recently and left a verbal request that I should . . . I should supervise her until she came of age, or married. She is not penniless."

"Nor is she rich?"

"Far from it."

"I could give her shelter in my little house until my Craskie returns and after that I could offer her a residential apprenticeship. After the first instruction, the work would be far from hard. They have an excellent midday meal and the workroom closes at nine in the evening. The quality come to my establishment and I would appreciate having Miss Pennyform around, to attend upon my chief milliner when she serves the quality."

"You close at nine o'clock, Madame, I doubt if Miss Pennyform would agree to that!"

"My ladies must be attended to at all hours. She can find her new hat unacceptable at three o'clock in the afternoon; it must be remade by ten the next morning. Present-day women are overautocratic and spoilt; I for one am a slave to the modern woman, but it is the only way in which I am enabled to continue to live, even in this

48

modest house next door. And mind you, Major, the hat would not be unacceptable because mistakes had been made in the making; oh, *mon Dieu non . . . c'est que . . .* she has changed her mind about the style!"

But now Miss Pennyform herself, fully awake, rat-tatted upon the front door and there was no alternative other than to tell her they had been discussing her future, and Emma explained shortly what had been suggested.

For a breath-holding moment they waited, watching the changing expressions on her face. "So you, Madame, have a kind of hostel for your employees?"

"Yes, we have now but nine staff and I could arrange for you to have a room to yourself." It was clever of her to avoid the words "worker" and "hands" by which her "staff" were known.

To the great relief of everybody present she accepted with what seemed at the time alacrity; she asked if she might first have a few days to look around and attend to the luggage. Since they were not to have her yoked to them, Emma's spirits rose and her heart warmed immeasurably toward the lass.

Madame said she would give her a day or two before she would expect her to start; she would provide her with breakfast and supper at nine, and Emma and Thomas would give her dinner with the family. Thomas' relief was such that he unexpectedly brought out the cherry brandy and they all drank to the amicable arrangements (much too soon, as it turned out).

Dear Mr. Melbury,

I should very much have liked to call upon you this morning but it is Saturday and you will not be at your office this afternoon. So I am writing at present to tell you what has happened; I do not know what my feelings regarding Miss Pennyform will be on Monday, but no doubt I will change my present attitude when I have had a talk with her.

I can only say that she frightens me, a curious admission but perhaps when you meet her you will be of the same opinion as I am.

There are so many questions to be answered: I believe she docked at Liverpool but why did she not come straight to you yesterday by coach, or even mention your name to me? Were you, in fact, expecting her? She has the sophistication of a woman of experience, are you satisfied that she is only eighteen?

Our neighbors on either side of us have been remarkably kind; one is giving her temporary house room and the other is keeping her inordinate amount of baggage for the moment.

I hope very much that you will be able to see me next week.

Yours sincerely,
Thomas Nateby-Dyce

Overheard in the Far East Club:

—This new member whose name I see up on the board: Nateby-Dyce? Who is 'e, anybody know?
—His father was Dyce of Scinde-Khelat, thirty-five years service; Star of India.
—But *Nateby*-Dyce, hyphen.
—Same Dyce, Nateby for inheritance probably, Mother's side, eh?
—Did you know 'im?
—Same station for a bit, he was Bombay Grenadiers. A hell of a beautiful wife!

—*(Casually:)* You met 'er?

—Met her? We had that misfortune. A feudal kind of bitch.

—Eh?

—A swell. Daughter of an Earl, seventh or so and couldn't forget it. She laid in to poor Dyce so he had to take it out on her, killing natives in battle. He was as brave as they come, we always used to say in his own mind he was killing her! A bit mean, wasn't it?

—*(Grunts.)*

—Is he around?

—Course, became "one of us" last week.

—You don't say! *(Long, long pause during which brain ticks over.)* By Gad! *(Another long pause.)* They do say that in the end she went the way of the rest.

—What rest?

—All the Brahoes he'd killed.

—You're not serious?

—'Pends what you mean by serious. "They said . . ." doesn't mean it's the dead truth, it's just: "they said." They said, let them go on saying! *(Long pause.)* It isn't as though they can prove anything. *(Long pause.)* Not at this date anyway. By Gad!

—What happened?

—I wasn't there.

—Where?

—On the voyage home on leave. You remember that famous mail ship. Depart Bombay third? I know it by heart: Bombay December third, sailed five-forty on the dot; Muscat December eighth ten fifteen; London January eighteenth; the *Berenice* via Persian Gulf and we thought that marvelous quick. *(Long pause.)*

—Well?

—He goes ashore at Muscat. Captain says *don't*. He's

seen going. It's the seaport of Oman, as you know. Grape place.

—Eh?

—I said *grape* place.

—Oh, I thought you said great place.

—Far from it but it's the residence of the British consul for Oman. Anyway . . . Dyce out all day, did not turn up at ten fifteen sailing time. An awful row . . . he'd evidently taken her sight-seeing. *(Great burst of laughter.)* Ship searched. Quay searched. Quay searched twice. Dyce found drunk, leaning against bollard, so they said. Lady Mary gone, vanished, disappeared.

—*(Opens eyes wider than usual but remains wordless.)*

—And he said. . . .

—Yes?

—He said she had died suddenly from cholera. Well, as everyone knows cholera isn't exactly instantaneous: He could not think of any other excuse, that was it. They asked him if he had gone to the consul and he said he had but by the time the ship was back in London it was all forgotten more or less. People hadn't time to remember the nine days' wonder on board; I don't know. Back from leave on the station a year later, people chewed it over, especially when we heard he had sent in his papers. Well, you know the sort of thing; in the narrowness of station social life you get this small-town gossip. I don't for a moment suggest that all was forgotten; it was simply a case of all *was not remembered*, which is different. Eleven years later he crops up and people start remembering. The reason I know anything about it is that the wife and children of a chap in my regiment were traveling home in the *Berenice* on that trip. She did not actually say in so many words that they were relieved to be spared Lady

Mary Dyce but she implied it and there was quite a bit of worry in case someone started up with cholera. In fact, they were more worried about that than about the lady's disappearance. The Captain of the *Berenice* himself was killed out hunting that winter; whether or not he started an inquiry one does not know. If the Captain is not there to start an inquiry . . . well, who else would?

—You are against the man, Dyce, I observe.

—Not at all, on the contrary. Why should I be? I hardly know him. It is merely, well, interest if you like.

—Was there a notice in the *Times* obit? Lady Mary Dyce, suddenly in Oman?

—Not that I know of. But to be fair, there was a lot of cholera about and no great rush to explore the town of Oman on the part of the transit passengers.

—Have you discussed this with anyone other than the chap in your regiment?

—*(Looking thoughtfully through the high windows at the white London sky:)* It was hell at the end of thirty; I was sent up into the Punjab where we had this frightful rout with the Sikhs. There were some Bombay Grenadiers who were newly back from home leave. You know how it went in the Punjab; frightful disorganization amongst the natives; huddled in our tiny mess, I suppose gossip was an escape. Old Dyce and others getting chewed over by his old chums, you know the kind of thing. We Indian Army warriors chattered away like a tight troup of prattling spinsters in the Pump Room in Bath. Jabber, jabber; it took our minds off the horrors of the Punjab that Christmas, 1830, by gad!

—Well, there he goes!

—*(Startled.)* Who?

—The man we've just been discussing.

Together they watched Thomas Nateby-Dyce cross the room from fireplace to further door with his friend Albert Niton. The gossips' heads and eyes moved simultaneously from north to south. One said "Well, I'm damned!"

V

SO far Nokomis had behaved like a young lady, whatever she may have looked like. Father, Mother and Amelia walked down the hill to church with Amelia and Nokomis in front, Amelia carrying her prayer book and Nokomis carrying Amelia's second-best one. They walked up Downshire Hill, past Amelia's chapel school, to the Church of St. John on the corner of Downshire Hill and the leafy lane where once Keats lived and wrote his poems. Nokomis' shining black hair was pulled so tightly from her face that her features were almost distorted. Lace-edged pantaloons appeared discreetly beneath her skirt and were the envy of Amelia, who was later to bring up the subject with her mother. She said she had bought them in New York on her way through, together with the capelet which she wore across her shoulders fastened at the neck with a brave fall of satin ribbon. She tripped light-footed, and Amelia took careful note of everything and tried to do likewise.

When the service was over they encountered on the path outside, the mother and father of Roderick with their five children. While the elders were talking Amelia made haste to make Roderick known to Nokomis, but it was disappointing that Nokomis was, or appeared to be, unimpressed by Amelia's best friend, who did, in fact, look smaller than Amelia believed him to be. He felt smaller, somehow, in her presence because she barely paid him attention and was looking at Mr. Daniel Ramble-Smith in whose house she had left her baggage.

He, too, was looking at her as best he could as he climbed into the carriage and pair of his great-aunts with whom he was having dinner presently. In fact, he had three elderly ladies on his hands, his great-aunts and a friend, and his hands were full as he helped them to mount, with his head screwed round in the direction of Nokomis rather than toward his task.

Having humbly prayed for guidance in church, Thomas now walked alone a few paces from his chattering family, head bent and gloved hands clasped behind his back. He would have given a great deal to have avoided the serious interview with Nokomis that he knew he must have. The feeling of horror he had had on first meeting her was as acute as ever, but now he was deeply confused because he had entered the area of thinking when common sense becomes fantasy. He could not see her as a girl at all and kept asking himself if she was an imposter, a woman of thirty posing as Miss Pennyform for reasons of her own.

If he were Mr. Melbury, he might, with reason, ask for proof of identification, and he must make sure that Melbury did this as he had done it to Thomas himself with the Inguta jewel. But in the meantime how could he unobtrusively assure himself that she was in fact who she was said to be.

Said to be?

That was nonsense, who, other than herself said she was Nokomis Pennyform? Thomas felt himself to be one who was both deaf and blind; he had no conception of what his mother's life had been like, or on what sort of terms she was with the Pennyforms. Thirty years of absolute silence lay between them and his mother had become a total stranger. He could think of no way of proving the identity of the girl to his own satisfaction. Unless . . .

He would have to unwrap himself, peel off all the feelings he had about the girl, obliterate his dislike, step out of his simple self and become one of those "cunning men that pass for wise."

Fifteen minutes later, with the smell of roasting beef permeating Number 2 Buck's Walk, he poured a Marsala for himself only. By prearrangement Emma and Amelia were going to visit an old lady of ninety in Hampstead Square.

He sat down in his own armchair feeling himself in the full penetrating glare of the great eyes upon him.

"Tomorrow being Monday, this coming week you will have to pay a visit to Mr. Melbury, he and young Mr. Melbury are solicitors of repute whom, no doubt, your solicitors in America have told you about."

Oh, yes, certainly, she knew all about them; the American solicitors had been personal friends of the Pennyforms and had everything to do with the wills of both Mr. *and* Mrs. Pennyform who had had much to do with them.

"This is the position as explained to me. . . ."

"Would it not be better if I were to explain to you, Major? There was so much hate against my poor mother who ran away; anything you have been told from the Pennyform angle you will have been misinformed. She was stabbed to death by my father after some years together and my grandfather told me when I was six. He told me that there was wild blood in me and that I would have to be more good than other people."

"More what?"

"More *good*!"

"Did he mean . . . holy?"

She nodded. "Of course the result was I was more naughty. If it had not been for Eleanor Pennyform I should have been sent away to a school of correction."

"Eleanor?"

"Your mother."

Thomas lost touch with all the fine resolutions and decisions about the "cunning men that pass for wise." He stared at her with, it must be admitted, his mouth slightly open. He realized for the first time that here was someone who had actually known his mother, had seen her within months.

"But perhaps," she said, "it might have been better if I had been sent to an orphanage."

"Why?"

"I might then have escaped the attentions of my uncle."

"Uncle?"

"My mother's brother." And for once there was no trace of that wide smile upon her face.

Thomas leaned forward. "Tell me about my mother."

"She was very kind to me. She was not holy and good, like the Pennyforms; I admired her so much because she would never, she often told me, become a Pennyform in actual fact. She often said she had made a fool of herself once in her life like my own mother, she had run away from security, and she was not going to repeat it. She was glad when Mr. Pennyform died, we both were."

Thomas was shocked, he was winded with shock.

"Mr. Pennyform called it gifts to God."

"Called what?"

"They could have lived in great style, but they lived in a small clapboard house and Mr. Pennyform gave all the money he made in selling land he bought when he was a

58

young man, prospecting, he gave it all to parsons to build more chapels and to use it for building houses for the poor."

"But surely that immediately causes one to think him a good man."

"That depends what you call 'good,' " she returned sulkily. "Eleanor had to go along with him in all this and she hated it. She said it was all her own fault so she went on doing what *he* wanted always. She said that *he* thought the more money he gave away the more he believed he would be sure to go to heaven. But Eleanor said she did not think it cost money to get to heaven; she would keep her money for her son Thomas and would not worry about heaven since it was a hopeless ambition as far as she was concerned."

Thomas laughed and at the same time tears poured down his face. That was his mother all right . . . over the acres and acres of years . . . there she was, saying it!

There was now not the slightest doubt in his mind that Nokomis was who she purported to be. This did not make his heart warm to her because her voice was still intolerable, she still writhed and smiled in the same revolting manner. But now he knew that he must do his best for her, as, quite evidently, his mother had, at least, befriended her.

He was strengthened beyond uncertainty by knowing that he was hearing the truth. He remained quite un-moved even when she splashed it out in an untidy and unseemly burst of giggles, that she had been ravished by her uncle when she was thirteen (though she did not use that dignified word). It was then that "Eleanor" took her under her wing: "She was the only person who ever loved me or took an interest in me and the only person I have ever loved. I lived with her for nearly two years . . . till she died, she was a lovely lady. . . ." she ended sadly.

She then told Thomas what he already knew that the solicitors back home had provided her with the money for her passage and furnished all the information regarding the solicitors in Red Lion Square. They had also given the address of Major Dyce to whom she would be sent by the London solicitors. "But I came straight to you," she said cheerfully, "because I knew you were expecting me." She was trying to cooperate.

Thomas and Emma were not; they had dismissed all unpleasant thoughts from their minds, in the state of euphory in which they had been living. Thomas said in his efforts to make up for his undoubted lack of care and attention, that he would take her to the solicitors this week and they would be able to give her details of the monetary arrangements that had been provided for her. It was going to be "enough" he said but "not too much" and he hoped that she would benefit from the plan for her future which had been made with Madame Mirabelle. He said he was sorry their accommodation was so restricted, but if she were to accept Madame Mirabelle's offer of a room, she would be able to keep all her possessions together and relieve the young man next door of housing them any longer.

The weekend passed without incident, but Thomas had a strange feeling that he did not wish to discuss the girl with Emma; he felt the uncertainty that a skater feels, having been warned that the ice is thin in places and may give way. He was edgy and he was quiet. He went down to his club but he was not wholly happy there. Sensitive to an unusually high degree he could define nothing more than a "feeling in the air." He noticed members' eyes resting thoughtfully upon him and when he went into the whist room there were several invitations to him to play.

A note told him that Messrs. Melbury would see him

on Tuesday morning at ten with their client Miss Nokomis Pennyform. "Emma, my dear, I have a feeling that I am unable to explain, that I should prefer to be alone with Nokomis on our visit to Mr. Melbury this time. Are you agreeable to this?"

Emma was agreeable; she neither liked nor disliked the girl, she only felt a great thankfulness that she was not sleeping in the house, which she too, on her part, found inexplicable.

All went well in the office in Red Lion Square, for twenty minutes or so, while the position was made quite clear to the girl. There were several documents to sign, which she did in big sprawling handwriting with Mr. Melbury junior coming in from the next-door office to witness the signatures. At the end Mr. Melbury senior said: "My dear Major, I have an apology to make." He drew from his desk drawer the worn-looking velvet case containing the pearl necklace that he had been shown upon his first visit to the office. Mr. Melbury opened it and showed the contents to remind Thomas. And astonishingly Nokomis leaned over in front of Thomas and said, putting out her hand, "Mine!"

Mr. Melbury snapped it shut, glaring at the girl for her lack of manners. "No," he said curtly, "not yours, I am afraid. . . ." He put down the case on the desk and from among other papers he drew an already prepared sheet upon which was a short statement to the effect that he had handed over the pearls, until recently the possession of Eleanor Dyce, known as Pennyform, to her son Thomas Nateby-Dyce. As he was passing it across to Thomas and reaching for the quill in order that he might sign at the bottom of the sheet, Nokomis' hand shot out and snatched up the case. She clasped it to her breast and pirouetted round the room while Mr. Melbury stared at her in indignant astonishment.

"Mine, mine, mine," she hummed. "Eleanor lent them

61

to me once, she said they would be mine. She said so. She said the Inguta moonstone would be mine, too. Where is it, Mr. Solicitor?"

Mr. Melbury took no notice but calmly wrote some memoranda for himself.

Dear God! The Inguta moonstone! Thomas knew where it was but he also knew where it should be: in the strong room of Messrs. Dixon, Brooks & Dixon in Chancery Lane.

Mr. Melbury held out his hand coldly. "Give them to me please." She said nothing but swerved evasively away. Mr. Melbury's temper was rising. He came out from behind his desk and approached her, but she gave him a violent push for which he was very far from being prepared; the force of the propulsion and astonishment sent him flying backward into the clerk's standing desk that stood out a little way from the wall. The desk went crashing back against the wall with a great clatter and Mr. Melbury junior and a clerk came rushing in to find Mr. Melbury senior lying backward across his desk in disarray and severe shock.

But the girl, expecting a blow from the angry young men, threw herself at him in full combat and there was suddenly a surprising state of affray. Thomas being of the school that "never raises his hand against a woman" kicked the case of pearls across the room out of the way and endeavored to pull Mr. Melbury from beneath the struggle which had assumed an aspect of indecency.

To Thomas it was more distressing than anything that happened at the town of Dadur when Major Dyce's party advanced upon the assaulting Brahoes; to him, that was normal, but this fracas was freakish.

She had been laughing hysterically but now that the timid clerk had applied himself to helping Mr. Melbury senior to extricate himself, her laughter turned to shouts and the shouts to screams. She was slippery, but as Mr. Melbury senior hobbled to his swivel desk chair the clerk was released to help Mr. Melbury junior. "Take her away," Mr. Melbury shouted above the din, "lock her in the outhouse!"

This sent her into full-scale hysteria, but now two other members of the staff appeared and the four men carried her, like a sack of potatoes and showing an immoderate amount of limbs and underwear, from the room.

For a few moments Mr. Melbury seemed undone, his elbows upon the desk and his head in his hands. "Never," he was murmuring, "never in all my sixty-one years at this desk . . . never . . . except once. . . ." He raised his head and looked at Thomas who had righted the clerk's desk and was endeavoring to collect the papers that had been scattered about when the lid flew back.

"I am afraid, my good Major, that the girl is mentally deranged. Think you not? We have been given no intimation of this, have we? No. Too bad! I am afraid you have a most serious problem on your hands."

He enunciated the adjective clearly and Thomas was not slow to note it. He said that she had been here nearly a week and during that time there had been no sign of the condition they had witnessed. Their neighbors on either side of them in Buck's Walk had, indeed, taken to the girl, one had given her temporary sleeping accommodation and the offer of work in her millinery showroom and the other, a young man who lived next door but one, had housed her baggage at great inconvenience to himself. "I should be deeply grieved if these kind neighbors were to be subjected to the same treatment as your good self," Thomas said anxiously.

He noticed the velvet-covered case of the pearl necklace lying on the floor and retrieved it, putting it on the desk beside Mr. Melbury who opened it, and as he stared down at the pearls he mopped his face with the spotless pocket handkerchief he had drawn from his breast pocket. "Would your mother have lent these pearls to the girl?"

Thomas leaned over and looked at them closely. "Strings of pearls greatly resemble one another," he said, "I think that these are the pearls my mother always wore from the onyx clasp. She was given some by my father's relations in Hampstead when she was twenty-one . . . but I could not swear to it in a court of law. I cannot see my mother, even at this distance in time, taking them off and lending them to anybody."

This in no way cheered Mr. Melbury, he was intensely gloomy but explained that in the course of his career he had had one such client, a lively woman and good enough in her way when she was behaving normally. "But unfortunately she was a prey to what in those days was often referred to as 'possession by the devil' and had to be 'put away' for months at a time, poor woman. Alas, the poor soul lived to a ripe old age. In the end the devil possessed her entirely; she was never able to walk abroad by herself and finally she was locked away for good. I was a very young man when this decision was made and I had to deal with the power of attorney; I have never been able to forget it."

"This Nokomis is going to become an apprentice in the workroom of my neighbor, a French woman who took refuge here after her family were guillotined in ninety-four. I could not bear for her kind offer to be rewarded by a scene such as we have just witnessed. Madame Mirabelle is in her eighties. I feel sure we must cancel this plan, but what can I do with the girl as an alternative?"

Mr. Melbury had carefully folded his handkerchief

and slipped it neatly back into his breast pocket; he was recovering rapidly, Thomas was relieved to notice.

He reached for the quill again and handed it to Thomas: "Take these pearls, anyway."

"I would like to give them to my wife," Thomas said as he sanded his signature.

"I would not do that for the moment, Major, were I in your position. The sight of the necklace on another woman's throat might spark off a scene such as we have just experienced, think you not?"

Slowly and thoughtfully Thomas slipped them into his tail pocketm

"I must not keep you any longer, my good sir. I can but thank you for your forbearance; we have had more than our fair amount of your time this morning. As I see it now, this girl is my problem; I have inherited much that is good. I feel that I must treat her as an inheritance and that I must take the bad with the good." He bowed himself out and as he crossed the hall to the clerk's office he saw the office boy letting in the next clients at the front door.

He looked round the clerk's office. Young Melbury was there, looking for something in a file. "Our clerk is out in the square searching for Miss Pennyform."

With great dignity, almost as though he had been expecting what had occurred, Thomas let himself out of the door and stood for a moment or two at the top of the steps, looking out over the square. In medieval times was there a knight, whose banner bore the red lion, stabbed to death in the square, Thomas thought idly? Or was there an ale house of that name established there in the days of Chaucer? There was no young girl about, demented or otherwise.

He set off for Hampstead on this delightful morning;

it had all been a nightmare and now he was free. He had no doubts; she had passed as a nightmare passes. He knew that the important thing about nightmares was that they *did* pass; they went, as the night dissolves into the day.

He dropped into a secondhand bookshop in Campden Town, a shop which, over the years, he would drag himself past, longing to enter but knowing he could not afford to do so. This morning he brooded for an hour and finally bought for Amelia a copy of a book about a little boy in India, *Little Henry and his Bearer* by Mary Martha Sherwood, which she would much enjoy, being passionately interested in what she thought of as that magic land.

Dear Amelia, he thought as he mounted the final steep slope to Buck's Walk. For the six days of the nightmare, Amelia's mouth had literally hung open slightly in admiration (as her father's had for some minutes but not in admiration) of Miss Pennyform. She had overheard from her parents that the girl was partly Red Indian and the name Pennyform thrown in, as it were, amused her greatly.

As he approached his homestead he remembered about the baggage, still stacked there against the wall of the obliging young businessman. They must no longer take advantage of his good nature; he would pay to have the baggage removed to a storeroom; he had in fact this morning passed one such warehouse in Campden Town that he had himself used on his return from India for several months, the months of courting Emma, in fact.

He knocked upon Mr. Ramble-Smith's front door to tell him that the baggage would be called for, but of course there was no answer because he was at work and the man servant came only in the evenings when the master was there.

There was a satisfactory smell of roasting as he entered his own home and Emma sat in the back garden with her work.

"Ah, you are back, my dearest . . . and. . . ?"

Smiling, Thomas hitched the knees of his splendid new trousers carefully before sitting on the garden seat. He threw up a hand and clicked his fingers, saying nothing but sufficiently demonstrating that Nokomis was no longer with them. And how he respected her when she made no reply, adhering admirably to their pact of not talking about her, of not lashing themselves into discussion as to whether or not she was a suitable companion for Amelia.

She smiled too, the same kind of smile as Thomas' own, as though she had known all along that it was a nightmare and that it had passed.

She went on with her work and Thomas reached for the *Times* and opened it.

In the evening it poured with rain and against the kitchen wall from the kitchen on the other side came tapping. Bess, washing up the supper dishes, ran into the drawing room wiping her hands on her apron, "Madame Mirabelle; she is tapping, tapping." The old lady had done this only once in Bess' time and it was when she fell and twisted her ankle. It must be urgent.

Both Thomas and Emma went in, thinking that she would be in the same sort of trouble and thus not discussing first what their answer would be if it concerned the visitor. She reported that Nokomis was not with her, was she with them? They exchanged glances, Emma leaving it to Thomas to answer. Thomas was sure there was nothing to be gained by not telling the truth and he did so. But not the whole truth. There had been "something of a scene" this morning at the solicitors. Nokomis had become upset, indeed hysterical. She had not waited for Thomas to accompany her but had excitably rushed out into the square alone. Thomas had looked for her in the square, but she was not to be found. "I feared she was being naughty and it appears that she is not yet recovered."

"But if she does not return she will be a young woman, a stranger to the streets of London, wandering around and prey to any of these unruly characters we have on the streets after dark."

Thomas said the thought made him wretched, tomorrow he would go to Bow Street and ask that the constables be on the lookout for this striking-looking American.

"Tomorrow, Major!" Madame Mirabelle cried. "Tonight, surely!"

Avoiding Emma's shocked look, he said he would go at once; there would be no omnibus at this hour, but he would put on his waterproof cape and walk down the hill, possibly he would pick up a hackney at South End Green.

Thus Thomas, wearing his old trousers, returning home soaking wet about the legs and feet after midnight, was able to salve his own conscience and, better still, satisfy Madame Mirabelle as to the efforts made on behalf of his "relative."

Nokomis remained invisible while her "anxious relatives" almost forgot her existence. Thomas gave Emma the pearls in the case and said he hoped she would wear them always, as his mother had done. This was not in truth a serious wish and Emma considered it a sentimental and transient fancy of the kind to which gentlemen are prone. Still, she was pleased with the pearls and at once put them around her neck.

Amelia had wanted to know, of course, where Nokomis was, immediately.

"She has left us, Amelia."

"But why, Mama?"

"She cannot like us. She is a wild girl who has been left much on her own, neglected by her parents and befriended by your papa's mama only, an old lady. I do not think she can have had much sport in her short life."

"Do you mean, Mama, that she has gone off, on her own?"

"I would fain be able to tell you where she is gone, dearest girl, but I, and your papa, are completely at a loss. She vanished from the office of Mr. Melbury, the solicitors."

This was all relayed to her friend Roderick as they walked down the hill to school. "Mind you, Roddy, I can quite understand her not liking being with us. We lead very dull, quiet lives." Amelia could write on Roderick's mind as upon a slate, he had few ideas of his own but he thoroughly assimilated Amelia's ideas. Through constant keen observation of what went on in Amelia's mind he would never have said the Dyce family led dull and quiet lives.

"Besides," Amelia continued, "I daresay she had no wish to be a milliner despite the kindness of Madame Mirabelle."

"Is it not pleasant to be a milliner?"

"No!" Amelia screamed. "It is not. You work all day, all day, making hideous hats for frightful old women. And bonnets," she added. "They cost an awful lot of money. Girls do not buy hats like that but have to put up with simpler things, like this I have on, bought at Miss Helps in the village for five shillings!"

"But is it not of interest to work in a shop like that?"

"Of course not! Soon she would have to live there, with all the other girls, and some of them are riffraff, I heard Madame tell Mama. Riffraff, she said! And they have their meals there and go on working sometimes till nine o'clock at night when the customer wants a hat for the races next day!"

"Why do they not order them in time so that the girls do not work all day and night?"

Amelia shrieked with laughter at Roderick's naïveté as she so often did. Roderick's mother did not approve of him; when he asked questions, she told him nothing except to go away.

VI

NOW that Thomas had given up his work at the bookshop in St. Paul's Churchyard he had a good deal more time to spare since the new library plans were advancing but slowly and the work at present consisted in committee meetings to the extent of two a week and further subcommittees at which ideas were pooled under the auspices of the amazingly clever and lively Mr. Carlyle. So there was more time to spare for visits to the Far East Club, and Thomas was able to increase his acquaintanceship and spend some pleasant hours in the card room.

When nine days had passed without any news of Nokomis, Thomas had not quite forgotten her because he wanted to carry out his plan for removing her baggage from the care of young Mr. Ramble-Smith. That gentleman, however, was proving unaccountably hard to get. Time and time again Thomas knocked at his front door to put forward his suggestion regarding the storage of the baggage, but always there was no reply. The baggage was still there, in the little hall, because twice the door had been opened by the man servant who said the master was, first, away and next, out. As Thomas was unwilling to leave a message he slipped a note, later on, into the letter box suggesting that he, Thomas, remove the baggage at his own expense. But so far there had been no reply.

Thus he was not quite so entirely carefree regarding the wildcat Nokomis nine days after her disappearance as he had been the two days immediately afterward.

As he entered the club he followed Albert Niton and they greeted one another enthusiastically as they hung up their hats. Thomas resolved upon the moment to tell Albert about his problem; it might amuse him and he might even have some comment to make which would be helpful since it was understood between himself and Emma that they were not discussing the Nokomis subject at all.

"Good to see you, Thomas," Albert Niton said as he clapped Thomas upon the shoulder. "Come to the smoke room, old man, I want a word with you."

As they rolled their cigars between their fingers, lying back in their armchairs, Albert said: "What happened to that first wife of yours, Thomas? The Lady Mary of such beauteous appearance?" As a soldier of his quality Thomas had complete control over himself; there was not the slightest twitch of his fingers on the cigar, not the jerk of the foot on the leg crossed over the other leg. There was even a pause as he lighted his cigar from the proffered tinder.

"She died of cholera."

"Um?"

"On a voyage home on leave."

"Um, Oman, at the base of the Persian Gulf, South Arabia?"

"Muscat, to be precise. How did you know?"

"I heard."

"It's a hell of a place, but of course, you will know it as well as I do, coming home on that new mail steamer from Bombay."

"I never went ashore."

"I bet you didn't; it's not fit for man or beast, if you ask me. Not English man or beast anyway."

For a long silent minute neither spoke. Thomas stared at the tip of his cigar. "What about it?" he said at last.

"I'd like to say: nothing, and leave it at that. But I can't, Thomas."

"Why not?"

"Because, and I want you to believe it . . . we haven't seen one another for a long gap of time, but I feel the same way about you that I always have, ever since we were cadets together."

"For God's *sake*, Bertie, what's coming?"

"You may well ask. Thomas, I've got to say this; I hate it and so will you."

"Well, let's have it then!"

"Some drunken bored fool on that ship you came home on, the *Berenice*, was it not? He made up a ghastly little verse:

> Thomas Dyce
> He wasn't nice
> I'll say it twice
> He wasn't nice
> He pushed his Lady Mary
> in the Ocean.

I'm sorry, Thomas," he said hurriedly and leaned forward to put his hand on Thomas' knee.

Thomas looked round; two members were in the process of arguing in a far corner of the room and

73

another was absorbed in a book, but Albert had kept his voice low, nobody could have heard.

"It's catching, there lies the nastiness. Once you have caught it, you remember it, it floats into the mind unpremeditated; it is not a *thought*, Thomas, it is a *jingle*."

"Well, do you want to hear if I did or not?"

For a moment Albert looked wild, like a scared horse. He simply stammered and did not succeed in getting anything intelligible out of his mouth.

"I could well have done so," Thomas said calmly and knocked half an inch of ash off his cigar with the tip of his finger. "I know she was the most disliked woman on any station we ever went to. She had the quality of making other people feel . . . feel unremarkable, of no account to anyone. She was—not a nice woman. I thought she was a goddess when I was young. I worshipped her. After five years of marriage. . . ." There was a long pause.

"You saw the light?"

"Not suddenly. I fought it down."

"The truth?"

"Yes. I hit back at it; I was hitting back at the truth most of those five years. Not believing. Not believing." A long silence.

Would he never speak again? Albert spoke for him: "So you drowned her. Well, I would probably have taken half that time."

"But I did not drown her, Bertie. I . . . did . . . not . . . drown her. And nor would you have done when it came to the point. I was sorry for her."

"Why?"

"She was a lost soul, contrary to all appearances. But I shall not be disloyal to her again. I do not wish to speak of her anymore, Bertie."

"All right," Albert agreed readily. "You won't hear another word about it from me. But I shall stamp on that

74

dreadful little ditty next time I hear it. And if I hear it
once again after that next time. . . ."

"Yes?"

"I'll see the beggar who recited it has his teeth knocked
down his throat."

Long pause.

"How do you like these cigars, Thomas?"

"They're pleasant. And Albert. . . ."

"Yes?"

"Thank you!"

He walked all the way home, arriving after midnight.
All the way he thought about that trip home from India,
his last. The heat had been intolerable, many people
simply lay gasping on their bunks, but until evening it
was too hot to stay on deck which had inadequate protection from the sun for the whole passenger list. Thus a
mere handful of indifferent people wandered about the
decks for exercise and paid little attention to others.
Nobody, in that heat, in the Gulf of Oman cared where
the Lady Mary Dyce was, though she had been intimately
discussed and, indeed, watched during the crossing of
the Indian Ocean.

Sailing from Muscat on December 8, the ship arrived
in London on January 18, giving passengers time to
make lifelong friendships which were over and done
with as they sailed through the Straits of Dover. An
absurd and libelous ditty, however, could lurk in-
destructible and deathless. And from what source did
this ditty emanate? Why, from the obvious fact that the
Lady Mary was no longer a passenger upon the *Berenice*;
her husband sailed on from Muscat alone, her absence
being noted only when they had sailed out of the really
destructive heat into cooler climes.

She died of cholera in Muscat and was buried quickly

there they understood. She had had the symptoms for several days, just after leaving Bombay, in fact, but being the valiant and tenacious woman she undoubtedly was, she endured it. But how was it possible to endure cholera standing up? Eating meals? Strolling about the decks? Talking to Thomas . . . so in the amoeba of an otherwise empty mind, and there were dozens of empty minds on that vessel, this deathless fugue germinated.

> Thomas Dyce
> He wasn't nice
> I'll say it twice. . . .

He had heard it once, accidentally, of course. And that was why, later, he sent in his papers, left the army and changed his name. He even invented a dirge for himself:

> I'm Thomas Nateby
> Please don't hate me
> I did not throw my Lady
> In the Ocean.

But how could it be proved, yea or nay?

And then his reason was saved by a bath chair. He went to Sidmouth between cliffs beside the south coast of Devon to try and think up a plan for his future in that soft healing air. Emma was staying with her great-aunt at the Bedford Hotel; pushing the chair with Great-Aunt in it up the western slope out of the town, a stone of very small size entered Emma's pretty slipper and hurt. She stooped to take off her slipper and toss the pebble out and in doing so let go of the handle of the bath chair for a moment, a split second only and the chariot was off down the hill with the gallant major walking up, there to stop it and also Great-Aunt's screams of fright at the moment when it reeled on one wheel prior to tipping over.

That was how it started and within three months there was a pretty wedding at Sidmouth Church with a reception at the Bedford Hotel to which all Great-Aunt's old friends were asked; no one had any doubt whatever that Thomas and Emma would live happily ever after. And for the first eleven years they did live very happily indeed at Number 2 Buck's Walk.

Thomas, who had trudged through London home from the Far East Club with his head bent and his hands behind his back, looked, as he approached, at his delightful row of cottages in the moonlight. The window of Number 4 showed that there was a light inside, and as he stood fumbling in his pocket for the key of his own house, he heard peels of hysterical laughter mixed with louder male laughs. Mr. Ramble-Smith plus a wild oat, no doubt. There was something hideously familiar about that laugh, but Thomas did what he so often recently had been obliged to do, he dismissed the thought from his mind. And other thoughts, too, which had been similarly dismissed for much longer time than this one.

Next day was another pleasant day and Emma was spending the most of it with a friend, so Thomas took the omnibus into town, called at the British Museum for some catalogues he needed, called in at The Lamb for a meal of port and oysters, then set forth on the walk back home. The day warmed up considerably, and he had not been sitting long in the garden before his head went against the back of the rattan chair he had brought from India, and he fell asleep.

He was awakened by a kiss upon the forehead and a hand smoothing his hair. "Guess who?" He felt violently irritated; he was sitting in full view of the kitchen window through which Bess would undoubtedly be watching and the tiny garden was overlooked, at an angle, by the houses on either side. She jumped eagerly round in front of him and he made a poor attempt at being pleased to see her. But to appear annoyed or angry would not do.

"Well, here I am and I do hope I have caused you no distress, dearest Uncle."

"Do not call me uncle," he snapped, "since I am not your uncle, nor anything near your uncle or uncle by marriage or even by adoption."

"I see you are cross with me," she murmured contritely. She sank down upon the grass; she was wearing a gown of silk taffeta in a loud check with a vest of net, a high collar and a tiny black velvet ribbon round her throat. She arranged her skirt so that her pantaloons just showed and the tips of both her red slippers.

"I know perfectly well with whom you have been, Nokomis, but I do not wish either that my wife Emma or my daughter Amelia should know. I beg of you not to tell them."

"You cannot know where I have been all this time, for we have been in Brighton for a week; Mr. Ramble-Smith took a week off from his employment and we went on the Brighton Coach. There was no time to tell you and as each day I intended to return, there was no sense in writing to say I was coming when I would be there before the letter."

"I am going to wash my hands of you, Nokomis, because I am in no mind to look after you, even if this would be contrary to my poor mother's wishes. Indeed, my poor mother could not know the circumstances in which I live, with a wife so much younger than myself, still a girl, in fact, and a daughter of eleven."

Nokomis sat looking sulky, fiddling with a scrap of loose skin round her thumbnail.

"And furthermore, I do not for one moment believe that you are only eighteen. I believe you are every day of thirty." If it did not frighten Nokomis, his remark frightened himself, it came suddenly out of his mouth, straight from his instinct and he had not intended it. He waited for an explosion; there was none, though her face was riven with an ugly grimace. "You are cruel!"

He had not really meant thirty, but he did not correct himself. Instead he said that he did not know at all why she was here and he would seriously like to know her intentions. He would gladly pay her fare back to where she came from.

". . . And the pearls?" she asked with a sly sideways look.

Yes, he would willingly have "thrown in" the pearls for good measure, but as he had rather formally and grandly endowed Emma with them he could not now reverse his gesture and ask for them to be returned, even though Emma did not, evidently, treasure them greatly. There was always the Inguta moonstone gem (where was it, by the way—oh, in his collar box in the left-hand top drawer of his dressing chest) by which he was exceedingly impressed. He would, however, much prefer not to have the gem if it meant not having Nokomis with them. On the other hand, he would like to keep it out of respect for and in memory of his father. Though he and Emma had but one ewe lamb between them, she was a sturdy one to whom they might well look for a strong line in posterity.

"The pearls belong to my wife, by my mother's wish. You think you can put anything that comes into your head down to my mother's wish, do you not? You can invent a pack of lies that can never be repudiated, so you think you have a hold over me. In fact, I believe I can turn you from my house by law since there is the fact that

79

as a woman of loose morals you are endangering the morals of my daughter, or would, if I allowed you to stay."

Nokomis sat back on her heels, rearranging herself; she was quite calm, but the expression on her face was malicious in the extreme; she was hitting back with a vengeance that was destructive. "I cannot go back home . . . I have been deported but because of the respect due to my grandfather Pennyform back home, it has been done inconspicuously, as they call it. And also owing to my age, and I am under twenty-one, whatever you say; I can prove it with the copy of my birth certificate they gave me; it was written up by those clever lawyers in America that I was 'sent to be in the care of relatives in England.' "

"Why was I not informed?"

Nokomis threw back her head and laughed scornfully. "I said they were clever! Would you have accepted me if you had been told?"

Thomas scowled deeply and wondered whether the Melburys had been party to this cunning scheme. If this affair had degenerated into a matter of guile, then Thomas must play it with corresponding treachery if he could, indeed, summon even more to his aid.

Upon the whole, it must be said with reservations: Good soldiers make poor cheats. Though by no means aware of this, he made a try, however, and now brimming with determination, did not know how to start.

His suggestion, no, command, that Nokomis should be sent round to Madame Mirabelle as soon as the fly brought her back from work, and, almost upon her knees, beg forgiveness for her deplorable behavior in the face of Madame's kindness, was agreed. It was also, surprisingly, agreed that Nokomis would beg that she could start boarding at the shop rather than sleeping in

80

Madame's house until Miss Craskie had returned from her convalescence.

"As good neighbors, I shall ask that our servant Bess be allowed to take your place in the next door house, during the hours of darkness. She will make a much better job of it than poor old Craskie anyway," he added. "If she makes any bones about it, Madame Mirabelle I mean, tell her you will ask me to come in and explain to her."

Nokomis leaned forward with yet another hideous grimace upon her overmobile face: "You don't mean you'll tell her. . . ?"

"Leave it to my discretion," Thomas snapped.

"Very well," she returned. "I quite understand you, Unk, I mean Major. You may as well understand me."

"Pray continue." Thomas' lip curled with a most unusually sinister sneer.

"I shall put all the cards I have upon the table. I intend to marry Dandylion, so there!"

Thomas cleared his throat which gave him time to see the point which, not inexplicably, he had missed. Fortunately this extra moment helped and he realized that the name of the Oxford graduate next door was Daniel, the name Dandylion doubtless born of love play.

"I wish you luck," he said with dignity and rose from the cane chair, and as he made the few steps toward the house he turned and said: "But I should be aware of the lions, if I were you." His remark was not without point because Daniel Ramble-Smith had a veritable troop of possessive relatives, not only aunts, but great-aunts whose only beloved nephew and heir their Daniel was. Nothing less than marriage into the aristocracy would be allowed. He entered his domain by the garden door and shut it very gently without the slightest smile upon his face.

81

The clock was striking four and he put on his hat and went out of the front door and down the lane to meet Amelia and Roderick whom he could see far down the hill approaching very slowly and playing a game of bumping into one another with their school satchels.

"Papa, why is Nokomis sleeping in the house next door but one, and why does she not spend the day with Mama now?"

"Because she prefers to sleep next door but one on the other side and I have left her at our house now." Thomas did not hesitate a second before answering the question. Amelia was undoubtedly an enfant terrible, but he and Emma took great pains not to allow her to think so. The more awful the question, the more quickly and soberly and uninterestingly was it answered by her parents.

"Oh," she said and turned her full penetrating gaze upon her father. To forestall a further question Thomas chatted on about Nokomis missing the company of people her own age and how it was possible that she would join Madame Mirabelle's establishment at once and would start to learn a trade. She must understand that though Nokomis spoke a kind of English she was a foreign girl and she must realize that foreigners had different habits of life from ourselves; neither better nor worse but different. And it was important that someone of Amelia's age should realize these differences and tolerate them.

"What is tolerate?"

"To put up with. That is to *understand* and put up with."

"Why?"

"Because that is decent behavior. And don't ask me why one should behave decently, think it out for yourself."

82

She turned to Roderick: "You see, Roderick?" as though she had proved something.

"Are you putting up with Nokomis sleeping with Mr. Ramble-Smith?"

"Nokomis is grown-up, she belongs to herself, not to your mama and me."

"Then she may do as she pleases?"

"Up to a point."

"What point?"

"We are back to the decent behavior point, Amelia. It is very bad manners that Nokomis should have removed herself from the kind services of Madame Mirabelle without, as I understand it, any warning. I have left the house at present to give Nokomis a chance, when Madame's fly arrives, to make her sincere apologies to Madame, and I hope she does so, but I shall sit down here on the grass for another half hour or so." He pulled a periodical from his pocket and said that he had today bought it and he would, if they would like it, read the last installment of *Master Humphrey's Clock* to them.

They would like it and sat down upon the turf beside the stony footpath with their arms wrapped round their knees, and listened.

The Far East Club did not stand directly upon the flagged pavement of the square, a semicircular gravel drive entered by a large wrought-iron gate stood between the building and the pavement. There were posts to which the horses of members who were not staying long in the club could be tied, and mounting stones. A few members had brought their grooms with them from India. Some had become so attached to their masters that they had left their native land forever to follow their masters to retirement in England. Rarely more than one or two would be seen squatting, small colorful objects, cross-legged upon the gravel beside their master's horse.

One of these syces knew Thomas and each time he passed would have his damson eyes fixed upon his as he entered the drive and walked in front of him to the steps. These grooms were very similar in appearance, but Thomas knew he had seen this one before if only because of the piercing look he gave Thomas. But he had no idea when or where; what interested him more was whose syce was he?

"I trust, Thomas," Albert Niton said one evening when they were alone in the washroom, "I sincerely hope you have not given too much thought to what I said to you the other night. I meant it when I said I should never mention it again and the very next time I see you, here I am, talking about it still."

"None of us ex-Anglo-Indians can cut ourselves clear of that subcontinent, that's the truth; it gets hold of a man; we sit round yarning and anecdoting like a gaggle of old spinsters who have been at the same boarding school. There's a syce out there now, stares at me as though I'd risen from the dead."

"Probably thinks you have!"

They were strolling across the hall now.

Albert laughed. "What price he was on duty and took part in that awful pigsticking route at Loodianah? By gad! Out hunting with the Quorn this winter I couldn't help thinking what a mild and gentlemanly sport I was at, after Loodianah, eh?"

VII

AN old lady of eighty-two might well be tired out after a long day flattering her customers, scolding her staff, pinning ribbon, roses, bunches of flowers and fruit on to hats, then tearing them off because they did not suit the customer or looked ugly. During the day she had drunk tea three times and eaten some crystalized fruit from a box given her by a customer who did not like them. She was now ready for one of the dainty but appetizing little dinners that Miss Craskie would have prepared for her had she been there. Since Miss Craskie was not quite recovered, she had to forego her meal and now sat perched upon a thronelike Louis XV chair, her legs being much too short to reach the ground from it; she placed her tiny feet daintily on a French embroidered footstool, folded her hands and waited for an explanation from Nokomis Pennyform.

This poured out in the particularly fulsome manner which Nokomis thought (erroneously as it happened) suitable to the occasion. She regretted so very much having to leave Madame's hospitable shelter without any explanation. Very many smooth and creamy words went into this, however, while the little old lady steadily regarded her with exceptionally bright eyes shining out

85

at her from the gray, wrinkled little face. She was clearly not satisfied.

But, Nokomis went on, fortunately there were kind and observant people in this hard cold world and Mr. Ramble-Smith was one who had observed the suffering she endured.

"Suffering?"

"From the Major, from Major Dyce. Major Nateby-Dyce . . ." She endeavored to wipe the total noncomprehension from Madame's face by adding, "Your neighbor, I mean."

"*Suffering?*" Madame frowned, still puzzled. "I do not understand."

"Ah Madame, is your own youth so far away that you cannot remember? But as a pretty girl, you must have been, from time to time, molested."

Madame repeated the word in French to make sure she had heard aright. *"Mais non!"* she exclaimed, *"jamais de la vie! Molestir? Non!"*

Nokomis shrugged then allowed her hand to fall open upon her knees still clad in their checked taffetas.

"Tell me more."

"Poor man, that cold fish of a wife, Emma. I bear him no grudge, I understand." Nokomis looked down sympathetically at her own pretty hands. "Mr. Ramble-Smith took me away from the danger; we went to Brighton and he showed me how, just how, I should fend off the Major's attacks."

"Indeed. It might also be helpful to me to learn how to resist these violent . . . sexual attacks."

"Sexual?" Nokomis shuddered with distaste.

Madame pulled a handkerchief from her belt and touched her eyes with it.

"But I was really frightened," Nokomis assured her. "With his reputation. . . ."

Madame stopped dabbing her eyes lest she should miss one syllable. "Reputation?"

"Throwing his wife overboard like that in the Indian Ocean! The Lady Mary!"

Madame nodded sympathetically. "Oh, yes. Yes, indeed. So, so *méchant!*"

"You knew?"

"Of course."

Nokomis was suddenly washed out, like an empty gun she had no more ammunition left for the moment. She wilted. She murmured that since Madame had accepted her apology she hoped she might be allowed to stay. . . .

But the little old lady interrupted her to say that now she had revealed herself, Nokomis, that is, Madame thought it a better plan that a mature young woman should have more freedom than was available in this little enclave. She suggested that the fly be recalled from the stables along in Willow Road and that she be driven to her house adjoining the millinery establishment in the West End at once with her immediate requirements. She would arrange for her baggage from Mr. Ramble-Smith's care to be sent down later by wagon. She was convinced that Nokomis would be much happier with girls of . . . her own age. They would be there now, her apprentices, about to partake of their supper, so she advised Nokomis to hurry. And Nokomis, surprised that Madame had found it in her to forgive her behavior to date, thought it discreet to do exactly what Madame suggested . . . for the present.

Emotionally she snatched at Madame's hand, fondled it for a moment then kissed it. Madame drew her hand back and used it to press her handkerchief to her face and Nokomis hurried from the room.

Madame put both her hands to her face. But she was not crying, she was weeping with laughter.

Though she had known them and loved them for eleven years, Madame Mirabelle had never referred to her neighbors as Thomas and Emma but always as Major and Mrs. Dyce. Some of her French friends, in an attempt to keep up with the times, would address one another as *citoyen*, but Madame hoped the detested word would never pass her own lips. She now appraised aloud to Emma the situation from her bedroom window. It was that Miss Pennyform would be taking up her residence this evening at her, Madame's, establishment in Oxford Street and that she would be starting at once her apprenticeship. That Madame would order a wagon to call for her baggage and thus that young gentleman, Mr. Ramble-Smith, would be relieved of the baggage which he had kindly stored.

Mr. Ramble-Smith overheard all this but such a coward soul was his that he dared not do other than stand out of sight by his window allowing his inamorata to be pushed hither and thither at the hands of bossy women in much the same way as he was himself. Alas, it was by no means the first of his affairs that had been quickly and competently dissipated. Every time he would issue to himself the comforting little valedictory amen: "It was lovely while it lasted."

The Misses Eglingtons, between the Nateby-Dyces' and Mr. Ramble-Smith, could not both together see, from the extreme edge of their window, exactly what was happening. But they would take it in turn to report as best they could, correctly, upon events. Number 1 heard Madame Mirabelle's voice and Number 2 could just discern her fly. Neither saw nor heard Mr. Ramble-Smith and assumed that Madame Mirabelle was taking it upon herself to protect Mr. Ramble-Smith's interests and dismiss the American girl whose voice came so piercingly through the party wall. They both assumed that the

88

young couple next door had been found *in flagrante delicto* and enjoyed their salacious thoughts thoroughly. And when the fly passed the window on the way back into Well Walk to town, they saw Miss Pennyform looking meek as she was driven away; they felt deflated.

Later Thomas and Emma went to bed, drawing their curtains round the bed more closely than ever and, whispering, talked the situation out. At last, after keeping silence all these days, they came together mentally. And when they had chewed the situation to rags and it was two o'clock in the morning, they were still not ready for sleep. What would happen next? Though Madame Mirabelle had been a wonderful friend to them, they were still quite unable to see the situation developing into an ordinary affair, with Nokomis Pennyform settling down into merely "one of the girls in the showroom." What worried them most was the effect she was having upon Amelia who reacted almost instantaneously to atmosphere. Hand in hand they lay staring up into the darkness, the working of their brains almost audible.

"I must tell you, dearest," Emma whispered, "I would rather be as we were. . . ."

"As we were when?"

"Before."

"I had this premonition, Emma. I had seen the advertisement for Thomas Dyce, as you know; I tried to ignore it because I knew . . . I felt . . ."

"What?"

"I cannot say quite what but I knew I was happy *then* and I know that with our new circumstances, I am not happy *now*. Something has, do not laugh, but I can only say . . . befouled our nest."

He longed wretchedly to be able to tell her what he had vowed never to tell her. The story of that last journey home from India in the mail steamer *Berenice*. Before their marriage he had long consulted himself as to whether he would say more than that his first wife had died of cholera. He decided finally against it because Emma was an exceptionally happy and contented person and he wished nothing to cloud this in the new start he was making by marrying her.

To tell her all now might be to cloud her life over with a worry which up to now had been unnecessary; to pull over her such dread and pessimism as he had gradually cast off as he put time between them and himself. But still he longed to tell her, to recite that hideous little ditty which had recently been told to him and so share, selfishly, his anguish.

Emma said, "I do not believe in curses but I think I believe that the stars, in their courses, may stand in one's favor or to one's great advantage . . . as may be, this way or that way. And if that is so, oh Thomas! we are enduring a bad patch now. My string of lovely pearls, your Indian Inguta jewel, your inheritance. . . . I would barter the lot to be as we were, to have you as plain Thomas Dyce, working again in the dear old bookshop in St. Paul's Churchyard."

"And not a sign that I am a member of a fine Far East Club?"

"Not that either, if it is part of us, as new people."

After a long pause Thomas, who had been weighing up the pros and cons agreed, even though he had remet one of his best friends, Albert Niton . . . No, not that either.

"There is one scrap of comfort," Emma remembered. "Only one year and a little over and we will be able to send Amelia to St. Agnes."

This was the school in Essex to which Emma's parents sent her and where she spent a happy four years. "It is understood that an only child can benefit very much from being at boarding school but now much more so than the average child, our Amelia who, in the last few weeks, has shown herself to be precocious in the extreme and imitative to a degree. She turns me cold in her unconscious manner of Nokomis."

"What would be best for us all were if Nokomis herself were to go to St. Agnes, but of course they would not have a girl of her age, whatever it may be. No, Emma, much as I abhor the idea of doing so, I must go again to see the Melburys and see if I can discover whether or not they had any idea that she was 'deported,' as she said. I doubt even whether they will receive me civilly after Nokomis' behavior."

VIII

PRIVATE AND PERSONAL

"My very dear Thomas,"

I am addressing you thus because your mother always spoke of you thus and for all the years she lived here, in this outskirt of New York City, I was her friend and counselor. I am a lawyer by profession and as a young man I came from Ireland as an immigrant to join my father who also came as an immigrant in the very early days. I have never returned to my country because the warfare, strife and sheer hunger by which that dear land of mine is riven, is unbearable.

I am not writing to you about your mother, and/or myself but I think it may interest you to hear that your mother bitterly regretted her departure from England and you, whom she said no longer needed her, in the wake of the adventure called Pennyform; she had ceased to love him even before they settled down together but in her own curious way she remained passionately loyal to him, though she would never marry him even when she was free to do so by her husband's death. She gave her life to the Pennyform family and she was finally left with not much money beyond her own, and the girl Nokomis, who is old Pennyform's ill-gotten grandchild.

I am given to understand that our old firm, Killarney, Gritley & Co. had deemed it the best plan to send this girl, in the absence of any other relative, to you. Eleanor died very quickly after a chill, a matter of two days; she had always had her Will prepared for the event and it seems that she was far too ill to discuss the future of Nokomis at any length.

So it is regarding this girl that I am writing to you, having requested your address from K.G. & Co. This child has led a fearful life, a to-and-fro tussle between a Red Indian tribe to which her father belonged and the Pennyforms whose "millions" they believed Nokomis should inherit, as the only living Pennyform offspring of any kind, legitimate or illegitimate. These Pennyform "millions" were, and still are, a myth. The old man had the bare bones of an astute business man but they were clad in far too many weaknesses, dishonesties and sheer silliness to have come to anything. He bought up the wildernesses but both wisely and foolish-ly; bedeviled, too, by the belief that one can buy good conditions HEREAFTER quite im-poverished him; in his very old age Eleanor had to keep him. R.I.P.

The appearance of the girl Nokomis is that of a grown woman approaching middle age; at fifteen she was already leading the life of, I cannot bring myself to write the word but I mean *woman of the world* you understand? The bit of education she had was not bad; during a period the Pennyforms gave her a home she was sent to a convent school, but in the end she had to leave because it was requested by the Mother Superior owing to "danger to other girls." When your mother finally rescued her she was badly damaged goods and the work your mother put into the eighteen months or so Nokomis was with her contributed to her weak state which culminated in her death from pneumonia.

Your mother insisted up to the last minute of her life that Nokomis was not wholly bad. She slips very easily into the role of Lady of Leisure and is only too ready to be waited upon and this should be heavily discouraged. It is essential that she be employed and kept at it and it is also essential to pay no attention to her own belief in her gentle origins. She is loud and vulgar, selfish, greedy, inconsiderate, dishonest, mercenary and ugly at times. But she is not stupid and her heart is not wholly hard. I think, given good conditions and some luck, she just might possibly survive in your world. She shows some talent in the matters of women's attire, I must tell you. From what I know of you "my very dear Thomas" you may be able to make something of her.

Having reached this point on my voyage through this letter, I have said what I set out to say, mainly for your guidance. But there is something else merely for your interest which has passed through my mind often during the days since Eleanor's death. It is that marvelous moonstone jewel given to her by your father. She would sometimes wear it when she was very low to remind her of "the happy times." And now I clearly remember that from time to time recently she had made remarks that were not like her at all. One was when she took it off after we had supper together one evening and held it up to the light: "I never had asthma," she said, "until I wore this." And once recently when she was feeling very low she said she had never really had any normal good fortune in this world after she was twenty-five. "I am ashamed of my very dear Thomas' mother. I hope he thinks I am dead, if he thinks of me at all." And again she said twice that she thought the Inguta moonstone was evil for all its beauty, she must see that it does not go to him when she was gone as she had previously willed it. She said she would auction it and in her last hours, when I saw her, she was raving before she gently died and she used a few of those words, moonstone and auction amongst them, I heard them.

I am assured by the Gritleys that the Inguta moonstone must go to you and I feel I should appraise you of this curious state of mind your mother was in regarding it. I know of no evil implications with this marvelous jewel. The Maharaja gave it to your father as a gesture of, shall we say, admiration and gratitude? So many Government officials failed to understand the natives, being too national for them. But your father saw things from their point of view, your mother said. "He had a heart," she told me.

95

It has taken me three days to complete this letter, I hope you will be able to read my shaky writing. If you hear no more from me you may know I shall have gone to join my dear Eleanor whom I was never wholly allowed in life. I am eighty-two. Perhaps I should inform you that the firm of Killarney, Gritley & Co. is the firm originated and founded by my father, whom I joined. Gritley came into the business through descendants of my sister who married a Gritley.

Next week Nokomis and I are to bid farewell. I shall not see her again in this life. I wish you well of her! I have hopes that time will quieten her and a happy marriage would be a Godsend.

With my good wishes, "my very dear Thomas," Sir,

Brian Killarney

This letter was addressed to Major Dyce at the solicitor's address in Red Lion Square and readdressed to him at Buck's Walk, Hampstead. It was undated. Thomas read it through three times carefully before showing it to Emma. "Keep it carefully, my dearest," Emma advised, "this may be of use to us."

"But shall I answer it?"

Emma considered. "It would appear to me that it would not be possible to answer it satisfactorily as things are at present. Have you noticed the expression upon the face of Madame Mirabelle? Like a pussycat."

"In what way, my love?"

"As though she harbored some secret satisfaction. I declare she is avoiding me as though she does not wish to discuss the wild girl with us."

"Not for the present, perhaps. But, Emma, my dear girl, what kindness that old woman is doing us! I cannot conceive or imagine how we should act in the predicament of our having Nokomis on our hands. I declare we have had the greatest good fortune in having our excellent neighbor so interested in our unwelcome visitor!"

"As we have not yet any means of knowing whether or not we are out of the wood, you must needs treasure this marvelously, indeed miraculously pertinent letter. Hide it, Thomas, hide it."

"I shall take it to the club and lock it in my locker in the portfolio in which I have stowed away all my personal papers, my dear."

Emma agreed that he should do that, but as she stitched away with bent head at her work she murmured that she could not yet feel they were free. In her prayers she thanked God every night for their friend Madame Mirabelle, but she also asked her Maker to keep a friendly eye upon them anent further ill fortune mingling with all the good fortune He had blessed them with.

But as she strolled along upon her morning visit to the village, carrying her shopping basket, Emma mused upon their condition and was uneasy. She could not throw off her vexation of spirit, she was in a highly sensitive state.

Yesterday the Misses Eglington had advanced toward her along Well Walk; they were wearing their pattens against a possible shower of rain and as Emma approached them they became engrossed in the possible behavior of their pattens, which could, upon occasion, throw their passenger down upon the mud. They passed her without a glance.

Why should they?

They had been neighbors upon stiffly bowing terms for ten years now.

And Mr. Ramble-Smith had now been away for a fortnight, as long a period as had elapsed since Nokomis' baggage had been removed from his hall. He had been away for as long a period before, of course, but Emma could not avoid the feeling that his departure might have something to do with Nokomis' removal to Oxford Street and subsequent silence.

It followed without the slightest doubt that if Nokomis had vanished from the millinery establishment, Thomas and Emma would have been the first to be informed by Madame Mirabelle.

But would they?

Was there something in the behavior of Thomas and Emma toward Nokomis that had upset the girl and caused her to sever all connection with them? Had she not been able to tolerate all Thomas had said to her in his serious talk with her? And, if this were so, would Madame Mirabelle align herself with the girl? Madame Mirabelle was a woman of the world and Emma, she coolly reminded herself, was not. Emma was one of those fortunates with a husband who treasured and sheltered her, and kept her free from the worse aspects of life.

Fortunate?

Yes, fortunate.

Having reached this point in her rumination, Emma stood waiting her turn for oysters, her basket upon her arm, in Cockles, the fishmongers, at the crossroads where the steep ascent to the White Stone Pond started. This fishmonger always depressed her; his fish was excellent but instead of a left hand he had an iron hook. She used to pity greatly his disability until the day he well-meaningly, but inadvisedly, stroked the top of

Amelia's bare golden, eight-month head with his hook as she sat chortling to herself in her bassinet at the entrance to his shop. Emma had felt a frisson of horror shake her then which she had never been able to throw off in over ten years, though Amelia would now bound into his shop in her hobbledehoyish way and anyone might be excused for thinking Mr. Cockles was in greater danger than she.

Emma would always hurry out of the shop without any pleasantries and this day she rounded the corner into Flask Walk at speed, and swung into the chemist to buy a packet of sulfur tablets, when she literally ran into the fifth inhabitant of Buck's Walk, Miss Blockley.

It was she who always endeavored to avoid Miss Blockley because she was one of the worst gossips in the neighborhood. She gave cookery lessons to young girls who were the orphaned children of serving soldiers in the ranks and cared for in an establishment near Chalk Farm. Miss Blockley was about the same age as Emma but a man hater; she was short and sharp and swiftly moving, like a malevolent mouse, and she was greatly disliked by the soldier's daughters whom she would constantly rap over the fingers with a not too blunt knife when they were slicing clumsily. With her scratchy sharp claws she clutched Emma's gloved hands: "Oh, Mrs. Dyce, dear. You should leave him. No point in thinking about it, just do it, dear; I could give you some idea as to where you might go, you and dear Amelia. . . ."

She spoke in swift conspiratorial tones as a matter of course, but this time it was even more urgent than usual. Emma stared blankly at her; she had no idea what she was talking about. She pushed past her toward the counter with a slight smile, murmuring that she was busy.

Miss Blockley hissed that she would "pop in and see you, dear, when I'm sure he's not there. I can help you, don't worry." And as Emma stood waiting for her tablets she had the nerve to wait around and to approach her again when she had received her purchase from the hands of the shopkeeper and was leaving the shop.

"You have a friend in me, you are not to worry now, promise. . . ?" In the absence of any response whatever from Emma, Miss Blockley whipped out of the shop with a "Bye-bye!" and Emma exchanged an exasperated smile with the shop assistant.

It had been a depressing expedition.

Emma hurried home, carrying her oysters and her tablets in her basket. She snatched up the *Times* and glanced hurriedly and anxiously up and down every likely or unlikely column.

Why?

Because from what is loosely called "the back of her mind" there came crowding the latent fears, the fears that could barely be termed fears. The tenuous thoughts, rather, that had always lurked, unvoiced, unnamed, indeed, unformed in that mental region on the border of hell where pre-Christian just men and unbaptized infants are confined.

It was connected with the life of Thomas Dyce before she had met him. She adored Thomas and the years she had spent as his wife solidified that love into something more valuable than an infatuation. She saw his faults and she pointed out her own faults to him. She realized that Thomas was too easygoing and lacked any sort of ambition to advance himself in life. She saw herself as lazy, a poor cook and lacking sporting achievements. He was of a literary turn of mind and she would often sadly complain that she was no scholar. He would wrap his arms round her and say that he liked her as she was.

But if Emma lacked brains she did not lack intelligence

and wit; she was mentally alert and attentive, she missed nothing. Thus she did not fail to notice how very little Thomas discussed his past, or related events in his past, such as the battle of Dadur. Recently, since he had joined the Far East Club, he made mention of his friend Albert Niton quite a good deal and this talk about the past was unusual. There was an area of sadness, she decided, in Thomas' mind which she connected with his mother and she also came to the conclusion that the sudden disappearance from his life, mysterious and unexplained and the lack of any communication at all with her, accounted for this faint sadness.

Or was there "something else," she was obliged to ask herself from time to time. And now she lay motionless upon her bed, with seething mind, for somewhat over an hour. Then she decided she must go and see Miss Blockley. It was just possible that there was good intention behind her behavior in the chemist.

She had flung her bonnet down with her new spring cloak when she came back from her shopping. And now, to show that her visit to her neighbor would not last for long, she placed her pretty net and lace cap on her hair, where it perched like a transient butterfly.

Hoping she was not observed but keeping her eyes to the ground, she passed the Eglingtons' little house, and Mr. Ramble-Smith's and lightly tapped Miss Blockley's front door.

"There you are, dear! I felt sure you would come round, once you had recovered from the shock! Come in!" She shut her front door gently behind the visitor and beckoned her into the parlor. "Pray sit down, dear Mrs. Dyce. Now I regret having to distress you!" (Not true) "I so very much dislike spreading unpleasant news but in this case I am not spreading it, I am doing what I feel to be my duty." And she slipped from the pocket of her black satin apron, the poison-pen letter. It was written in capital letters:

YOU MAY BE INTERESTED TO HEAR THAT MAJOR DYCE IS A WIFE KILLER.
BEWARE.

Emma's behavior was exemplary and disappointing to Miss Blockley who was hoping for an attack of hysterics at least.

With a cool, contemptuous look Emma quickly handed it back, rapidly flicking her fingers together as though removing some filth from them. "I am surprised at you, Miss Blockley!"

"Surprised!" Miss Blockley, unable to hide her disappointment, lowered her eyes to refold the note in the exact folds in which she had received it, addressed simply to Miss Blockley and no address upon the envelope, so obviously delivered by hand.

"This sort of thing happens to the best of us, does it not? And someone of my dear husband's distinction would inevitably be liable to be picked out for some sleazy blackmailer's attentions." She paused. "I find it childish. The 'beware' is a non sequitur."

g"i am afraid I cannot follow your highbrow Latin quotations, Mrs. Dyce."

"It means it does not follow. The 'beware' does not arise from the warning. Since if Major Dyce is a wife killer it would seem pointless to utter a warning to a neighbor living three doors away." Emma rose and walked toward the door: "But thank you for showing it to me, Miss Blockley, it is right that you should have done so. This communication is, in fact, of no importance because I am well aware of who sent it. A childish and pointless prank."

With great dignity and some speed, Emma returned to her own house because she was beginning to tremble so violently that it was becoming evident. She had spoken bravely and she did, in fact, know or thought she knew, who had sent the missive but that in no way diminished her terror.

In the years she had lived with him Thomas had never had an enemy; he now had one; it could only be the girl Nokomis, envious and angry because she was both dependent and deprived. Thomas' mother had been kind to Nokomis and, in the manner of people of Nokomis' frame of mind, the girl had overestimated that kindness, expecting Thomas' mother to die leaving all her worldly goods to Nokomis, no doubt.

It was explicable so far but the frightening aspect was: How did Nokomis come to use that accusation? Everybody knows about poison-pen letters, but how came it that Nokomis picked upon that particular form of denunciation?

The state of Emma's mind was only too explicable. Right from the start of their love affair, Thomas had made it plain that he did not want to discuss his past, more especially the people in his past. His father, his mother and his first wife; indeed his life in the army. This was by no means abnormal, but when the subject of his first wife or his mother arose there was a look of great distaste upon the face of Thomas. He was proud of his father and if his father were mentioned at all, no involuntary cloud appeared. It was the women folk who upset him, and before their marriage he had told Emma in a few curt words the outline of his past. Emma had at first thought that he had greatly loved his wife and very much missed her, still sad at her untimely death from cholera, but over the years she came to the conclusion that this was not so: He hated her, and his mother bewildered him because he had never had any tidings of her and now that she had died he had no longer any hope of communication.

She and Thomas could talk together for hours about their innermost wishes and thoughts. Thomas would even discuss the reveries and aspirations of his early youth with reference to his parents, but there was always silence about those years of his first marriage; a silence according to the mood of the listener. Now, Emma could not but find it sinister. She sat bewildered; then, not wishing that Thomas should come home and find her trembling, she went downstairs to the dining room sideboard for a tumbler into which she poured a little brandy. This had the effect of stopping her shuddering, but it in no way enlivened her because she had now, she reminded herself, become a secret drinker: That bottle of brandy had in no way decreased in content since Christmas, five months ago. She would have to fill it up with water lest Thomas should begin to suspect Bess of drinking. As she sat in misery in the parlor toying with her work, Thomas advanced up the hill toward his house. Amelia was playing at shuttlecock and battledore after the walk home from school with Roderick; the boy's twin sisters of six were acting as fielders out on the sloping green down to South End.

Thomas had not had a happy afternoon at his club. Since he joined he had had a great deal of pleasure but every now and then came the pinpricks and things were such that each pinprick was magnified into a stab of agony. He could not take the reminders of his last journey home from Bombay lightly. A man of temperament different from that of Thomas would laugh off the references not only to the journey but to the whole matter of leaving the army suddenly. He could not but imagine implications infesting the air like bats at sunset.

This time a man he had known vaguely from the Engineers, who had been on that ineradicable and ever-present journey home, had lunched alone, and Thomas had taken a seat beside him in the drawing room for coffee. Idle chat brought them to the subject; heat, to be precise. Did Thomas remember that appalling heat in the Gulf of Oman? "Well of course you remember it," he said, reddened; "if you don't mind my saying so, Major, some of us were of the opinion that your wife succumbed to heat apoplexy rather than cholera. Ninety-eight degrees in the shade and one day on the voyage it was over a hundred. Still . . ." he hunched himself over the stirring of his coffee, "what does it matter since dead is dead?"

"And gone is gone," Thomas absently echoed, and his friend gave him a quick sharp look to see if there was a trace of interest in his face. There was not. But why had he not thought of heat apoplexy? Thomas wondered. Strong men on the plains of India quite often died of heat apoplexy and no questions asked. Cholera was a slower, more complicated affair. In his shock he had thrown off the first fatal illness that occurred to him; his own cowardice shocked him. Bravery as a soldier was nothing compared with moral bravery. If he could just have shown a little moral bravery he might have lived happily ever after with his Emma.

Thus Thomas waved a vague hand to his child and her companions as he passed up the steep footpath. He was about to enter his own front door when Madame Mirabelle's fly turned into Buck's Walk and the groom jumped down to help her descend. She waved to

Thomas before descent and when firmly on the ground, hurried toward him.

"Dear Major, I have excellent reports of your relative Nokomis. Upon my word, I find her an asset to my showroom. Many of my customers have taken a liking to her; her manners are really charming and her looks, well, some people have called her striking. I am quite proud of her and you should be too."

Thomas lifted his hat and continued to hold it as he gravely listened to Madame Mirabelle. His troubles were too thick upon him to smile, but he nodded as he carefully listened. He said he was pleased to have this news, though he looked far from it.

Madame Mirabelle chattered along; she thought he had been quite right not to attempt to keep the girl in his own house, especially as Craskie was now recovered and back home again. Madame herself felt that she could really make something of such a biddable young woman who showed herself eager to excel. He stared thoughtfully at the Frenchwoman, feeling a great wonderment. One of the many things that had worried him was the great risk he considered Madame Mirabelle had taken by employing the girl Nokomis. He had lost sleep in the consideration of the ease with which he had let the great Nokomis burden slip from himself to this lively but frail and very aged lady.

"She is mature well beyond her years and to have kept her with you, if it had been possible, would have been a mistake from the child's point of view. Amelia herself is mature when she is not playing tig upon the green with other children. Constantly in her parents' company she has learnt a wisdom beyond her years and she would have been liable, perhaps, to pick up, shall we call it the tricks of the trade that Nokomis so excels in?"

So that was the way it went and it was a bewildered but relieved Thomas who hung up his hat on the hat stand and went in to join his wife.

IX

THEIR friends called Emma the Perfect Wife and as far as her own intents and purposes went . . . she was. At the start of their marriage she had convinced herself that a wife's duty was to cherish her husband; her every thought regarding him should be promotion of his well-being. His happiness and contentment should be her only anxiety. Emma put her whole self into this not too arduous task.

Her whole self, indeed, to the exclusion of the good fund of native intelligence that she possessed. So long as her Thomas was content she suppressed mental inquiry or complaint.

Thus, when Thomas entered the parlor, recovered from his depression and immensely encouraged as he was by the talk he had just had with Madame Mirabelle, he appeared moderately carefree. And Emma, greatly relieved but also affected by the brandy now frisking round in her veins, ignored all her morning's misery, fear and anguish, falling in instantly with his mood and only too ready to take everything that Madame Mirabelle had said at its face value.

What Madame Mirabelle had not said was of much greater importance, in fact. For reasons of her own she had not treated Nokomis as she treated her other

107

apprentices. She had meted out to this foreigner an inordinate amount of privilege, which under the true circumstances was grossly unfáir.

She had let her have a room of her own, and she had allowed her to finish work at the same time as she let out the two forewomen, who had been with her many years, while leaving the housekeeper who supervised the boarders attendant upon the workroom until nine o'clock. "My working hours are nine till nine," she would boast.

There was something special about the new girl and when the first period was over the rest of the staff were still unenlightened as to what this specialty of the newcomer was. Except for their thorough dislike of her.

No one was to guess that she was: bewildering Mr. Ramble-Smith; writing the odd poison-pen letter as the names and addresses of suitable recipients came to her; house-hunting for a place of her own which cost nothing.

She laughed and squirmed and rolled her eyes and shrieked pleasantries in her nerve-racking voice, the sound of which rose above the noise of the sewing machines in the workroom. And the customers tore their eyes from their images in the looking glasses and smiled at the lively new assistant Madame Mirabelle had taken on.

Knowing nothing of all this, Emma and her Thomas smiled at one another in their parlor. True, Thomas had anxiously noticed that Emma was not looking well, but Emma fell in with his own mood and at once reassured him, deliberately failing to kiss him and keeping her distance discreetly, so that he should not smell the brandy.

Madame Mirabelle's reassuring talk with him had given him the moral bravery the lack of which he had so recently deplored.

The house-hunting project of Nokomis was a fearsome business since she had no talent for finding her way about. Grandfather Pennyform, arriving in new country, had bought land regardless of where he pitched his camp; on the other hand her Red Indian ancestors annexed the places where they watered their overridden horses, as their own.

Nokomis walked in the opposite direction from Buck's Walk. She walked away from Hampstead, south, with her face to the sun, away from Oxford Street where the milliners were, to Westminster where the grandees must live around the Abbey and the Hall. Though she was revolted by the smell from the river, she had known worse in her day; she was shocked by the demolition mess, but she had known worse mess too; the confusion of building what was to be the new Houses of Parliament reminded her of Grandfather Pennyform's jerry-building in outer New York City.

In Westminster, west of the Bridge, there was no built-up waterfront; watermen lolled among their boats on the foreshore, and beyond, a brick wall protected the old Tudor houses or half protected them. Their end was clearly in sight. Standing upon Westminster Bridge Nokomis stared at the mess, barely enhanced by the light of the setting spring sun. No one could have called the Tudor houses slums, exactly; they had a fading air of past elegance. The gentry were fast leaving them and as she walked between them she saw that many of them were already abandoned and vandals had broken the windows. She walked to the end of the crumbling row by St. Stephen's, glancing from side to side, and as she turned round and walked back again she saw a small notice upon the front door of one. It was approached by three steps, and arrow-headed railings protected passersby from falling down into the basement, just.

109

Upon the card was written CARETAKER WANTED. And indeed, the inhabitants, if there were any, might well need a caretaker for the houses on either side were empty and ruin had set in. This house was protected by shutters in good condition, and it is not nearly so satisfying to throw half a brick through a shuttered window as it is through one unshuttered, as the wandering vandals had discovered.

She stood uncertainly upon the top step, biting skin at the side of her thumb. There was no one about and she gave a start when she saw the shutter to the left of the front door opening and a wrinkled old face looking out at her. The door was opened almost at once.

She was invited inside and found the house furnished with pleasant furniture of a century ago but in an unpolished condition, the carpets thin and worn and faded. The old man had been groom to the family all but one of whom had died. This solitary survivor was a member of the East India Company who now spent most of his time on that subcontinent and came home once in three years. This present caretaker had been ill, still was; he enlarged at length upon his illness which he convinced Nokomis was fatal. He must return to the country round Norwich where he was born and where his grandson lived and be looked after by his kind relations. In the absence of a rush of eager aspirants for the job of caretaking, he almost begged Nokomis to stay, but still she hesitated.

"The master's lawyers will see you are paid," he urged. "There is no work attached, but it must appear that the house is inhabited for the present until the master has made suitable arrangements for the contents. It will be knocked down with the rest in due course. What's going amiss with you?"

Nokomis was still biting her thumb.

"There's Charlies around all night, keeping an eye on

110

the place. The land is Crown property, they say, though I'm not sure of that. Just the job for a sturdy young woman like you, I'd have thought. Any husband?"

"Yes," Nokomis said firmly. "It's the smell," she said after further consideration, "I don't know if we can put up with it. It's the sort of smell you get where there's cholera."

"Oh, come on lass! There's cholera everywhere. You just don't have to drink the water unboiled!"

But there was a smell of some kind all over the London river, Nokomis mused. "Can I see the rest of the house?" As she followed him up the linoleum-covered staircase he cackled unamused, saying: "There's no locked room with dotty granddad being fed through a tube, if that's what you're thinking."

"I was not thinking anything of the sort, but I am wondering if I'm expected to keep it clean, even though you said 'no work attached!' "

"Up to a point you are, yes. But there's a hefty navvy comes in on Thursdays and cleans from top to bottom. It's shabby but it's clean."

The houses did not face the river but were built facing a similar row in equally bad condition. The backs overlooked a small area which could barely be called a garden, so choked as it was with weeds, the high brick wall and beyond the foreshore. From the front windows the great shadow of the rising new House of Parliament had begun to show above the opposite houses.

The caretaker had selected the best room in the house for his own use; on the first floor, it had a fine four-poster and the three long narrow windows across the back of the house had deep window seats which overlooked the squalid foreshore and a splendid double washhand stand, fully equipped. Nokomis asked him if he had been here long and he answered, a year. Then

Nokomis said that was not long, and he answered that the housekeeper before him was his own aunt, recently died. She had been with the family forty-three years. And her mother before her had served them from the day they first moved into the brand new house, the same year Queen Anne died. This grandmother was here only a short time because her husband was killed in the battle of Ramillies. "They been married just four years. She went back home with her babe, that was my aunt, to iive with her mother, it broke her heart."

So it was a one-family house and Nokomis imagined a cozy quality about it. She was now slightly fettered by having said she had a husband. To avoid getting herself into deeper waters by saying he was a soldier or a sailor she said vaguely that he was away a great deal. She invented a name quickly, Mary Burnish, and wrote it down twice, once for her own reminder and once for the lawyers in charge of the property. The caretaker wrapped a shabby old cloak around him, drew a hairy green hat down over his face and demanded that he take Mrs. Burnish to them at once at their office in Maiden Lane and the transfer of responsibility would then be complete.

In the lawyer's office either fortuitously or purposely he was doubled up with a devastating attack of coughing evidently brought on by the long walk from Westminster, which went on for an unimaginable length of time, giving verisimilitude to his plea of being unfit to be in that low-lying damp house all alone.

In front of the lawyers Nokomis, alias Mary Burnish, was handed and had to sign for, the front door key. She was also obliged to go back to the house with the caretaker and stay while he collected his possessions. She would then have the sole responsibility for the key, and one of the lawyers sternly reminded her of this as they left.

She wandered about the house while he packed a large basket with his personal things. "You must be on the lookout for those folk in Maiden Lane," the caretaker said as he staggered into the hall with his basket. "They turn up anytime, anytime. You can hear that great key they have, like the one you have now, and it's morning, noon or night. Sole responsibility, eh? Don't you believe it." He tumbled the basket down the steps and went to find a man with a handcart. "Good day to you!" he waved and as she closed the door after him, Nokomis thought she heard wild haggish laughter, but no, it was only a wagon disposing of a load of gravel on the building site.

She could not yet fetch her baggage so she now sat in the window and thought about the Melburys. How could she have lost control of herself to such an extent as to make a visit to them now out of the question? She wanted to ask Mr. Melbury senior to allow her to handle her allowance from home herself. What possible chance was there of Mr. Melbury complying with this request after her terrible behavior the first and only time she was in his office?

And then there was the delicate question of young Mr. Melbury. Where young men were concerned she had total confidence in herself; she could, without fail, captivate any male under thirty.

She was less confident about the older men and, of course, she had no confidence at all in a young man who apparently started to avoid her as the wretch Daniel Ramble-Smith had done. That he should absent himself from Buck's Walk and from the London Discount House to take a sudden spring holiday with his rich relative at the exact moment when she was setting about bewitching him into marrying her, was maddening. She had had to revise her schemes, and to start with she packed her bags and disappeared from the millinery establishment of Madame Mirabelle at almost the same time that Madame Mirabelle was singing her praises to her neighbor.

She now considered that the weeks she had spent at Madame Mirabelle's establishment were a foolish waste of time, waste of effort to be charming, too. Not once in her waking hours did she see a man there of any kind at all, young or old, rich or poor. She had arrived in this country, which was quite new to her, full of ambition, no, more than ambition, certainty that she was going to marry a rich man and become of importance upon whatever social scene she could attach herself. She had had hopes when it was decided back home that she should go to the Dyce family. "Army people!" she would think cheerfully, a great step up from the Pennyforms who were mere tradesmen; the society in which the Pennyforms moved looked up at Eleanor Pennyform, or Dyce, as the only "real lady" of their acquaintance.

Nokomis had imitated her speech and manners as best she could in an endeavor to be a "real lady" too. Unfortunately she was her own worst enemy because she frequently smashed up the "real lady" image suddenly and without any provocation, in the manner of her frightful behavior in front of young Mr. Melbury. Grandfather Pennyform, who detested her, had once rounded upon her and cried that she could not expect to be a woman who put her body to infamous use and a "real lady" at the same time. Nokomis could have torn his eyes out and might have, had they been alone. But he had not dared to say it in the presence of his Eleanor.

As if it were not enough to have inherited her wild father's temperament, she was richly endowed with her grandfather Pennyform's violent antipathies too. She hugged this "real lady" aspiration around her like a woolen shawl, protecting her from the chilly realities of her own black bile.

And now, as she sat watching the filthy river swelling in, she realized she had once again acted true to form and thrown everything to the four winds; her so-called "relations" the Nateby-Dyces, the young graduate who had fallen so quickly for her and as hastily recovered, the lawyers in Red Lion Square who were responsible for her welfare, the regard of the old lady with the milliner's establishment. She had stripped herself bare of esteem and as surely as her father had stabbed her mother, she had stabbed Major Nateby-Dyce to the heart by posting the letters she had so eagerly penned a few days ago in her dismal attic room in the millinery boarding house.

The present looked dangerously black, but she was not without hope. The poison-pen letters she had written would cause disarray, to say the least of it, in the Nateby-Dyce household; it would separate husband and wife; it would render Emma more accessible to her, perhaps, and the whereabouts of the Inguta jewel might be revealed accidently or even purposely.

If Eleanor Dyce had known that old Mr. Killarney had talked to Nokomis about the moonstone, something might have been put down in writing on the lines of really wishing Nokomis to have it. Nobody was going to agree that by rights it was hers. She would create havoc until she had it in her possession. Mr. Killarney's indiscretions, too, were a marvelous weapon. That garrulous old man having told Nokomis when she first came to live with Eleanor, that Eleanor's son had married into the aristocracy and it ended in disaster when she died, or maybe as rumor said, he pushed her overboard on the way home from India.

Eleanor Dyce had heard this in a letter from the

Hampstead relative with whom she was in constant communication and that was why she had never written to her son or tried to get in touch with him, perhaps. After Eleanor's death Mr. Killarney's visits had not ceased, he haunted Nokomis as he had haunted Eleanor forever; he needed to talk about her incessantly, he had nothing else to do but talk, talk, talk—

Quietly thinking things over, Nokomis found without doubt some circumstances in her favor. When the river had swelled so that the water's edge was now out of view below the wall, it deposited its burden of dead cats, drift wood, putrefied fruit, vegetables and offal as it started to withdraw along the water line.

Best of all she thought she was now in sole possession of a roof over her head. She had been given five pounds as payment for six months' residence in advance, so she was secure in tenure, at least for that length of time, longer if she gave no cause for complaint. The manner in which she had found it was extraordinarily fortunate: Because not knowing her way around London and walking in the opposite direction from Hampstead and the small village shop in which she had seen the letting advertisements displayed, she might have been lost; but she had walked right out of the district where there could be found small stores advertising lodgings, into the realms of gentlefolk and nobility, members of Parliament and Prime Ministers, Kings too! And on the front door of this simple crumbling but eminently respectable abode was pinned the notice waiting for *her*. The finger of fortune was pointing to it.

Her packed luggage had been sitting in the bedroom she had left scrupulously neat; she had quit before the rest were up and about. They would have been dismayed at her disappearance, and all day Madame would have run through to the boarding house to see if she had

116

returned. At ten o'clock Nokomis would find a one-horse hackney and a youngish jarvey who would carry down her baggage; she would wait a few doors away and join him after he had drawn away from the boardinghouse, leaving the key behind; he would drive her "home" and when he had carried in her things, if he insisted, she would let him stay the night.

X

"LOOK, Amelia!"

With a steel fly-button on a piece of string, Roderick was demonstrating the wonders of his new magnet as they walked down the hill to school. "And do you know, I took Mama's pin box from her workbasket and . . . Amelia, you're not listening!"

"No Roddy, I'm sorry but I have a lot on my mind."

"Out with it then."

"It's too private.

Long pause. "Oh, go on Amelia, we have always shared our troubles."

"But this is. . . ."

"Yes. What?"

"It's a family affair."

"Well, go on. . . ."

"I do not know, Roddy, what is wrong, but it is something very bad because they are not talking to each other. Not even in bed."

Roddy carefully rolled the string on two fingers and secured it against unraveling itself. He put the button, string and magnet in his pocket and gave his whole attention to his friend. "Go on."

"Well, it is something to do with . . . I do not quite know."

"Nokomis?"

"Perhaps. She has gone . . . just gone. . . ."

"But she went ages ago."

"I mean she has gone from Madame Mirabelle's."

"I should have thought they would be pleased."

"But there is something more . . . at the back of it all . . . there is something but I cannot make out what. It is such lovely spring weather outside." She looked round at the sky and the trees and the city of London which seemed this morning almost to shine with the great dome of St. Paul's like a jewel set in its midst. "But at home it is cold and gray and we do not speak to one another, not even to pass the marmalade, since Papa and Mama are not eating breakfast, and all they say is: 'Hurry up Amelia,' or, 'Have you a clean pocket handkerchief,' or 'Do not forget your satchel, child!' *Child!* Why do they not tell me? Families should share their troubles."

"My family do," Roderick said smugly, "if Mama's new gown does not fit, everybody in the house knows, or if Papa has misplaced his diary the blame is on us all."

"That is not quite what I mean." They turned into Downshire Hill.

"Will you help me, Roddy?"

"Yes," he returned with instant enthusiasm and after a pause added: "but how?"

It was only when they were within a few steps of the school that Amelia answered. "By finding out what is really wrong with Mama and Papa."

"How?"

"Talk to other people . . . not only me. . . ."

Roddy curled up his nose with his finger, looked aghast and grumbled.

"Do not be merely silly, Amelia. Me, a gossip!"

119

"You said you would help, so do not give up before we start. We must be a couple of spies and report upon our findings to one another every day, or even twice a day!"

"Oh I say!"

"I can't do it on my own, Roddy. Girls cannot be spies easily."

"Oh, I don't know. . . ." He pulled his button, string and magnet out of his pocket. He had thought there was some fun about. With Amelia there usually was; now she was too serious.

At twelve o'clock there was an hour-long break after which school was continued until four o'clock when the children left school to join the family dinner. But every child brought a small packet of food with them in their satchels to consume at twelve together with a provided mug of milk: pasties and pies, sandwiches, slices of plain bread and toast; they would eat in the playground if fine and in the assembly room if wet, the boys separate from the girls but not by rule of the school, by choice.

One close little group of four boys had their heads together over their refreshments for some time before they broke apart, and Roderick, alone now, leaned against the wall and stared hard at the group in which Amelia was now giggling. He was trying unsuccessfully to catch Amelia's eye. But he had to wait for her attention until they broke up for the day. Pulling her away from her friends, he hissed his news to her long before they had reached the corner of Downshire Hill, which was just as well because Amelia found the tidings so overwhelming that she had to sit down on the half wall. For once she was rendered speechless. Lying in bed last night, she had overheard whispers in the next-door garden between the Misses Eglington; they would never have whispered if they had not been talking about their neighbors. Her instructions to Roddy had been all too apt, frighteningly so.

"And it is all over Hampstead," Roderick assured her, clearly quoting and delighted with his success. He fiddled with his magnet until she recovered from her shock somewhat.

"But it is not true! My papa would never . . . no, Roddy, no!" She did not exactly consciously quote St. Matthew's gospel but maybe the words came from it involuntarily: "An enemy has done this, Roddy! Someone who hated my father." Pause. "But how could anyone hate him?"

"I like him," Roddy volunteered.

"And so does everybody, oh Roddy! Do stop fidgeting with that steel button and string. I must think!"

Presently they were walking with heads close together and slowly up the grassy slope. "If we are to discover anything, we must pretend . . . pretend."

"Pretend what?"

"Pretend that we are stupid little kids who do not care."

"Care what?"

"Care if our parents are miserable or not. Your parents don't care anyway, do they?"

Roddy agreed they did not. They might care what Major Nateby-Dyce had done, but they did not much care what Roddy did so long as he kept out of sight.

"Well then!" she said.

"Well then what?" Roddy wanted to know.

"It means you can help me and you will help me, will you not, Roddy?"

"To do what? But of course I'll help."

"To help my papa, to find out that Papa did not do it. He did not push my first mama in the sea. No, I do not mean that; I mean the first lady he married before my mama, of course."

121

"What shall we do?"

"I must think. You think too, Roddy. Think hard. But first I shall go home and ask him."

Roderick was aghast: "You cannot do that."

"But how can I start discovering if I don't?"

Yes, how? Roddy's brow was wrinkled with the strain of thinking. He opted out of it. "You do the thinking and I will do what you say."

When Amelia asked him, he wished he were dead. Mama was in the little back garden and Papa was sitting with a pad in his hand upon which he was making notes from a reference book; it was something that referred to the work he was doing for Mr. Carlyle. Amelia stood in front of him and asked gently, as opposed to demanding roughly, whether it was true that he had pushed his first wife into the ocean on the way home from India.

He did not even look up, he went on writing, saying: "What do you think Amelia?" This put her to great shame; she burst into tears and went on crying while he continued with his writing. Emotionally she flung herself round his neck, knocking the pad and pencil from his hand.

"I'm sorry, I'm sorry, darling Papa. Forgive me, sir, forgive me. I know you did not." And after she had ceased to cry and had mopped up her face with the handkerchief he handed her she wailed, "But why do they say so?"

"They?"

"At school they are saying so. They have heard their fathers and mothers talking about it. Papa . . . was it an accident?" Thomas smiled, upon the edge of laughter. He was proud of Amelia; his child had a mind of her own and he prayed that she should use it and not allow it to fall into decay, assuming that reasoning was not for a

122

woman but to be left to the gentlemen, as so many women did.

Was it an accident, he thought bitterly.

How easy it would be to say, Yes, Amelia, it was an accident.

But still he was not able to say, No, Amelia, it was not an accident.

Yet, with a child of her quality of mind it would not end there. He took what he considered to be the coward's way out; he had no alternative.

"I do not wish to speak about it, dearest child." He only just managed not to add, So run away and play! He was not even able to add something about When you are old enough. . . . His dear wife was old enough and yet he could not talk to Emma about it. He suffered from a true, ingrown inability to tell anyone what actually happened that night in the Gulf of Oman. There was only one person in the whole wide world he just possibly could discuss it with and that was Madame Mirabelle.

Once that *grande dame* had said to him: *"Mon très cher monsieur, vous êtes né dans une époque quand votre société était louche, n'est-ce pas?* And yet fifty years after your birth your country has achieved (if that is the word I need) so strict a social code *upon the surface* that a man cannot or may not discuss the sex act with his wife, even after marriage. As a people, you English are a mass of astonishing contradictions!"

She had thoughtfully said it all in French that Thomas could understand; otherwise he would have been embarrassed and confused.

Like a few other French words *louche* is untranslatable; figuratively it means eyes which look both ways, but the nearest English word to it is in "equivocal" and the meaning she tried to convey was that at the time of Thomas' birth, ten years before the start of the exciting nineteenth

123

century, society was altogether gayer and more free beneath the superficial code of behavior. But she was compelled to finish saying what she felt at the time was an unfortunate one-sided discussion: "You bring your God into your everyday life in a manner that is not wholly admirable, though it seems to be so upon the surface, and so many of you believe that going three times in one day to church is a passport to everlasting life."

Like a governess, he thought irritably and unfairly, Amelia stood before him, waiting for an answer.

He might say: Amelia, if you must know, at the beginning I adored my first wife, at eighteen she was a gay, warm, passionate girl; no one could have been happier than she made me. But parental influence impressed upon her that she was, as they say, "Not as other women are": She belonged to the nobility. And that changed her. I watched her and before my eyes she became, as I thought, condescending; she appeared, I believed quite unwittingly, to yield to my attentions only as a favor. I was so greatly wounded that I . . . that I withdrew from her. But then I was wrong, terribly lacking in perception. She was still the warm, marvelous girl beneath, but my mind poisoned my body, and I could no longer make love to her. I was so greatly repelled I could not bear her near me; it was like an illness.

It was not true! But, of course, he could not and did not say all that. It was a preposterous and even obscene thought that he should discuss the matter at all with the bewildered child standing before him. He considered that his mind must have become very adversely affected.

Still, he thought it might make the situation more acceptable were he able to do so. How many decades would have to pass before one could be upon the terms of talking thus with one's daughter, herself standing upon the edge of puberty, who would listen with sympathy and store the information away as wisdom that might one day prove helpful to her?

Amelia stood staring down at one of her feet emerging from below the frill of her new pantaloons. "Well, Papa. You may not wish to speak about it and nor do I. But I shall if it is mentioned before me. I could not help it. I shall say my papa would never, could not possibly, cause the death of anybody who was not the enemy."

Not the enemy! Aye, there was the rub. He was born a soldier, so they said, and was a ruthless killer. We are all God's creatures, so how could he ask God kindly to discriminate? As he slashed through the enemy cutting people to pieces with his saber, would he be crying: Look, dear Lord, they are only Brahoes? (But Brahoes, of course, might equally reasonably be crying to their god: Look, Shiva, they are only British.) Life was really too complicated for a man to live it as God intended. And the Old Testament was not much help either . . . *and they shall draw their swords against Egypt, and fill the land with the slain.* It depressed him to read the Old Testament; Ezekiel was one long yell of revenge.

"There speaks the soldier's daughter," Thomas said sadly. "Not the enemy! Who is to say who is the enemy and who is not, when in the long term it may be man's own self?"

"Oh, Papa, *don't* speak like that!" And Amelia stamped the foot at which she had been staring so balefully.

Thomas' mood might have sent them both into deep water or an inextricable clash of opinion had not the situation been rescued by the figure of Mr. Daniel Ramble-Smith from next door but one. Amelia ran to open the door because he was a favorite of hers and she was greatly relieved to see him.

He entered the parlor and they were joined by Emma with her trowel slipped into the long pocket of her

125

gardening apron. He came in holding a version of the poison-pen letter; the shock of receiving it had caused him to rush into his neighbors without folding it and putting it tactfully in his pocket before coming in to see them.

He held it up excitedly: "It was dropped through my letter box during the night; it was not there last night when I went to bed. Sir, can you tolerate this? What has happened?"

Emma and Thomas were staring at one another as though they could never look away.

"One of my great-great-aunts is at death's door and I have been obliged to be with her, but as it now seems she is somewhat better I have returned only on condition that I am recalled at once if necessary. She is a hundred and one," he added in explanation. "Where is Nokomis Pennyform, sir?"

Thomas told him that a few days ago Nokomis disappeared with all her baggage from the employment and care of Madame Mirabelle. That Madame herself was greatly upset since Nokomis was doing excellently at her employment. He thanked Mr. Ramble-Smith for bringing in the disgraceful communication so quickly and told him that this was the kind of thing that sometimes happens and that they would all have to "live it out." He looked around, holding his hands apart and wearing upon his face that very endearing expression of bewilderment that was his wont.

The young man did not sit down so much as collapse into a chair. He still held the letter, hanging dejectedly between his knees. He looked at Amelia. He looked from her, first to her mother, then her father. Neither noticed his discomfort; each was wordlessly saying to the other unsayable things.

Mr. Ramble-Smith cleared his throat, but it had no visible effect.

He said: "Er."

"Daniel wants to say something," Amelia said helpfully.

The young man ran a finger round his neckcloth.

Since neither of her parents seemed to be with them in spirit, Amelia said she had been thinking. She took the letter from Mr. Ramble-Smith and studied it. "I think I know. . . ." she said.

"Amelia!" Her mother finally sprang to life. When Amelia suddenly turned on her enfant terrible act, it was every man for himself.

"Leave the room please." With Mama like that Amelia had no alternative but meekly to obey. She left the room on tiptoe and closed the door after her without a sound.

"A man has every right to have a mistress," Mr. Ramble-Smith complained when he had told them about his family's reaction to Nokomis Pennyform. "So long as he can keep her and doesn't expect any of his elderly relatives to subscribe to the intention. As I told them most forcibly, *'I am not the Prince of Wales.'* (It was a ten-year-old allusion caught from his parents who had had their Prince of Wales for well-nigh fifty years.) As though he had proved something by these impenetrable words he went on that he was just an ordinary person with a number of very old great-great-aunts who had no one to whom they could leave their money but his wretched self.

"And I have repeatedly pointed out to them that there are quite a lot of poor around. They had only to glance about them to discover that the poor abounded. But they are not interested in the poor, even like old Mr.

Pennyform, as a means of getting straight to heaven. They believe much more firmly in leaving their money in the family and their family now consist mainly in my married sister, herself well-provided for . . . and wretched me!" He looked round the room crossly. "It was just unfortunate that my very old great-great-Aunt Emily should have been declared to be at death's door just when I was enjoying the company of Miss Pennyform in my house and at Brighton. However, I have not come to see you about my problems. I am aghast at this communication and my reason for rushing in so unrestrainedly to see you regarding it is that I feel I might be able to help run to ground the ruffian who has so evilly written it. Now, sir, is there any way in which I can help? Some dismissed servant who feels him or herself ill done by; perhaps, I might look them up for you? A wretch of a soldier from your army days? Your batman?"

He looked expectantly at both Emma and Thomas. "Well, I can sense you are deeply worried as, indeed, I should feel myself. But I should, were I in the same unfortunate position which I *well* might be, I would endeavor to throw it off, sir. Only a wretchedly unhappy person could do such an unpleasant deed as to write this communication, and they can finally only bring remorse upon themselves."

He stood up, bowed to Thomas, kissed Emma's hand and was off as quickly as he had appeared.

"An endearing youth," Thomas said.

Whether or not Mr. Carlyle had heard of or had even received the poison-pen communication regarding Thomas, he had no time for such trivia. Occupied with writing *Past and Present*, he had still found time to give his attention to the plans for the new London Library. To Thomas' great pleasure he was entrusted with a good

128

deal of investigation and research, which included staggering away from the British Museum library with heavy books and lists of books.

It also meant hours of quiet study at home. During these three weeks he was too busy to notice a falling off of their social life in Hampstead. His mind was too occupied to question the disappearance of Nokomis Pennyform or what steps Mr. Ramble-Smith was taking to find her. Emma had lost her air of patient quiet endurance, and he failed to notice that Amelia wore rather conspicuously a mien of one who bears a burden, spiced with another manner, that of conspiracy. This latter she wore particularly at the weekends.

She and Roderick were burdened with knowledge the importance of which could be attributed to a State secret. They were constantly together during the long light evenings; the green sward down to the village of South End was sprinkled with young people, playing shuttlecock and battledore, practicing walking on stilts, playing ball, lying upon the grass reading; pastimes, in fact, commensurate with the long light, and above all, warm evenings.

Amelia and Roderick's occupation could not be recognized instantly as that of spying because it was well concealed. But that, in fact, was what they were up to. They and they alone were in possession of the knowledge that Miss Nokomis Pennyform was, as Roderick excitingly put it, "haunting the district."

At first they thought she was "watching" the Nateby-Dyces, but later they decided she was spying upon Daniel Ramble-Smith. Amelia was secretly rather distressed that her parents were comparatively unperceptive. There could be as many young people as fifty or so, some accompanied by grown-ups and some not on the green at a time, and often Nokomis wandered among them and never once had her father or her mother noticed her or seen her from their windows overlooking the slope. But as Mama had gradually lost the terribly strained expression upon her face and Papa was occupied closely with his work, the atmosphere at home had improved. In the evening Papa would go into the garden for a smoke.

Before "all this happened" as Amelia referred to the letters, Papa had bought himself a purple velvet jacket and cap with a tassle hanging from it which he kept in his locker at his club. This was his smoking jacket and cap and was used for the purpose of protecting his clothes and hair from the contamination of tobacco smoke. Until recently Papa had never been able to afford to smoke but now, with the kind permission of Emma, he was allowed to smoke as much as he wished, so long as it was out of doors.

Thus Papa would stroll round and round the tiny back garden, musing. After six in the evening when the sun had lost its sting, Nokomis Pennyform could be discerned by the observant, sometimes concealing herself in the coppice which grew on the other side of the lane and at the same level as Buck's Walk. It was not thickly planted, so she could see, through the bushes and between the trunks of the silver birches, Buck's Walk and Parliament Hill Fields and away down across the city to the docks.

One evening Roderick and Amelia lay upon the grass on their stomachs side by side about a hundred yards from Buck's Walk. Roderick was reading a schoolboy's story and Amelia was simply watching, her bonnet pulled well down so her eyes were only just visible and no one could see at what exactly she was looking. But she was watching Nokomis and Nokomis was watching her; she was wearing an absurdly large bonnet which almost hid her face, and certainly hid her whole head; to anyone taller than herself it would be like looking down at a mushroom.

"If we just keep on like that," Amelia remarked, "I know we shall find out why she comes and comes every fine night to watch. But I'll tell you something you haven't thought of, Roddy. Have you noticed that she always goes before the last omnibus leaves from South End? No, you haven't, have you?"

Roderick grunted. But Amelia went on: "And do you not think it strange that she should be called Pennyform?"

"Shaped like a penny? No, I do not think it strange as all that or funny."

"But *penna* is the Latin for feather!" Amelia rolled about laughing at the strangeness of it and when she saw that Roderick was slightly irritated she explained: "Her father is supposed to have been a Red Indian, and the Red Indians wear lots of feathers, do they not? Her mother was a squaw and squaws are Red Indians' wives and they only wear one feather. . . . Mama told me so, about the Latin *and* about squaws!"

Emma had in fact told her so, but she had been careful not to tell her things that would not have been good for her to know, such as, that Nokomis' mama was not married to a Red Indian but was decimated by one.

And as Amelia was still chuckling, a horseman rode up to their house, dismounted and looked around for the tethering post, tied his horse to it, went to the front door and soundly banged the knocker.

"Now I wonder who that is and what they want?"

After twenty minutes or so, Emma came out of the front door and beckoned Amelia and as Amelia ran toward her she cast a sideways glance and noticed that Nokomis Pennyform was no longer in the coppice.

"Dearest. . . ." Emma handed her sixpence. "Please,

131

child, go down to the dairy for me and buy some cream. Saturday evening it will still be open. Bess is making some cream pancakes for supper for Papa's friend from his club, Colonel Niton. And you may sup with us. Send Roderick home, it is his suppertime too. Make haste. . . ." She handed her the cream crock.

"Niton, n-i-t-o-n? *No*, n-i-g-h-t-o-n, *no* . . . n-y-t-o-n?" Amelia was muttering to herself as she sped down the hill path to South End.

And as she was about to enter the shop Nokomis came out, peering past Amelia to see if the omnibus still stood waiting for passengers.

"Hallo, Amelia."

Amelia looked falsely astonished: "Nokomis? What are you doing here?"

"It is pleasant out here in the fresh air. The smells down by the river sicken me; I feel better here. I am looking for Mr. Ramble-Smith and I have been for some time. . . . Where is he, do you know?"

"I see him sometimes," Amelia returned, "but he is not sleeping here because his family needs him at present. Why have you left Madame, Nokomis? She will never forgive you or take you back."

Nokomis writhed and squirmed and widened her great mouth so it was as disproportionately large and as ugly as that of a fledgling, newly burst from the egg upon hearing the approaching parent, carrying food to thrust down its throat.

"I was a servant and was treated as such, she must have understood that; do this, do that, run and fetch this or that! No, not for me!"

"Why did you not let her know you would leave?"

"Oh, *whoiee* to that!" She clicked her fingers.

"My papa and my mama are your guardians, Nokomis. They are very upset."

132

"*Whoiee!* to that, too," she snapped. "I am far too old to have a couple of old caretakers!"

"*Old!*" Amelia gasped.

"Shall I come and see you?"

Amelia felt she must say yes and did so but without enthusiasm.

"What day?"

Amelia had been surprised, now she was even more so. "Oh, any day."

"When the guardians are out?"

Now she was shocked but withal flattered. "They go to the Camden Town Music Circle on Wednesdays."

"Wednesday evening then. . . .Why are you in such a hurry, Amelia?"

"I have come for some cream; Bess is making cream pancakes since Colonel Niton is for supper."

"Who is he?"

"A friend of Papa's from his club."

"What club?"

"The Far East Club in St. James' Square."

"Niton? How do you spell it?"

"Night . . . maybe a *K* . . . yes . . . Knightown. . . ." Amelia was only too capable of amusing herself thus. "Nokomis, I must run, they are waiting for the cream. . . ."

"Not a word about Wednesday mind!"

She had forgotten already. She frowned: "Wednesday?"

"I'm coming. And mind . . . do not tell a soul. A secret, yes? You may whisper it to Daniel Ramble-Smith if you see him. But no one else!" She clutched to her breasts the bag of buns she had purchased and bit into the apple she had bought as she hurried to the omnibus stop.

Amelia went more slowly up the hill carrying the cream crock than she had come down it. She practiced the strange *whoiee* that Nokomis had uttered twice. It resembled the Swiss yodel, she thought, but less friendly, less a call to comrades across the ravine than a battle cry. She gave a very creditable imitation.

Back home she handed the cream to Bess and went up to brush her hair and put on a prettier, clean apron. She came downstairs and tripped into the parlor looking, as her grandmother would have said, "as mim as a May puddick." She gave a little bob of a curtsy to the visitor and sat meekly down on a low embroidered footstool, hands folded, as though she were about to pray.

Neither parent had ever told Amelia she may be seen but not heard. But she was discreet regarding her entries into the conversation. She waited for a lull and broke in gently: "How do you spell your name, sir?" He bent toward her, charmed by her gentle manner and small voice.

"It is spelt N-i-t-o-n, and it comes from the name of a small village in the Isle of Wight where, I daresay, my ancestors lived when they painted themselves with woad."

Amelia's eyes were enormous when she rolled them round to him and said: "Woad, what is that?" Both the men laughed and exchanged glances, but Amelia's appearance had given the little assembly the feeling of a party.

He left after the cream pancakes flavored with Marsala. He bowed to the ladies and Thomas accompanied him into the narrow hall and out to the tethering post to the horse.

Colonel Niton turned to Thomas with a sober air. "My good Thomas," he said, "it has been noticed that you have not put in an appearance of late at the club. You have friends there in St. James' Square, you know, old man. And my real reason for coming this evening was to

134

assure you that your problem has been discussed and there are very few, a half dozen or so amongst all the men with whom it has been debated who have made light of it. 'There, but for the Grace of God, go I . . .' has been the general opinion. We are as though we were still in the mess, Thomas; we speak our minds, we argue things out. We are a very different society from the group of people flung together on a long voyage and suffering acutely from ennui! Puny gossip is all they have; fortunately, this is not so in our club. Besides, we are all people in glass houses and none of us wishes to be the one to cast the first stone."

Why had he brought up the subject in a veiled manner when he had resolved never to mention it again?

Later, when the horse was watered and he was about to leave, Thomas said, "Tell me, Albert, those few native syce one is apt to see squatting in the drive at the club with the waiting horses. . ."

"Yes?"

"There is one whose face haunts me!"

"My dear chap, they all look alike to me, alike as white ants, only they are brown."

"I know what you mean, but there is one with huge dark eyes."

"They all have huge dark eyes."

Thomas tried again. "This one is a Hindu. He shows a singular interest in myself, and I, on my part, know I have seen him before. But where?" He paused. "He's old. Could he have been one of our servants thirteen years ago?"

"Does it matter?" Albert asked as he fitted his foot into his stirrup.

"Everything that happened in India matters to me now, somehow."

"Don't let it," Albert said as he swung into the saddle and was away.

XI

EMMA stared down at the zinc figure of Wellington which she had bought out of wedding-present money; she decided she had grown out of it, so she picked it up and carried it into the little garden where she arranged it to her satisfaction against a small bush of scarlet rhododendrons they had recently bought; he looked well in his new situation.

"Mama?"

She turned: "Do you like this here, Amelia?"

"Yes, Mama. Are you and Papa going to the Camden Town Music Circle on Wednesday evening?"

"Yes, dear. Why?"

Amelia knew some of her own failings, she was grown-up enough for that. But, on the other hand, she was not grown-up enough to deceive her parents or carry about with her, intact, information which might be of importance. Some people might call her too blatantly honest, but she called herself cowardly.

She stood childishly on one leg and said that Nokomis Pennyform would be calling and Emma, without looking up, again asked, "Why?"

"Because she loves Daniel and he seems to be avoiding her."

136

"Are you sure you should interfere, dear?"

"*Interfere!*" Amelia was hurt. "I'm nearly grown-up," she said crossly. "You ought to have had more children, you and Papa; why did you not? All your love of children is centered upon me and I'm not a child any longer."

Emma looked grieved and Amelia was at once sorry. She adored her mother, but she wished to be more forceful than she. It was a terrible strain for Amelia to be meek as she knew ladies should be. Even her mother's reply was dull and stereotyped: "The good Lord did not bless us with any more children, Amelia."

"Oh!" Amelia said, brightening up, "then let us keep our fingers crossed." Tears came into Emma's eyes but not of sorrow, tears of laughter and the effort of not laughing.

At last she said, "Nokomis is not a suitable companion for you, Amelia. The Americans are a newly established country compared with ourselves; they lead a harder, indeed, more of a striving way of life; Nokomis had grown up much more quickly than an English girl of her own age; she is one who has seen, well, the seamy side of life."

"What is that, *seamy* side?"

"Well it is . . . oh, Amelia, you must see that she is not . . . not. . . ." She stood with her trowel hanging from her hand, looking helplessly at Amelia. "You know perfectly well what I mean."

"But can she come?" Amelia insisted, purely out of habit.

"How can we stop her if you do not know where she lives?"

Amelia stood upon the other foot and looked vaguely about her, which told Emma that she did not know where Nokomis was lodged. This would be of interest to Madame Mirabelle, who constantly mourned her lack of information regarding Nokomis' whereabouts since she wished to see her and verbally tear her up. And since Emma believed that this would be a good thing, she said nothing regarding Nokomis being kept out of sight of Madame Mirabelle when she came. And since Amelia had confidence in herself her mother decided to let her handle this situation as best she could and learn by experience.

If on Wednesday evening there were unforeseen incidents of any kind, the Misses Eglington would be the first to arrive with shining eyes upon her doorstep to report it and Miss Blockley would be waiting just behind her curtains to follow on when they had left. Nothing could occur secretly in Buck's Walk.

At the actual time, however, Nokomis was clever enough to let herself in by the back entrance used by Bess. She crept soundlessly across the tiny lawn and tapped upon the kitchen window where Bess started violently because she was beating eggs for a sponge and could not hear the tap. She saw just the adderlike face and from where she stood, slightly below the sight of the top of Nokomis' head, she could see no hair at all; it was frightening.

Amelia, on the lookout for her, skipped out of the garden door to welcome her. "Come in," she cried gaily. "But he's not there!"

"Let us sit in the parlor window and watch for his approach."

And this they did for a few minutes until Nokomis said that she was very hungry. What was Bess making? And Amelia said she was making a caramel custard for dinner tomorrow and a sponge.

"Oh, if only we could have some cream pancakes."

"I haven't any money," Amelia said. "Otherwise I would ask Bess to make some and we could run down to

South End and get the cream—they stay open till eight."

Nokomis fished about for her reticule, which was hidden about her person, and produced sixpence. They both went into the kitchen and asked Bess to make the pancakes, which she agreed to do as they took only a very short time and the top of the range was still hot enough.

"Run and get some cream," Nokomis urged.

Amelia flew down the bank as fast as her voluminous skirt and her new pantaloons would allow. And Nokomis held up her own skirt and sped upstairs to search, unsuccessfully as she might have guessed.

Thomas had thrown the Inguta moonstone into his collar drawer, but Emma had begged that it be removed to a hiding place with more guile. When Amelia returned Nokomis was sitting as she had been when she left the house ten minutes ago but more disconsolate. She gobbled her warm brandy-flavored cream pancakes in a manner certainly not befitting a young lady, while Amelia watched her amazed, eating but two pancakes herself while Nokomis devoured, there is no other word for it, nine.

"I am sorry I have heard the terrible news of the letters your father has been receiving," Nokomis said as she wiped her greasy mouth and flung her crumpled napkin down. "It is all over the town. But I am afraid it is all part of the curse."

"Curse?" Amelia croaked.

"The Inguta curse my grandmother related to me."

"*Your* grandmother?"

"Grandmother Pennyform."

"She's not your grandmother but she is, was, mine. Papa says I am very like her. She was a Dyce, not a Pennyform."

"She was certainly *my* grandmother!"

"Mine! Mine!"

Nokomis studied Amelia sullenly for a moment or two and decided against going to war about it. "Well, a maharaja in India gave it to your papa's papa, Thomas Henry Dyce. Well, he did not really give it, he threw it away, in fact, because he could not bear to have it any longer I guess!"

"Why not?"

"Because it brings the owner such devilish bad luck."

"But Thomas Henry Dyce married *my* grandmother and gave it to her as a betrothal gift."

"Exactly. That is why she told me. She said she had worked it out."

"Worked what out?"

"The awful luck she had had. She told me about her life and how it had all gone wrong and that now, in her old age, she had at last realized what had caused it. She said she was putting the blame on the Inguta moonstone because she had tried always to be good and do the Right Thing and God had been against her, she said."

"Oh, tell me, tell me!" Amelia said eagerly.

"Well. Your grandfather—he gave her the jewel in London, and on the way back to India he suffered the most terrible storm in the Indian Ocean and several people were injured and one man was washed overboard, and at the same time at home Eleanor Dyce broke her leg and was unable to move about for a long time." Nokomis murmured thoughtfully that her grandmother had never really recovered from that leg injury; she had a very slight limp and it had been painful at times right up to the day she died.

"Oh, there were lots and lots of great troubles that befell her! She had always been healthy and then . . . almost as soon as she had arrived in India as a bride she started with asthma. . . . There were many misfortunes fell upon that lady, Amelia; she would tell me about them

140

as we sat together in the evenings at our work. Now that she was old, she remembered things which during her life she had no time to recall and now she felt it all started with the Inguta jewel. It seems the maharaja's two sons had tried to kill their father. One of the wives of one of the sons was said to be a sorceress; she was herself murdered in her bed and there was a horrible mix-up of murders. The maharaja himself either stole or inherited the moonstone, but he gave it to your grandpapa and as a result died a peaceful death in his old age. So you see!"

Very far from it! She might well be making it all up.

Even Amelia thought the whole thing lacked authenticity. She wanted to believe it because it was, as she thought, interesting and would make good repetition, but it closely concerned her papa and his welfare and therefore it was important that she should not treat it as though it were a kind of game that she and Roddy might play. ("I'm an old witch and I'm going to put a spell on you, Roddy." And Roddy would shriek and hold his head and roll in the grass.)

Then Amelia thought of a way of showing up Nokomis' powers of invention.

"But what is it like, *this* jewel?"

"You haven't *seen* it?"

Amelia shook her head firmly, which is not really *telling* a lie.

"It is quite big. About so big." Nokomis made a circle with her thumb and forefinger. "That's why it is special. Moonstones abound, so they say, in India, but it is the size of this that made it important. That and the diamonds all round, huge ones. And it can be fixed on to a long kind of hairpin so that on great occasions you can wear it in your piled-up hair and it shakes slightly and so the French call it a *tremblante,* and why it is called that in French is because they were fashionable when Napoleon was

141

young and used to give these marvelous balls in Paris every time he won a battle."

"You have seen it then?"

"Of course, how would I know what it looked like if I hadn't?" A slight boost to Amelia's credibility.

There was a long pause which Nokomis broke by saying, "You know where it is, do you not?" Amelia knew where it ought to be, which was in the Bank: Dixon, Brooks & Dixon, 25 Chancery Lane. Papa had said he would take it there. But it was not there. It was here and now Amelia's mind turned to the great misfortune that had befallen them all. That Papa's name should be banded about so that "everybody knows" Papa was a wife exterminator. That this should be said about such a dear, harmless, beloved person was an evil and unnatural thing, and if there were any curse-causing object at large, to bedevil such an innocent man as Papa is just the kind of thing it would do. A wicked man would be immune; a good man would be vulnerable.

Papa had been about to take the jewel down to Chancery Lane; he had taken it out of his collar box and slipped the case in his pocket. Something had happened during the morning when she was at school regarding Mama receiving one of those terrible letters herself, and Papa had put the jewel . . . had put it . . . for the time being. . . .

Amelia could not take her eyes off an old tea caddy, one which Mama had inherited from an elderly relative. She liked it but they had never used it because Mama had a more practical one. The one that Amelia could not take her eyes off stood on top of the walnut tallboy and was quite big enough to hold the case in which the jewel was kept because the central division with which it was once fitted was no longer there. It was made of mother-of-pearl in small squares and two of those squares were

142

missing from the side. Amelia was not thinking, she was acting entirely automatically when she pulled the footstool up to the tallboy and lifted down the tea caddy. She must have noticed Papa or Mama touching it recently or heard something said that she could not recall.

She brought out the case, opened it and held the jewel before Nokomis' eyes.

"That's right," Nokomis murmured casually, but she could not hide the fact that she was deeply impressed. "You knew it was there all the time."

"No, I did not," Amelia said firmly. "The devil in it told me!"

Nokomis, toying lovingly with it, laughed and her laugh had a nasty edge to it. "Silly little thing, believing in devils!"

She caught, at the stop in the village, the Highgate bus to Charing Cross, downhill all the way, and alighted at Charring Cross where she had to walk a quarter of a mile or so, through the demolitions which were proceeding and over which, during working hours, dust whirled in the manner of a sandstorm in the desert. Seen from this side the destruction was moving rapidly westward of Westminster Bridge and it might be that one morning the workmen would start with their axes upon her present shelter. But she comforted herself by remembering that she would have some kind of warning because the house could not be demolished with the furniture still in it. But how soon would the smell be dealt with and how could the country have been governed at all with the fearful odors permeating the old Westminster Hall where Parliament now sat?

Had it been less crestfallen and clearly obsolete, she would have been proud to run up those Queen Anne steps with their elegant spearheaded railings and put the key into the lock of "her house." As it was she did this hurriedly, as though she did not wish to be seen. She slammed the front door and there was a corresponding crash from near at hand which gave her a shock so that she jumped and shuddered. Every time she entered there was noise of a kind. Had the house already started to fall? She peered into the parlor from which the sound had come and saw at once that a large oriental vase had fallen from the pedestal upon which it stood and was on the thin carpet in smithereens. Had banging the front door caused this?

She stood looking down at it. Did this mean that she would be held responsible? If so had she not better get in touch with the owner's lawyers and point out to them that the house was so fragile that the closing of the front door could cause disruption to this extent?

She went upstairs and sat down on a window seat. She opened the jewel case. Gloatingly she stared down at the Inguta *tremblante.* She counted the diamonds: eleven fine specimens. One single one of these could keep a person for life if they were to use it with proportionate care. She would start off by selling one. If Daniel Ramble-Smith was going to be difficult she might have to spend the proceeds of that first one in getting another rich husband.

To catch a titled man might cost her, well, half the proceeds? A Lord . . . to win a Lord from nothing . . . might cost a whole diamond. She sat musing, nervously nibbling a corner of her thumbnail. And who was the best jeweler in town to whom to take the jewel? She would pay him well, but only if he were to allow her to watch him at his task. What jeweler would allow that? No reputable one; he would be affronted at having it suggested to him.

Two long, gilt console mirrors filled the strips of wall

which divided the three windows from ceiling to floor. Nokomis jumped up and pinned the jewel to the silk between her breasts. She swung this way, that way; the effect was breathtaking. "Hell and damnation," she swore and, "the devil damn thee black, thou cream-faced loon!" The latter was an expression used frequently by Grandfather Pennyform, who knew not from where the expression came but who liked the length of the abuse. Neither had Nokomis any idea who invented the expression, but she intended it for Daniel Ramble-Smith, who was behaving in a pixilated manner and would not be captured. Perhaps, after all her experience, Nokomis was wondering whether, in the end one did not benefit from refraining from jumping into any and every available male bed. Was it possible that the hackneyed warning to wantons that her virginity was a girl's greatest asset was, in fact, true? She brushed aside the debilitating thought.

There was no one, no presentable male, no unmarried male anywhere either on this side of the Atlantic or on the other side, to whom Nokomis could turn in her determination to marry a rich man. She had no particular sentimental wish to "live happily ever after." She just needed to be safe in his arms and behind his name. She fingered the *tremblante* lovingly; this, *this* gorgeous thing could solve her problems, but was she really going to have to mangle it in the process?

She rummaged into her luggage and brought out her manicure set which contained a small but exact pair of pinchers with which she firmly grasped the tiny gold claw which secured, with three others, one of the diamonds in its setting. Though fragile, it was extremely rigid and she could not bend it at all. Perhaps it was as well, since the diamonds had to be secured into a safe setting.

She had now less than one gold sovereign left of

Grandmama Pennyform's allowance, but the next installment would have arrived at Messrs. Melbury in Red Lion Square.

At this thought she felt more cheerful; whatever happened, however great their dislike of handing it over to the girl who had shown herself capable of such abominable behavior, they would be compelled to by law.

No, she would bravely march into the offices of Melbury & Son and demand her allowance. If they made her go to Hampstead to Thomas Nateby-Dyce for his signature, she would not perhaps be able to escape too easily.

Above all, she thought as she took off her stays preparatory to going to bed, above all, she must remain free, and she cast her stays from her to show herself just how free she intended to be. She had had wonderful good fortune after her vain attempts to enter the house in Buck's Walk when everybody was out; she had "retrieved" what she said was her own property and, very far from having to steal it, it had been put into her hands. And at this she laughed gaily as she cast off the last garment, being her chemise; it was almost beyond belief that fortune should reward her in such a manner because it had seemed that fortune was always against her. She climbed into the huge bed with the moonstone jewel in her hand and slipped it beneath her pillow before she drew the curtains close, then blew out the candle upon its little shelf.

She went to sleep.

But not for long.

It was as though some great fiend were ripping a sheet from top to bottom, or was it more of an eldritch scream whistling from where to where? Across the city? Across the street? Across the house? Through her bed?

Or just through her ears?

It was beyond being a mere sound, it was a happening which ended with a giant sound of cracking.

Nokomis hid her head under the clothes and clutched herself.

And the absolute silence which followed was almost as bad as the preceding sound. After minutes had passed and the terror seemed also to have moved on, one arm came out from under the clothes and felt for the jewel. Finally her fingers touched it and she lighted the candle. She peered out between the curtains on the door side and could see nothing out of the ordinary. But when she peered out upon the other side she saw the consol mirror, which was between the windows on the further side from the one nearer the bed, had broken into tiny fragments which lay all about between the floor and the bed so that if she were to have jumped out of bed on that side the soles of her feet would have been torn in shreds.

The candle was burning low. What if it were to go out, as it soon would do? She did not dare to leave her bed and once the candle had burned out she would be in the dark, and alone.

But it was nearing the summer solstice when the sun is farthest from the equator in winter and in summer, a time when the light or the dark seem to stand still for a while. Now it was the light which came through the bed curtains at the thickness of a page from the Bible, and seemed to save the reason of the shuddering woman. The candle had gone long ago and now was she able to sleep; but only until the wagons started to groan past, spreading their load of grit.

After a restless while, brave with the light, she flung back her bed curtains and leaped naked from the bed on the door side. It was none too warm; snatching up the bedcover, she wrapped it around herself and gave her attention to her still unpacked trunk by the door. With

147

the bedcover wrapped round her waist she snatched clothes one by one from the trunk, held them up and cast them aside. Apart from her face, which wore a disagreeable look upon it, she was more beautiful than the dawn; a firm, large, wondrously smooth young woman. To see her was to be reminded of the Danaïdes of whom she might well be one; a fine specimen of the fifty daughters of the King of Argos, beautiful creatures who all married their cousins, and each one murdered each husband upon the nuptial night with a dagger given to every one by their papa.

As Eleanor Dyce had died there were people present in her room, two lawyers and old Mr. Killarney, the retired lawyer from the same brotherhood who never let Eleanor out of his sight for long . . . and Nokomis. And when Eleanor had finally died Mr. Killarney flung himself upon the bed and buried his face beside her in the pillow; the two lawyers had taken her pearls from her neck and her Inguta jewel from the top drawer of her dressing table before departing. And while old Mr. Killarney had continued to moan into the pillow, Nokomis had had a quick look through Eleanor's wardrobe. Too quick, as it happened, because she now discovered that in her haste she had brought a number of dresses and petticoats which would neither fit her nor suit her.

But the first article she had grabbed and stuffed into the bottom of the trunk was a wildlooking racoon fur coat, ground length and intolerably heavy but miraculously warm; the coat of a lifetime. Nokomis slipped off the bedcover and naked, pulled the coat around her. She waltzed up and down the room, the skirt of the coat flying out on a parallel with her black, black hair. Had it not been a large room, she would have suffered agonies on the broken glass.

148

Prudence slowed her down and sent her out of the door in search of a broom. Now was the time for her "Dandylion" to knock upon her front door, but what a fantasy thought that was; there was nothing less likely, and besides, she was after more solid prey. Business first and frolicking afterwards.

A breakfast brought to her on a tray would have been pleasant; all she had was the three buns left from those she had purchased before meeting Amelia at the shop at South End. Having cleared up the glass after a fashion and poured the fragments into an empty cardboard hatbox from the dustpan and moved the box out of sight into the closet, she threw everything but the fur coat into the trunk and slammed the lid. On the lid was a dull brass medallion with the entwined initials of Eleanor Dyce; it had been in use a long time; it must have gone out to India when she was a girl and back home on the long, long voyage more than once. She was glad she had it; furthermore, she was sure Eleanor would be glad she had it.

She sat on the window seat to which the sun was now creeping around and thought about Eleanor Dyce, the only person who had ever loved her, and she imagined the heat of the fur coat on this spring morning was Eleanor's blessing. She must try to adjust some of the clothes she had taken to her own proportions, but in the meantime today she would wear the checked taffetas she had bought in New York, with the new pantaloons and slippers. She slipped off the coat and dressed with extra care, turning this way and that in front of the remaining mirror. She put the jewel case in her reticule and drew on her black silk mittens. Then she let herself out of the front door into all the noise and dust, making sure the door key was safely in beside the jewel case.

It was Thursday.

149

They knew that in Amelia they had a strange child. Emma so deeply wished for another and prayed to God to send her one since there seemed no reason why He should not. But it was bad for Amelia or any other child that her parents should pay too much attention to her and discuss her at length. In the circumstances it was difficult not to do so; she differed so much from other children they knew. It was not that she was too clever that worried them; many children achieved an inordinate cleverness in early youth; that could founder upon the rocks of adolescence. It was that Amelia seemed unnaturally adult and Emma blamed her continued childlessness for this and encouraged the school friendships. "The more she sees of other children, the better!" she frequently said, both to herself and to Thomas.

Thomas' anger had had a long vacation; it was a long time since he had felt anything more than mildly cross, but now with Amelia standing in front of them looking inordinately pleased with herself, he felt anger rising. She had lifted the tea caddy down from the top of the walnut chest and was holding the box in one hand and the lid in the other, explaining how she was "saving" her parents from the influences that had been therein.

"God damn it, Amelia!" Thomas struck the top of the fragile loo table with his fist and one of the three little legs broke off, which made him even more angry. "How dare you interfere?"

Any other child might well have rushed weeping from the room at this totally unexpected reaction, but Amelia bravely stood her ground; looking down at the caddy ruefully she carefully replaced the lid and thoughtfully ran a finger over the inlaid pieces of mother-of-pearl. "Somebody has to help you, Papa."

"Help *me* . . . what on earth are you talking about?"

"You are so 'up in the clouds,' Papa."

"This is the most infernal impertinence and leaves me totally bewildered! The Nokomis woman has behaved abominably; she has no right whatever to come here at all, since she has clearly washed her hands of us once. And now . . ." He clutched his neckcloth as though he were being strangled. "*Will* you leave the room, Amelia?"

She walked slowly past him with lowered head and replaced the tea caddy upon the top of the walnut tallboy, which she could only just reach on tiptoe. She repassed him within a foot or so and opened the door, through which she disappeared, only to push her head back into the room: "You have not permitted me to have my say. It is your belief, as you have often told me, that in a clash of opinions one should always allow the other person to have their say, till they have said everything they wish to tell."

As the door was quietly closed he looked red-faced and furious at Emma. At first Emma could have laughed, but now the situation was too serious; she looked bewildered and slightly shriveled. She opened her hands as though to demonstrate that she had nothing to subscribe to the scene. But as Thomas fumed up and down the small parlor and finally gave a vicious kick to the broken table, which landed in the empty fireplace, she said, "We must be rational! Would it not be wise to take yourself for a walk, dear? When you return you could have an amiable talk with her, perhaps."

There was a long pause before Thomas answered. "Where have we gone wrong, Emma, you and I?"

"I think we have behaved childishly, Thomas. A kind of 'jam for tea' condition has overtaken us since that

151

memorable day when we decided to go to the Melburys in Red Lion Square." She stopped for a moment and examined her fingernails, careful of what she would say. "*Either* we should have told Amelia everything, not making too much of it, *or*. . . ."

"Yes? Or. . . ."

"Or we should have told her nothing at all and been very careful indeed not to allow her to think there was anything extraordinary in the air."

There was another long pause before Emma said, "And your mother, Thomas, of whom you have spoken so little. Can it really be that she made a friend of Nokomis to the extent of telling her about, for instance, the Inguta gem, not to mention a number of other instances of her life in India?"

"Yes, I am learning now what I never worried about when I knew her. In all my life with her I never asked myself what sort of woman she was; in those days (and I really believe in these days too), one's parents were never criticized, one accepted them as they were and gave thanks to God for the great blessing of them." He said this bitterly and angrily as though enraged with himself for his own stupidity. "She probably left me because I bored her."

At which Emma buried her face in her hands and wept with laughter, and Thomas gave a kind of snort and slammed out of the room, very nearly tripping over the broken little table.

Emma stopped laughing instantly and reprimanded herself for her constant uncontrolled laughter. She sat on the floor and attempted to fit the severed leg back into place, trying it first this way, and then that way, but having no success.

The door opened a fragment. "He's gone out, Amelia. Oh, you bad girl to so enrage him!"

Amelia crept up and sat down on the hearth rug beside her mother. "I quite know you do not understand, Mama. But you did leave the house, you and Papa, and Nokomis and I here at home while you went here, there and everywhere, buying things and seeing your friends. So I did spend a lot of time with her . . . we could not sit in separate rooms! She did not like going for a walk on the Heath with me *and* Roddy, so I told Roddy I had to go with Nokomis because she was lonely, and he understood. So she talked on our walks and told me all sorts of things. . . ."

Amelia looked dreamily out of the window, and Emma's heart, in spite of her recent laughter, sank even lower.

"And Mama . . . have you not observed how everything has changed for us?"

She nodded, expecting elucidation.

"We were always so happy. . . ."

She nodded again.

"We have not been so, recently, have we?"

"No!" Emma said emphatically, but she would not encourage Amelia to continue.

"Ever since we had the moonstone," Amelia said triumphantly. "Papa said he would take it to Chancery Lane to the vaults of the Bank there, but he did not. I saw him put it in the tea caddy, I remember now, I saw him from the hall. Nokomis only wanted one thing of us, no, two things, your pearls that you are wearing now, Mama, and, much more, the moonstone. I have asked people if moonstones are supposed to be unlucky; the teachers at school said yes, and Roddy's father, and the man in the fish shop in the village and everybody said either they did not know or they said *yes,* very unlucky."

Emma looked so uneasy that Amelia added, "Of course I did not tell them why I wanted to know. Anyway,

Mama, you can cheer up now because Nokomis has taken it away and we shall never see her again and the bad luck that has been all around . . . gone!" And she threw her arms up in the air to show just how gone all the bad luck was.

But the bad luck dogged them still because Papa had taken himself and his anger against his young daughter with him after he had stamped out of the room upon hearing Amelia's confession. Seeing the stage in the High Street about to start for the West End, he jumped on it and presently entered his club. As always now when he entered the club he looked automatically for the squatting Hindu syce, who this afternoon was not there. But Albert Niton was there; he got up as soon as Thomas entered the smoking room and they went into the library where there was no one.

Albert took the note from his pocket and Thomas knew with sinking heart exactly what the envelope contained. "Not another!" he exclaimed. "Those poisonous notes! What does it say this time?"

"So you're still a wife killer," Albert said as he handed it to Thomas with a sickened little laugh. "Thomas! You are the last person to have an enemy. For God's sake what has taken place for this absurdity to happen to you, of *all* men? It is crippling, however untrue it may be. It must not be allowed to continue. The first time it can be disregarded, the second time too, perhaps. But if it goes on, Thomas . . . if it is hammered in . . . there are those who begin to believe, or, if not quite to believe, to begin to ask themselves." He clasped his hands and shook them as though he were wringing a neck. "If only, *if only*, there were a witness!"

"How could there be?" Midship. Midnight. Midway.

154

Alone with a she-cat. Screened even from the last solitary drinker in the light of the last solitary lantern in the saloon, by the longboat.

So *how could there be?* They could find no answer so they kept silent for several minutes while Albert sullenly cleaned out the fragments of burned tobacco that had remained from his smoking recently in the right place, which was the club smoking room.

But for a moment Thomas' eyes were riveted to the envelope. He pointed: "K-n-i-g-h-t-o-n? You see how it is spelled?" He knew the writing, it was that of Nokomis, a kind of print. He was quite sure of it now, though he had seen it only once when she had written a shopping list when Emma had asked them to shop for her in the village. He had found it lying upon the parlor floor later.

Albert was looking at him keenly. "Do you know the writing?"

"I am not sure but if I am sure, then it is not so bad, not so bad."

They sat on in silence until Albert said, "How I envy you that little girl of yours, Thomas. I married too early; I am now a grandfather. To have a child of your Amelia's age keeps you young, by Jove!"

Thomas did not actually laugh, but his face wore an expression of observing the oddities of his remark. "This very day, this very afternoon," he said, "I have for the first time in my life, seriously lost my temper with her. I do not mean I was cross. No, I was bitterly angry. There seems, these last two months, a change came over our otherwise happy family. These letters. . . ."

"It will pass, old man."

"But will it? My Amelia seems, or has seemed, a perfectly normal child. But now, of a sudden, she seems older than us. Observing us. Even critical. I have the feeling that I do not know where I am with her. I am afraid that since I left the army I have let my brain slowly rot."

"Rot? *Rot!*"

"Oh, I have kept myself competent enough to organize a library, for instance, but I cannot think quickly . . . in the way Amelia does. I do not and cannot spring to rapid and correct conclusions. In fact, I do not spring to conclusions at all, to be honest," he said, though he had just done so regarding the envelope.

"Do not worry, dear good Thomas; my own daughters are houris who take charge of everything, including the old folk, that is, my wife and myself. I rather enjoy it; they save us a lot of trouble. Mark you, we were never ones to lock up our daughters; we gave them their heads. And I feel sure your Amelia is the same kind of child as they were. It is always best to accept the child God picks out for you, and be thankful. Come and have supper with me downstairs and I shall feed you a bottle of wine; just what you need tonight."

And because he had drunk most of the Vouvray that Albert bought him, when he left the club to catch the last Highgate stage, he turned round on his way out of the club drive and, running his eyes over the waiting syce, this time he saw the one who was familiar to him and nodded to him with a "Good night," in Urdu. The syce, sprang to his feet and saluted: "Good night, Dyce-Sahib," also in Urdu.

XII

MAMA had said the grass was damp, so Amelia took out her book into the front and sat on the grass beyond the footpath with her back to the holly bush so that she could not be seen from the house, and Mama would not call her to do anything for her because Amelia was gulping down great undigested lumps of *Castle Rackrent,* a novel about Ireland which she was much enjoying; words like *abatements* and *drafts* were beyond her, but if she slid over them, the meaning would be evident within several lines. And it would have been impossible for her to read aloud because, though she knew for instance what the written word *sign* meant, she did not know how to pronounce it; though she was both deaf and dumb to the contents of her book, her eyes sped over the pages in complete absorption.

"Heyday, Miss Nateby-Dyce!" Mr. Daniel Ramble-Smith cried. He came closer and tried again.

She started, then jumped up and made a slight curtsy, being the good-mannered child she was. "Good evening, sir. Where have you been all this time? Are you back; or are you here to rush away again?"

"It depends upon my great-great-aunt. It is as though

157

God calls her, but she is not ready to go, as it were. She finds her little life too absorbing to bear leaving it. But, of course, her time is up. What say you?"

Amelia made some entirely suitable remarks about the old lady and then he inquired about Nokomis Penny-form, and Amelia asked at what stage he had last seen her. But he put a misty, far-distant expression upon his face and said that he was afraid he had not kept up with home affairs. What was the latest news about her?

Amelia said she hoped they had seen the last of her, which remark shocked the young man as it was intended to do. Amelia said that since Nokomis had rejected Madame Mirabelle's great kindness she, Amelia, could not find it in her to think kindly of her. None of them knew where she was now living but, and Amelia relented now, she had been "around here" upon several evenings last week, looking for him.

"For me?" He seemed delighted. "Then where is she now?"

Amelia shook her head. "I do not know."

He was as shocked as he had been delighted. But Major Nateby-Dyce held the part of guardian to that foreigner to these shores, was not that so?

Indeed, yes. But Papa had washed his hands of her. Amelia knew quite well that this was not the kind of remark that Papa would approve, and, of course, Amelia would never have said it had he been there. Nor would he approve of the rest of what she said.

It was not the way a child of her age should speak, but Amelia found the greatest difficulty in being anyone other than herself in her speech, though she did bow to convention in her manners. "She has upset everybody; she is just an absolute nuisance! I know you like her and I am sure she loves you because you're nearer her own age and . . . and nice and kind to her. But I am sure she hated it here and I know she hated it at Madame's shop, only she tried to behave well there. She could not support it. You have to remember . . ." and Amelia was enjoying herself very much, "you have to remember, dear sir, that she is half Red Indian, *half*!"

Mr. Ramble-Smith looked embarrassed; he must have known that this was not the way he should be talking to Amelia, but he had done so before and he would do so again. Amelia was different from other children; she was more grown-up than her parents, he considered. Still, his own importunity embarrassed him.

Flattered and entranced by the attention being shown her, Amelia knew without doubt that she was about to transgress and promptly did so.

She said, "She has stolen the Indian jewel that my grandmama left to my papa. Well, I mean, I showed her where it was," this said with a trace of pride.

Mr. Ramble-Smith was aghast, but he hitched up the knees of his excellent trousers and came down to her level, squatting upon his toes and thus wobbling slightly to keep his balance. "Go on."

"Papa was going to put it in the bank but he kept putting off the day when he took it to Chancery Lane and I just, *just* happened to be passing the parlor door as he shut it away in an old tea caddy, instead of leaving it lying about in his collar drawer." Pause, then: "Well, you *see*, Nokomis says it was really hers, but Papa's mama in America died quite quickly; she told Nokomis it was hers to keep and Mama's pearls too. But then, when the old lady was dead, they brought out the wills she had made so long ago and nobody believed Nokomis of course. Grandmama would have altered the will if she had managed to live long enough to get someone to give her ink and a quill, but she died too quick. She was annoyed with Papa anyway."

Amelia stopped. She knew she was going too far. But was she going *much* too far? Yes, she was. "She was annoyed with him because he pushed or threw or tossed the first Mrs. Dyce out of the ship they were in and she was eaten by sharks." In her "wisdom" Amelia added: "I mean . . . probably."

"I see," Mr. Ramble-Smith said, as he scratched at a tiny spot of something on the knee of his trousers, still beside her and down at her level upon the grass, from whence, by the way, he could not be seen from Number 2.

"I see. So she's gone off with the loot?"

"The what?"

"I mean the . . . er . . . the jewels."

"Not the pearls. Mama is wearing those; have you not noticed them?"

"And what about her baggage?"

"What about it?"

"Where is it?"

"Gone."

"Gone! Lock, stock and barrel?"

Amelia thought for a moment: "Not barrel but . . . but everything else."

"And you don't know where."

Amelia shook her head firmly. She was fully aware that she had acted meanly and in a way which would not please her mother. She could not now retract anything, but she deemed it better not to add injury to injury by enlarging any further upon the subject. To end upon a happier note, she said, "But Nokomis needs help, I know she does. She needs you to help her for why did she come, time and again I saw her, in the trees, and . . . well, about . . . and once coming out of the milk shop down there at South End Green. Yes, she needs you."

Surely, that would put everything all right with Him to whom the parson at St. John's Chapel referred to as a Jealous God?

"What was this, this jewel like?"

"She would not be wearing it if you met her in the street."

"Why?"

"It is this size! It has a moonstone in the center and it is surrounded by big, big twinkling glass stones . . . diamonds, are they called? And round these huge diamonds are tiny ones, like picture frames to the big ones. And at the bottom part of the case is a big gold pin and you screw this into a little, little screwy thing fixed to the frame and you pin that in your hair and so it shivers and shakes and catches the light, specially at night by candlelights. It's for wearing at a ball. Nobody would wear it in Oxford Street. Or even Regent Street, though sometimes Mama takes me there and we have a look at the shop windows. I have never seen anything quite like that in them, so *big*. . . !"

She paused. "There's Mama calling me for dinner. . . ." She shut her book and stood up. She gave a little bob, said she enjoyed their talk, and scampered off and Mr. Ramble-Smith remained hidden from view for a few moments, partly because he wished not to be seen and partly because he felt he had barely the strength to rise.

Upon the little table which he had had to move aside to accommodate the luggage of Nokomis weeks ago in his little hall, there stood a silver salver now entirely obliterated by correspondence which had been put through the letter box in the absence of the owner of the

161

house, and laid tidily upon the table by the assiduous manservant (who, incidentally, served two gentlemen, the second one living on the other side of the hill, hence his frequent absences).

He found the opened envelope for which he was looking with the large printed lettering on the front of the envelope, which was one of the type upon which the stamp is printed. (Though it had a penny stamp imprinted, it was not one of the famous penny blacks.)

The note inside, folded once, bore the hackneyed message regarding the murdering propensities of Thomas Nateby-Dyce from an anonymous well-wisher. It was neat, careful printing and large. He stared at it at some length; then he drew another envelope from his pocket, addressed to him at Buck's Walk, because he had picked it up off the floor where it had been awaiting his arrival home. He had already read the note, but he read it again:

Dearly beloved Dandylion,

When shall we meet again? Have you no longer any wish to see me? On Saturday afternoon will you meet me to walk in St. James' Park and bring a bottle of cherry brandy? I shall wait for you in Piccadilly where the new stages leave, the White Horse cellar at 2 o'clock. I X you X X X

Nokomis X

The writing was larger than average and sprawling; it had been written with an uncertain quill which had twice crossed with a splutter. He carried both notes into the parlor, through the window of which he had a better light. He held them side by side and studied them closely. The resemblance was too tenuous to get excited about, but it was worthy of note and something to remember.

He felt in his pocket for the folded and gummed cover of the corrupt letter into which he intended to slip back the letter, but he was at once arrested when he held the envelope in his hand because it was an exact replica of the second (and love) letter.

They were identical even to the postmarks, which were both *London*. It was by no means impossible that two different correspondents might write to him in a cover with the self-contained stamp and identical postmark, especially when it is *London*, but the fact remained that it was barely a coincidence. It was something that was almost unremarkable and required no exclamation of surprise.

It had never crossed his mind that Nokomis had written the envenomed and perverted letter regarding Major Nateby-Dyce: Why should it?

It still never crossed his mind when, weeks later, he opened a very different kind of letter in exactly the same type of envelope.

Only now, minutes after he had had an extraordinary conversation with the Nateby-Dyce's girl, was his mind polluted sufficiently to remark, at the very least, the likeness.

Still, it was no mortal sin to send vile accusations through the post.

Or was it?

If they were true?

True of Major Nateby-Dyce?

Never, never! A gentle man, if ever there was one. And a gentleman to boot.

But even a gentleman, in pressing circumstances, has been known to raise his hand to his wife.

Unfaithfulness, perhaps. What about the *crime passionnel,* quite endorsed by that country just across the Straits of Dover, where a man may shoot his unfaithful wife and her lover too, and still not necessarily be guillotined or even, in some circumstances, deported?

Quite unmanned, Mr. Ramble-Smith searched among his miscellany of bottles in his dining room sideboard cupboard.

He was looking for the cherry brandy.

She felt dashing as she hurried along Whitehall, and she looked it. She was eyed by the workmen as she left the Westminster confusion behind her, but there were no catcalls after her because this morning she looked a lady. The sun was shining and everything was going to be all right, except that she felt very hungry. Looking as she did, it would be impossible for her to enter any eating place which she could afford.

There was a jeweler on a corner in Regent Street, a fine splendid shop with a dazzling display in the windows. This one would do. A uniformed porter had just arrived at his post, ready to open the carriages of the gentry as they came. He hurried to open the double doors, and Nokomis swept in, in the manner of Eleanor Dyce, which she had carefully observed and now imitated. She stood very upright by the glass-topped counter, tapping the counter with her gloved fingers as though she were in a great hurry, which indeed she was. If she did not have something to eat soon, she would quite simply fall down.

An assistant came up smiling and rubbing his hands. His face dropped only slightly when he saw her opening her reticule and bringing out the jewel case. It retained the smile however, when she opened the case; it might be said, in fact, that the smile became somewhat increased; and there was some effort made, it was plain, not to gasp with delighted surprise.

"Um," the assistant grunted, holding the Inguta jewel at arm's length and a becoming angle. "And what are your wishes regarding it, Madame?"

There was no doubt an office behind the showroom where one could put valuables in pawn, or even sell them. Sell she could not do, but pawn? That would mean an instant breakfast, of course, but that was not what she had primarily come for.

"I want one diamond taken from among the eleven big ones."

Instant consternation. Shocked exclamation. "But Madame. . . !"

"Could it not be replaced by a . . . by a false diamond of the same appearance?"

"Yes . . . yes," doubtfully, "it could be done . . . it would reduce the value of the *tremblante*, very much. . . ."

"Never mind, I must have that done. I would like to be present during the operation, of course."

And now the assistant was truly aghast. He looked wildly round. A senior member of the firm was eyeing him, so senior that he might have been Mr. So-and-So, the owner himself. Slow and stately, he approached. The assistant handed him the jewel, and Nokomis said she would like to have a sham diamond put in the place of one of these eleven big ones. She would like it done immediately and she would like to watch the operation.

Nothing she could have done would have been more shocking, but they remained exceedingly dignified, it was almost as though they were undertakers and Nokomis had suggested some unusual or even indecent antic regarding the body of the deceased. But the head man did the talking and so flattening was it that Nokomis could not stand it.

"Surely!" she said and now her voice had taken on the shrill edge and she started to writhe irritably. "Surely it is not unreasonable for me to ask that I might watch the proceedings?"

Unreasonable! It was completely and utterly unheard of.

Nokomis continued to argue, but he raised a placating hand. "In the first instance, to replace this great diamond, or any of these eleven, by an exact reproduction, would take weeks, since it would have to be procured from a maker, and many makers might have to be approached before the right size was found. It might even have to be made specially. In the second place—"

"Oh, for heaven's sake . . ." Nokomis stamped her foot, "if it is going to be like that, just take the blessed stone out for me and do not concern yourself with replacing it. I can have it done some other time, and *elsewhere*," she added nastily.

The head man closed the jewel case and handed it to her with a bow. He had come out from behind the counter in readiness to show her out (or, it might seem, kick her out).

There was no one else in the shop, and it was just as well because Nokomis' ladylikeness fell from her and had all her clothes suddenly fallen off, the effect could not have been more shocking. The two men who were attending to her and a reinforcement in the background were aghast, which only goaded her into shocking them even more. In her very worst accent (and when she wished it would be excrutiatingly horrible) she screeched: "You surely do not think I would let you lot take my jewel to bits and me not there to watch what you were up to, do you?" In a flash she was out in the street.

Surely, surely, she thought, in this country you do not have to hand in the thing you want to have repaired, and leave it with them to do what they like with, do you? And to test whether this was the case, or not, she entered the next jeweler she came to, one of equal splendor.

She stamped in, looking exactly what she was, a flustered and angry young woman off the street and not at all like Eleanor Dyce: "Say, would you take a diamond out of this here brooch for me, please. Just right here at the counter while I watch?"

These jewelers, too, kept their heads, but were a great deal brisker than the last. The assistant made a lightning sketch of it on a pad which lay on the counter before answering because he obviously thought it stolen. He would go far, this one. He then brought a lens out of his weskit pocket and studied it carefully through the glass. "Sorry, no," he said as he handed it back.

Nokomis looked round; there were four other customers in the shop. She leaned forward: "Please do. I will pay you well."

The assistant frowned as though he could not comprehend. "You wish me to . . . re . . . remove. . . ?"

"That's right. Lookee . . . I've tried to do it myself with my nail tweezers but these little grips which hold the diamond in place, they're much too strong; I cannot even bend one." She leaned forward, smiling, all her charm apparent, her ugly forehead hidden from view beneath her decorative bonnet. "Please."

She might just have succeeded if one of these bossy head men or managers had not hurried up. "Can I assist?" The first assistant told him quickly what was required. He also hurried out from behind the counter when Nokomis had, once again, tucked her jewel case into her reticule. Haste was necessary because his boss was struggling to achieve words which would meet the

167

occasion without accompanying abuse. And just as she was slouching past the first assistant as he held open the door she heard him hiss: "Try an ironmonger."

Try an ironmonger?

Was it a joke?

She walked slowly and dejectedly up the street under the arches.

She walked on till she reached the New Road. She turned right because she did not know what to do, and right meant as much to her as left. She, in fact, turned toward Soho where both cheap food and ironmongers were to be found.

The streets became narrow and dirty and packed; she turned up and down, backwards and forwards, choosing her shop; she was not many streets short of Seven Dials, which was the famous slum where people were taken who wished to be shown London at its worst, but she was bewildered by the chaos around her and thought rightly that it would be the act of a lunatic to take her brooch into any shop in this district. She also deemed it unwise to enter any of the eating places from which came such strange new smells; the jellied eel shops, the gin shops, fried fish shops, twopenny lodgings . . . she sought her way out; these were not for her. She met a tall peeler, evident by his hat among the crowd long before she caught him up.

"You want to git yourself back to Piccadilly, dear," he said pointing, and she set off in the direction he indicated though none too pleased at the peeler's familiar manner.

At the corner of the street she was walking down, only half in Piccadilly, there was a shop which put up a brave appearance, calling itself, STATIONERY AND FANCY GOODS. Looking in she saw that one of the two windows held a dazzling miscellany of fans, cheap snuff boxes, gaudy playthings, showy trifles, baubles, rings, brooches and sovereign purses.

No one in her senses would enter a shop of that standard with an ornament of the quality of the Inguta jewel, but Nokomis did not hesitate.

"A pretty bauble, is it not?"

The young man was delighted to see her, he could barely tear his eyes from her to look at what she was attempting to show him.

"What, what?" he exclaimed playfully. "Of course I will oblige, my dear!"

Nokomis was deeply wounded by his manner to her since she was feeling again her most ladylike. However, she would have to put up with it if she were to achieve her aim. And achieve it she did: first he took a small pair of pinchers from the drawer under the counter. Then, unsuccessful at making any impression upon the four small prongs holding the diamond in place, he put back the pincers and took out a larger pair of pliers. He was clearly not qualified to do a job of this kind and should never have attempted it, but the attitude was that of helping a member of the opposite sex, however idiotic her request; an inept and clumsy oaf playing Knight Errant. He made no impression upon the main jewel, which stood up to his handling marvelously, but with much twisting of his face and wrenching of his mouth, as though he were trying to transfix his left ear with his front teeth, he did manage to twist one of the grips out of place, and the next one very slightly, so that he was able to edge and urge the diamond into the palm of his hand.

"There, lady. . . ." He held it out on his open palm as though he were a conjurer (or had just decided to be).

Nokomis was effusive with thanks; she writhed and wriggled and giggled her way out backwards, the jewel

169

replaced in the case and the diamond clenched in her hand. She did not even stop to buy a packet of fancy envelopes, nor hesitate when she noticed, as she must have done, the enthusiasm fade from the features of the assistant. She sped into Piccadilly and slowed down.

Much building was going on there, with fine new premises, and shabby old ones, side by side. The next problem, which was to take the diamond to a pawnbroker, was quickly solved. A dear old gentleman with, clearly, no other thought than that of helping a lady took her down the side of St. James' Church, past the Turkish baths and down an alley to the unobtrusive shop with the three golden balls painted long ago on the wood of the humble entrance.

Nokomis fully intended to have the diamond valued professionally, but for the moment food was her ambition; she would leave the diamond in pawn for a few days and soon buy it back with money that she would earn . . . somehow. She was contemptuous now about her previous fears regarding someone exchanging her diamond for false ones; she saw how foolish they were.

With apparent indifference and as little interest as though she had brought in a Britannia metal mug to pawn, the assistant offered her one hundred guineas for the diamond and showed that he was not prepared to discuss it by tearing the pink pawn ticket off the roll and handing it to her after he had written upon it as he did so.

Nokomis slipped the ticket very carefully into her reticule, beside the jewel case, and stepped out into the street, virtually at the point which she would have chosen if she had been invited to choose.

Crockett's Oyster Bar.

She was tired now, emotionally wrung out from the strain she had been under. She tore off her bonnet and, letting her long straight hair fall around her shoulders, she asked for a pint of porter and a dozen oysters and had no eyes for anything else until she had finished, at least, the oysters but not the porter.

A group of young men had come in and were making a good deal of noise, clearly clerks escaped temporarily from their desks for perhaps half an hour. One, who was taller than the rest, with untidy hair and an unkempt neckcloth, lounged gracefully against the bar with his back to it, his mug of porter in his hand and a slightly teasing expression upon his face as he stared openly at Nokomis. This was to be expected because she was the only woman present in the bar.

Refreshed now she responded and almost at once he came and sat beside her while they exchanged badinage. Though neither of them gave any personal information to the other, each was provided with enough banter upon which to start an affair. When it was time for the group to leave, their flirtation was well on the way to fruition and she promised that at eight o'clock this evening she would be sitting upon this same bench at this same table and in this same bar. She waited until the group had left before counting out, from below the table top, the amount of money she needed to pay for her meal.

Later she thought that she would have asked him "home" this evening if she had known the address. She had a confused conversation with one of the navvies working on the building site, if site it could be called, because it seemed so much more extensive than a mere "site." The end of the street that had the name upon it had already been demolished, and at the other end was the Chapel of St. Stephen; the navvy finally had to admit he did not know the street's name.

She would have to be vigilant if she did decide to ask

her clerk-friend "home," making quite sure that she was certain of the way. If he were to ask where she lived, she would answer: "Westminster," and if pressed further, "down by the river," but were she to lose her way or seem uncertain of it, she would cause him to realize that she barely knew her way about. She walked the half mile or so from St. James' where the oyster bar was, back to her temporary habitation, slowly and carefully taking notice of direction.

It was a warm summer day, not hot but with a gentle breeze. She was, therefore, shocked and astonished to find as she stepped into the house that a strong wind blew through the hall, snatching the front doorknob from her hand and slamming the front door behind her; there was sound from upstairs and downstairs in the basement of doors slamming and one earsplitting crash from the basement which, she discovered, was a large copper preserving pan which had unaccountably fallen from the top of the dresser-plate shelves where it had been propped. Examining it, Nokomis found it covered with dust and cobwebs; it had clearly not been moved for many years and the color was greenish-brown, since it seemed never to have been polished.

She was overcome with a sudden weakness; she felt her legs would no longer carry her. She told herself she was ill, not admitting that she was badly frightened.

What caused the tiresome terror that weakened her was that the wind, which had sprung up as she entered, had died down completely within about fifty seconds.

Or was it the shuddering of the house?

So weak had she become that she could only ascend the staircase by pulling herself slowly up. She reached the bedroom and flung herself upon the bed, her reticule now bulging out of recognition with the newly acquired sovereigns. She lay on the coverlet with one arm folded back under her head and stared at the familiar article which served the purpose of a pocket. She emptied the contents out upon the coverlet. She opened the jewel case and stared at it almost as though she were examining it anew. The diamonds were not quite as big as cats' eyes but as big as the eyes of a kitten; she fingered the jagged points made by the removal of one diamond; the whole jewel looked as though it had sustained rather an unpleasant wound, as indeed it had.

If it had a grievance before, it now had much worse grounds for complaint. If it had wished to invoke misfortune to the owner up to the present, how much more so now that it had received this damaging wound in its vitals!

The porter and the oysters lulled her to sleep in a despairing mood, but four hours later she awoke with a feeling of elation. She had now, without difficulty up to date, carried out that which she had planned to achieve. She had the Inguta jewel; she had a roof over her head, for the time being at least; she was on her own, responsible to nobody, and she could do what she wished, when she wished.

Were the intentions of Daniel Ramble-Smith serious at all? Would the young insurance clerk meet her on Saturday in Piccadilly or not? There was no time to be lost; soon the house would become unhabitable and there would be trouble about all the breakages. Every opportunity that occurred would have to be pursued.

Her meeting this evening was not important, merely fun, but tomorrow she must become seriously attentive to her project.

She was certain she could, if she were careful and clever, marry Daniel Ramble-Smith and "make something of him." But first she must try for a richer man of some standing.

The urge to do this arose from her experience of her grandfather Pennyform. Since she had started to grow up, he had irritated her beyond endurance, not only because he disapproved of her and deprived her of what was her right, so she considered, but he was a lazy wastrel; he made money, but he did not use it to good effect; he allowed unsuitable people to sponge upon him (unsuitable as opposed to suitable people, *i.e.*, his granddaughter Nokomis).

In her anger and frustration Nokomis would attack him physically in a raging temper; this had happened quite frequently until the awful day when he had turned upon her, (a fragile girl of sixteen!) and beaten her "black and blue."

She ran away, but of course she was found and fetched back; there was nowhere else for her to go. He was a constant irritation to her and she to him. She was glad when he died, but he left her nothing. He was always quoting the Bible to her and one day he said at a meal, eyeing Nokomis over the top of his spectacles: "He that overcometh, I shall give him the morning star!" Nokomis had flung herself into near hysterics, screaming that she was a grown woman and what the hell would anyone want with the morning star? It was just the way he talked, droning on about biblical matters. . . . Grandmama Pennyform had to call the maids in to pull Nokomis off the old man when she snatched away his spectacles and made to tear his eyes out.

Even though he was now dead the urge to get the better of him somehow clung to her. She must *show him.*

She thought mistakenly she was free of all that. Wild and free. She jumped out of bed and sought water with which to sweeten herself and perfume with which to make herself desirable.

And before leaving the room she made the huge bed

174

with care, putting on the old Indian bedcover, made with thousands of tiny fragments of colored broken mirror sewn into the satin (reminding her of the broken console mirror).

Meanwhile the young insurance clerk who was to meet her at eight was having an idle afternoon. Outside the sun shone and inside he sat at his desk nibbling his nails and picturing the ecstasy he might be going to experience as the sun sank slowly in the cloudless sky. He kept looking at the clock and at seven all the clerks were free. They tidied their desks, brushed the dust off the top of their hats with their sleeves and made for freedom. It needed a whole hour to eight o'clock, but he and several others filled it drinking porter in an ale house. He was careful to drink only as much as would leave him with money to buy a bottle of German wine for the lovely young woman he was later to escort. But it was enough to make him feel brave, also bold and fairly bad.

Back in the oyster bar five minutes before meeting time, he hurriedly swallowed six oysters and another six. He greeted Nokomis, when she had arrived the prescribed half an hour late, as though he had spent the whole time since he last saw her at midday thirsting for her. Which indeed he had.

She was hatless now and wearing a different gown from this morning; this one was profuse in lace which blossomed out round her neck and at the wrists and round the skirt like May blossom on the bushes.

They were gay and happy; they chaffed one another and exchanged tiny slaps until the bottle of Rhine wine was empty. A dinner would have been pleasant then but it was too late, the oyster bar closed at ten. There was a doughnut stall on the corner of the Haymarket, commensurate with the young clerk's pocket; he generously

175

urged her to more and more; whether these would make good companions with the still undigested oysters was something which he left unconsidered.

To have had a serious thought might have wrecked the evening, since the average nineteenth-century man preferred his womenfolk totally brainless. Aware of this, Nokomis appeared to have all the trappings that a young man out for an evening's enjoyment could require.

"We had better not go to my diggings," he said when they were full of dough and jam.

"Let us go to my house," Nokomis suggested with a slight accent on the pronoun. He ran a quick look over her as though he had just had a thought: *her* house?

"Where is it?"

"Westminster."

"What street?" There it came. She avoided it.

"It is soon to be demolished," she said, "to make way for the new Houses of Parliament."

"Lor!" was his only comment, and he did not pursue the matter of the street's name.

Having ample pockets in her petticoats, Nokomis had left her reticule under her pillow with its contents. Giggling now, she fumbled about in her pockets for the front door key and opened the door. But once inside the hall and the door closed, she seemed to lose her breath and put a hand to her breast. She had, in fact, lost her breath from shock which was acute even though she had expected to be shocked. There was a knock, knock, knock, not a regular one but loud: an object against wood.

She wrung her hands gasping: "Oh God! Oh God!"

There were many other sounds coming up the basement stairs: her companion looked startled. "Do you live here alone?"

"Yes. . . ."

176

"Is the house haunted, or something?"

She nodded. "Yes. . . ."

"Is this a joke you are playing upon me?"

"Much more likely that someone is playing a joke upon me. . . ."

"How long has this been going on?"

"A long time . . ." she lied. Whereas previously her arrival and the excitement of it all had divided her mind so that she barely paid attention to the extraneous sounds, she was now terrified. She was not getting used to it, she was getting more frightened, not less so. Her fear infected her companion so that he stood uncertainly upon the doormat, longing now to depart; to take to his heels and leave the mysterious lady with the house of her own to her troubles.

They stood rigid, listening, when there was a few moments' silence. Then they heard footsteps and the sound of water, sloshing to and fro. Then the sound as of a bucket being thrown across the floor.

"You'd better go," Nokomis snapped. Whatever may have been happening it was certainly not the venue for a love scene such as both had had in mind.

He agreed readily and opened the front door: "Sure you are not. . . ?"

"No. Go, go!"

He just stopped himself before hurtling down the steps and turned: "Meet you again? At Crockett's tomorrow, yes? Same time?"

She nodded distractedly.

"Then you will tell me all about it?"

She was listening hard now, but not to him. Seeing that he no longer had her attention, he fled.

XIII

IT was still Thursday but not for long.

The navvy who came on Thursday to clean the house was on the verge of leaving, since it was now ten o'clock and dusk. He noisily climbed the bare wooden basement stairs to let himself out of the front door.

Nokomis was crouching against the door, visibly shaking. The man was for the moment more shocked than Nokomis, but he recovered. "Lor love us! thought you was the ghost at last!"

And then she remembered: the old caretaker had told her. A navvy from the building site had volunteered to come in after work and do the job of cleaning the house throughout.

"What . . . what day is it?"

"Thursday at present. You the lady the lawyers said was here as temporary caretaker? Scared, are you? Don't come from these parts meself, but the lady as was Misses here forty years since, she died of shock, so they told me. Never seen a thing meself."

Nokomis wept. "I knew, I knew there was something!"

He was inclined to be kind to this poor lonely frightened woman. He'd known there had been trouble, the mess was terrible: he'd not cleared it up, he'd brushed aside all he could and left the rest for the lawyers to see; never seen the like, he hadn't. He'd not come again—there would be trouble and no mistake! He'd known as soon as he came into the house that it was around. He'd not spend the night alone in this house, not he! He was sorry he had frightened her and tried to make up for it with comforting words about it would soon be gone. Then, throwing down the key and adding that he would love her and leave her, he hurriedly went.

"It!"
It?
Surely in this peaceful country there were not houses carrying a story of a murdering *it*? Rape? Arson? Poison? Hatred? Jealousy? It was with the idea of leaving all this kind of thing behind her in that new unsettled collection of States back home across the Atlantic where there were people like the new-rich Pennyforms that Nokomis had come hopefully to England. She thought all this while she slowly dragged herself up the stairs which she had so lightly and hopefully skipped down in the early evening. She opened the big bedroom door and the double washhand stand against the wall behind the door, motivated by an invisible power, "deliberately" fell forward and crashed on its face. The two large china basins and jugs slid off and smashed to pieces on the thin carpet, and the soap dishes and perforated trays fell with them so that there was a veritable pile of irretrievably broken china upon the floor.

Nokomis, face downwards upon the bed, abandoned herself to hysteria. Since there was no one who either knew or cared that she was in a state of major hysterics, it had to peter out unattended, and left her fit only for sleep.

But next morning Nokomis, as the caretaker-tenant of the house, who had said she was known as Mrs. Mary Burnish, burst into the lawyer's office in Maiden Lane and was attended by the lawyer who had supervised her signature upon the exchange of caretakers which had taken place recently. He was only partly interested, his mind upon more important things, but in connection with this particular house he used a word which Nokomis had never heard and which seemed to have very unpleasant connotations.

Well, yes, the house did have an ancient *poltergeist*. It had been there a long time before the present owner's occupation; it might even have haunted the site before the house was built. Certainly no one in it had died of shock. It was nothing whatever to worry about. He spoke as though it were a mere attack of milk fever in a favorite cow. "Never listen to casual gossip!"

"Mrs. Mary Burnish," as might be expected, quickly became overwrought declaring she could not endure to share a house with a poltergeist.

So far the lawyer had preserved the tact so requisite to his honorable profession, but now he summed up his client sufficiently well to be able to speak plainly and tell her the naked truth.

"Nobody knows," he said soberly, "anything about poltergeists, but clever professors have given their attention to the problem from time to time and it is well known that 'they,' if that is how one may refer to them, react according to the people who come in contact with them. Some people, a very few, rouse them to activities of a destructive nature and the majority . . . have no effect upon them at all."

It appeared that in the years that their client had owned that house, there had been no manifestation of destructive haunting whatever. But the legend remained

180

and the stories around it varied considerably and were obviously inventions, in the main. Then "Mrs. Mary Burnish" smartly and quickly said she had no intention whatever of paying for the damage.

The lawyer considered for quite a time. "My only comment, Madame, must be to ask you to quit, since your presence is evidently causing the . . . er . . . upheaval."

So frightened had she been, Nokomis had not thought of this. Surrounded as she was by her possessions in the roomy bedroom, she could not bear the idea of being turned out immediately, once more entirely homeless. She was sorry now she had rushed thoughtlessly to the lawyer's office in Maiden Lane, and tried to retract. She succeeded, up to a point, in that the lawyer did not suggest accompanying her back to the house. She would clearly have to endure the antics of the polter-whatever-it-was for the moment and get herself married and out of the house as quickly as possible.

She rose and said with dignity that she had registered her complaint and he must make a note that something entirely out of her control was damaging their client's property. "And good morning to you. . . ." she bowed and left.

It was the eighth of June and that night she knelt upon the window seat of her bedroom and watched the great fire which burned down Astley's Amphitheatre, a great horse stud and a popular place of amusement at the foot of Westminster Bridge. Though fifty horses and twenty-two zebras were saved, the owner went noisily mad. It was a frightening evening and drained Nokomis of more personal fear for the present. The psychic phenomena after the fearful washhand stand exhibition reduced it-self to mere triflings: a saucer flying across the room, the flour bag in the kitchen quietly leaking a thin stream of fine flour off the chimney piece until it was empty, the

181

kitchen cutlery falling about, the sashless old windows suddenly opening, a door banging for no reason, a shutter flying open . . . she endured it, but she left the damage to the washhand stand in the bedroom exactly as it was, skirting it carefully to make sure she did not stand upon some broken china. Anyone could see at a glance that it would be too heavy for a woman to pull or push over.

She now decided that she would avoid meeting again the handsome but untidy young insurance man she had met at Crockett's Oyster Bar, and at once seek something much more elegant.

She would have liked to spend money upon certain amusements, Madame Tussaud's Waxworks, for instance, and Tom Thumb at the Egyptian Hall, but all that must wait until she was, as she termed it, "established."

Mrs. Eleanor Dyce had told her that the Berkeley Hostelery on the corner of Berkeley Square was, in her day, one of the elegant places which she had frequented when a girl, and Nokomis set out to discover if it still existed. The march of progress was so evidently in full swing in the outskirts of the old city of London, and society itself was moving westward toward the old Court suburb of Kensington, via Piccadilly and the New Road to Oxford.

She could be seen emerging shortly before dinnertime in her very best robe, which she had purchased in New York. It was the last word in elegance, being a softly falling black muslin scattered with pink flowers and a small white straw bonnet tied beneath the chin with pink ribbons to match the flowers. She wore black mittens, but because the June evening became chilly, she hung over her arm the white shawl which Mrs. Eleanor Dyce had had as long as she had known her. She carried white gloves to draw over her mittens and hoped it would not rain. Finding Berkeley Square was a matter of asking a

182

number of people to direct her, and it was quite a long walk from Westminster. She entered the Berkeley Tavern.

There were still customers frequenting the place who were, at a glance, clearly of Mrs. Dyce's caliber and with an unworried expression she sat down gracefully with the evident appearance of a young lady with the intention of meeting friends, taking a seat until their arrival.

It was easy.

One hour and she had made her kill, choosing carefully between several gentlemen who were interested in the most gentlemanly way possible. Concern for her solitude was the only object of their interest, of course, because as time passed and no one joined her, she looked more and more lost and bewildered . . . and appealing.

Unfortunately, none of those interested were exactly young but, as she told herself, beggars cannot be choosers. (Though, of course, she was hardly a beggar now.) And, of course, if they had worn their titles upon their breasts, they would have been more easily chosen, but she had selected a seat from which she overlooked the entrance door and the arrival of carriages and could pick and choose from appearances, at her ease.

She answered anxious inquiries with the usual concern for her friends who had not arrived. She greatly feared their carriage may have had a mishap on the turnpike coming up from Windsor . . . it was all so prettily done. This was a new Nokomis, far removed from the wild girl known to the Nateby-Dyce family. They would barely have recognized her.

As Nokomis sat in the Berkeley Tavern wringing her hands at the nonappearance of her nonexistent friends from Windsor, Mr. Melbury senior and a gentleman a good deal younger were pacing along Well Walk from the village where they had alighted from the Highgate stage. Mr. Melbury knew his Hampstead reasonably well; he had enjoyed many a leafy walk upon the Heath.

Thomas sat in the garden with papers round his rattan chair as he made some final notes to his indexes. He was happy about his work, and there were great hopes that the new library would be open in this present year. Emma had her seamstress in for the day and both were at work upon alterations and repairs in Emma's bedroom.

Amelia was at school.

Madame Mirabelle was selling a variety of headgear for day and evening at her emporium in the West End.

Daniel Ramble-Smith was at his great-great-aunt's funeral, partaking of the baked meats which followed the interment.

Miss Blockley was scolding five wretched girls who had allowed a baked custard to burn to a cinder when, in fact, it should have been slowly thickening in an oven barely warm.

The Misses Eglington were at their window, nudging each other for the corner seat from which *one* could obtain a view of the entrance to Buck's Walk from Well Walk but not the *other*. Thus there was always a struggle for ascendancy; apart from eating and sleeping, it was almost the only thing they did. The one who, at this particular moment, achieved supremacy tossed comments back over her shoulder to her sister: "Two gentlemen have turned in. Beautifully appareled. Walking sticks. They are going . . . they are coming . . . next door . . . *do not push, Gertrude*. . . ."

Bess showed them into the parlor and brought Thomas in from the garden carrying his papers in a hurriedly-put-together bundle. Mr. Melbury introduced Mr. Gritley from New York, a partner of the firm of solicitors who had been dealing with the Pennyforms' affairs for many years.

"Messrs. Killarney, Gritley & Company," Thomas said at once, "Mr. Brian Killarney having honored me with a letter which I value very much. I gather he was an admirer of my late mother, Eleanor Dyce?"

Mr. Gritley admitted that this was so. He made his mark immediately, there was nothing devious about him; Thomas took to him at once. He spoke with an unfamiliar accent but with no hesitations; he said that he was here for a definite purpose, his time was limited and that he had Mr. Melbury's full permission to "talk straight, and fair and square" about a very vexed and tiresome subject indeed.

Nokomis Pennyform, who had been a problem from the very dark day she was born. . . . "Nay, between ourselves, from the day she was conceived! Old Mr. Pennyform said upon his deathbed that she had been the curse of his life. Unhappy words with which to face one's Maker. My brothers and myself . . . and by the way . . . I have a brother himself a lawyer, practicing in London and with whom I am at present lodged. My brothers and myself, as I saw it, are resolved upon solving, once and for all, this family problem. This is why I am here."

Thomas brought the cherry brandy bottle and the liqueur glasses, and as they sipped it appreciatively he told the story as far as he and his wife and daughter were concerned, not in detail but as quickly and lightly treated as he was able to make it. He very much disliked having to tell them of Amelia's final officious action because they would suspect Amelia of being, herself, as big a problem as Nokomis. That she should give her father's Inguta jewel to Nokomis was, superficially, nonsensical. They would never understand.

185

That Thomas and Emma themselves understood might well be a sign that they were doting, stupid parents. However, he told all. He ended by hoping that they would never see Nokomis again.

At which Mr. Gritley cried that he hoped, indeed, that this would not be so because he had come to England with the express purpose of returning with her to America. "She is to be questioned in court regarding, particularly, the death of Mr. Brian Killarney."

Thomas gave a great shout of dismay, and Mr. Gritley was in no way going to mitigate his distress. "We have every reason to suppose," (he rubbed it in) "that the young woman Nokomis caused his death!"

Thomas sighed. "I see." He was not at all surprised.

"He was an old man but very much in control of his senses, I may say. He was kindness itself to Nokomis. After Eleanor Dyce, your good mother, died so sadly, Mr. Killarney literally took charge of Nokomis. She behaved to him like a fishwife, and finally in one of her tempers we have every reason to believe she pushed him down the very steep stairway in Eleanor's house."

> (Thomas Dyce
> He was not nice
> He pushed his Lady Mary
> In the Ocean)

There was a very long pause indeed during which Thomas appeared to be struck dumb. He crossed the carpet to his visitors and refilled their glasses and finally sat down with one himself, his fingers covering the glass so that they could not see how much he had poured for himself.

The silence was becoming grim, somebody had to say something. Thomas spoke just for the sake of it, but was

186

shocked to hear his voice, which was a croak. "*Pushed!* Did anyone observe. . . ?"

"No."

"Then. . . ?"

"That is our problem."

(And mine too! Alas, mine too!)

It appeared that Mrs. Eleanor Dyce, in the weeks before her death, had several long discussions with old Mr. Killarney about the future of Nokomis, because as Eleanor had said in her practical way, living with an old lady alone in this none-too-cheerful old clapboard house was no kind of future for a girl of her caliber. And several times Eleanor had said that she would write to her "very dear Thomas" after all these years and ask if she might send Nokomis to London where Thomas could perhaps supervise her finding of employment with some seamstress or someone associated with ladies' fashions, since it was a matter in which Nokomis showed interest and some ability. This project was, in fact, still being discussed with the three of them when Mrs. Eleanor Dyce fell ill and Mr. Brian Killarney's distress and concern were such that he never brought himself to talk about Nokomis' future in the event of Eleanor's death.

After the death and the funeral had taken place, no one was resident in the house other than Nokomis, with two Negro servants living in adjacent huts. Messrs. Gritley removed from the house Eleanor's personal jewelery and certain items of silver, and Nokomis was free to help herself to anything she might fancy before the will was proved.

Mr. Killarney, with the best possible intentions regarding Nokomis, would ride across the two miles from his home to the Pennyform residence and spend the day there, ostensibly keeping Nokomis company. By this

187

time she had heard about the small amount of money Grandfather Pennyform had allotted as her portion and was resolved to leave at once for England. The money not yet forthcoming, she had helped herself to many things in the house, and more especially some of the private and personal possessions of her late benefactor.

It grieved Mr. Killarney that she was doing this without consultation with himself or anybody, and in the most fractious of moods. Within three weeks of Mrs. Dyce's death, there came a Sunday when the servants returned from a long session at church and found the house deserted and Mr. Killarney lying at the bottom of the stairs with his neck broken.

All the baggage which Miss Pennyform had been accumulating in the front hall was gone. The servants were found to have minded their own business rather too successfully for anybody's comfort; what had happened between Nokomis and Mr. Brian Killarney was only to be guessed at. The most that anyone could say with any certainty was that he "rode over every day and spent the time with her." And during this period she was "packing" in preparation for her journey to England.

Undoubtedly it was then old Mr. Killarney wrote his letter to Thomas; it was found some days later, the envelope stamped down, addressed to Thomas Dyce, but in the absence of any further address or stamp the Gritleys had sent it to be readdressed to the Melbury firm in London.

The servants saw nothing in the behavior of Nokomis Pennyform that was contrary to what would be done normally in any house the mistress of which had died. If they thought at all, they had assumed that the lawyers had left instructions that her personal property was to be dealt with by the only female left in the family. She was constantly pressing raiment with an iron in the sewing room and sorting out piles of clothes upon the big bed in which Mrs. Dyce had died. . . . That she claimed much of the material was no surprise to anyone, and she told the servants that anything she left upon the bed was to be "given to the poor."

Messrs. Gritley had written a letter to her informing her of the small allowance due to her now under her grandfather's will and also of their plans regarding her future, giving her the name and address of Major Dyce in London. They also asked her to call at their office to discuss these details with them before leaving, and they awaited her arrival, both before and after Mr. Brian Killarney's sudden death.

They were entirely puzzled by the behavior of this Pennyform woman; that she had always been an anxiety to anyone to whom she was responsible, had to be accepted. But in view of the circumstances of Mr. Killarney's death, they felt bound to make some attempts to discover her whereabouts and discuss her extraordinary departure (and upon a Sabbath!) with her.

They would also wish to know more about the circumstances of Mr. Killarney's death: Did he suffer any form of apoplexy? Did he previously complain of any physical discomfort? Did he appear hale and hearty, as he had certainly been when he had left his home that morning, according to the groom who brought him his horse?

Finally, Emma was brought into the parlor and was apprised of the extraordinary circumstances of the visit of the two lawyers as shortly as possible. As always, Emma's behavior was impeccable: She sat with folded hands and calm unworried face and listened, instead of interrupting and exclaiming in the manner of many a woman, and even when they had finished telling and waited for a comment, Emma kept silent for several minutes, thinking, and to some effect.

She said that Mr. Ramble-Smith, a young Oxford graduate working in a discount house in the city, who lived next door but one, during the period she had been with them had more to do with Nokomis Pennyform than any of them. Consulting no one, she had gone on a trip of over a week with him to Brighton. Emma was quiet for a moment while the full implication of this information was digested by the men of law.

"I would venture to say, sirs, that it is he who might know more about Nokomis than any of us; since her last disappearance he has been here many times to inquire for her but he has been occupied very much of late with family troubles of his own and has been away from his house a great deal among his relatives."

"If you will permit, we will call upon him."

"He is at present at the funeral of his great-great-aunt whose heir, we have been given to understand, he is. Nokomis disappeared last Tuesday fortnight and took with her the quite considerable amount of luggage she had stored in his hall. We understand from my young daughter Amelia that she spent several fine evenings in our purlieus, hoping to see him. But, sirs, we are not left with kindly feelings toward the girl, I regret to say. Our very kind French neighbor, an elderly lady, a refugee from the Revolution, who has for many years owned and managed a millinery establishment in the New Road, was most kind. Almost upon Nokomis' arrival, Madame Mirabelle offered her a position in her establishment, indeed, as a resident apprentice. She did this without any written reference for the girl but simply on the recommendation that she was a vague connection of my

190

husband. And within a short time, though she had made a promising start, Nokomis walked out of the millinery establishment without any word of thanks or apology."

The two gentlemen exchanged glances: That sounded very like Nokomis. Now, having spent quite a considerable time in Buck's Walk, they felt they must depart and talk over the information they had learned from their kind hostess: Mr. Gritley wrote down for them the address at which he would be staying in Bayswater. He would be in touch again very soon. He bade them good day.

Thomas and Emma were left facing one another in the parlor.

"So much has been left unsaid."

"And must remain unsaid, Emma dear."

"Those terrible notes she has been writing. . . ."

"All that."

"But Thomas!"

"If there is, alas, something vile I must carry throughout my life . . ." and the hateful little refrain ran through his mind, "there is something equally intolerable Nokomis will have to carry through her life. Like myself there is nobody who witnessed her crime or my questionable crime."

"To lose her temper with an elderly man whom we know felt the best of good wishes toward her, and to shove or thrust him down a steep staircase . . . did she even pause to see if she could assist as he lay there? Oh, Thomas, how could she live with this knowledge?"

"Easily. She will fill her life with all the luxuries the Inguta jewel will provide. Her conscience, if not already moribund, will shortly breathe its last. Whereas . . ."

191

Thomas paused and said infinitely sadly, "*whereas* my conscience in the eleven years of living with such a, such a lovely person as you, has thriven, grown sharper and more active . . . and will kill me yet."

Emma put her arms gently round his neck and wept.

XIV

IT was no good keeping anything from Amelia. Both gentlemen had brought walking sticks and taken them away with them, but one had absentmindedly left his gloves upon the hall table and neither Thomas nor Emma, in their ferment of mind, had noticed them. They had had no time to discuss whether or not they should talk things over with Amelia and if they agreed to do so, how much they would tell her.

It was something which greatly affected them all three, as a little family: They told her all. Emma could think of no valid reason why they should make sure she would not repeat everything to Roderick and, besides, she did not know how they could stop it anyway. She had decided that since they could not control Amelia it was better to bring her into their confidence; indeed, they might even benefit from it.

She was quiet for some time after they had finished telling her, until she said, "Then Nokomis must be found?"

"Yes. For her own good she must be found. She will have to be closely questioned and if she can assure everyone that she did not lay a finger upon the old man, in one of her fearful tantrums, well and good."

"And if not?"

"If not . . . not," Emma answered for Thomas, who was too pained to be able to answer.

"She will be hanged at the crossroads," Amelia said in a small weak voice.

"I do not know," Emma said with truth, "what they do with . . . with criminals in America, either with men or with women." And she looked questioningly at Thomas, who was standing looking out of the window with his back to her and did not answer.

"But I quite like Nokomis," Amelia said thoughtfully. "She was always nice to me. She called me her cousin Amelia and said that I reminded her of Eleanor, not in looks so much but in ways, she said. She had not any, any money, Papa. It may really be true that your mama wanted her to have the Inguta jewel."

"If, *if*, it is unlucky, as has seemed to have got around, why should Mrs. Dyce wish it to go to her son?"

"Or anyone else?" Thomas put in. "We must not make ourselves absurd talking about something which carries good or bad luck, a curse or a blessing with it. We are living in the nineteenth century, remember. We are as ridiculous as though we still believed in witches."

"I *do* believe in witches; Miss Pritt at school is one."

"Do not be absurd," Emma snapped. And then she went on: "If Nokomis really believed in the nonsense about the bad luck of the jewel, why was she so anxious to have it, that you kindly gave it her?"

"But my Grandmama Eleanor believed it too!" Amelia exclaimed, aggrieved. "We all believe it a bit, Papa. We cannot help believing it. You never hear about anything that carries with it a blessing, it is always a curse." She laughed but only a little: "A curse is really more interesting."

And now Emma's eyes filled with tears in the effort not

to laugh, which Amelia so often caused her unexpectedly to do. So far in her eleven years, Amelia had never tried to be funny but how long would that delightful unself-consciousness last?

Amelia got up and took her father's hand. "I hate to see you worried, Papa. You have been so happy about the library and your club and all that, all these last days that we have been without the Inguta jewel. You *have*, do not argue, I have been watching you specially, you really have been carefree, Papa, for at least a week."

"I am never carefree, Amelia." But he smiled over her head at Emma.

"We will find Nokomis," Amelia said, "somehow. Now I remember, she complained somewhat that it was so foully smelly *down by the river*."

"You might, you just might find her, Amelia, but I beg of you not to try. Within such a short distance of this peaceful spot there are some terrible districts. Not that I can see my lady Nokomis settling herself in any spot that was not reasonably salubrious, but what I do see is my darling girl getting herself accidentally into some dreadful squalid dockland slum; Petticoat Lane, Houndsditch Clothes Exchange, St. Giles, Drury Lane, Seven Dials. You do not have to set out to find a slum, you fall into them unexpectedly, at every turn."

"Papa, I promise you I will take care. Roddy will be with me and he knows London better than I. Nokomis loves shopping and we may meet her in Regent Street or among the shops in the New Road, or in Piccadilly and St. James'. Besides, Roddy wants to go and see the ruin of Astley's Amphitheatre at the foot of Westminster Bridge that was burned down last week . . . I said I would ask you if I could go."

Thomas wished to shout: "I forbid it!" But he wished even more not to be the new kind of stern papa who was emerging, a papa who was unreasonable and expected his children to do exactly what he wanted: "BECAUSE I SAY SO!"

"You let Roddy and me go to Baker Street for skating on artificial ice last year!" Amelia said reproachfully, "and that was really dangerous!"

But Thomas was not going to give her his blessing to the suggestion that they wander the streets in search of Nokomis. He walked out of the room, quietly closing the door after him in a way that conveyed his displeasure in an appealing way, he hoped.

"I'll tell you what, Mama, Nokomis may come here."

"Never! *Never* after she has taken the Inguta jewel in the meanest of circumstances."

"Not about the jewel, Mama. About Mr. Ramble-Smith. She loves him. She calls him her Dandylion," Amelia chuckled. "She wants to marry him," she chuckled richly, her amusement rising, "but she thinks she should marry a *Lord* more."

"Good gracious, Amelia, I should have thought Nokomis was much more grown-up than that! Marry a Lord! She may look very showy but no Lord would be able to stand her voice! Oh dear, how catty of me! I should say, I *hope* she succeeds in her ambition, because I would prefer that we should not have her living almost next door as Mrs. Ramble-Smith."

As it turned out, he who showed the most concern for the apparently bereft Nokomis was also the most elderly of those who sought to help at the Berkeley Tavern upon that delightful June morning; he arrived in a coach and pair and had both groom and footman; the two servants were, in fact, a necessity in helping him down to join his friends. A heraldic shield was blazoned upon the carriage door, but he disappointingly turned out to be a commoner, a Mr. Hetty (or Mr. Hetté), describing himself as a Frenchman and anglicized in the manner of Madame Mirabelle, Nokomis noticed, in that he had no wish to return to his country.

He bored Nokomis, but she could see that he had distinct possibilities as a protector; there was no need for her to lavish her best behavior upon him; he was just a kind old simpleton distressed by Nokomis' predicament, she, alone in the Berkeley Tavern, awaiting friends who did not come.

"Come and sit beside us," the old man called, patting a chair close by, "young lady!" And Nokomis did as she was bid, but she was not her usual self, being quiet and thoughtful. She was thinking hard how she might turn this encounter to her advantage, because clearly the situation was not going to be as she had planned. Some of the company were drinking brandy and water, and Nokomis noticed a lady drinking a warm steaming brew which seemed inappropriate for the summer morning; but when Nokomis was invited to partake of a glass of the negus, she agreed and sipped it thoughtfully. Her plans had seemed so easy to carry out when considered, but in practice they appeared so much more difficult.

She would have liked most of all to take her new acquaintance to "her" house in Westminster; rotten upon its foundations though it was, it had a faded elegance, standing between two empty houses even further gone in decay.

But how could the haunting be laughed off? Pray, sir, come and meet my poltergeist?

Up to that moment in her thoughts she was a young unmarried girl awaiting her reluctant friends, but now she suddenly saw that it would be a better plan, in the case of Mr. Hetty, to be a young married woman who had suffered ineffable cruelty in the hands of her rascal husband before he abandoned her.

The latter, in a way, seemed more convincing than the endless waiting for friends, a scheme to which she had not yet planned the alternative end; the idea of a young man wishing to marry her upon the instant.

The trouble was that she was not nearly clever enough, she did not pay enough attention to detail in her schemes. An idea flashing through her mind was enough to set her believing totally in it and giving up the sheer drudgery of thinking everything might not go smoothly, in favor of numerous frivolities such as going to theatres and dances and routs, always the belle of the ball, accompanied by a handsome gentleman of total devotion.

When the little crowd surrounding Mr. Hetty had drifted away, Nokomis was very conveniently seen to be quietly weeping; pity for herself and her predicament causing sad slow tears to fall, with some effect.

Mr. Hetty patted her hands and sent out a message to his carriage that they were to wait for him in Constitution Hill, since he would stroll in the Green Park for an hour. And in the Green Park, with the folds of her flimsy skirt billowing about her ankles, Nokomis took the arm of her protector and confided her troubles. Her mittens concealed her left hand without any wedding ring.

At four o'clock, great friends now, they dined at Sam's Chop House in the Strand. One third of Nokomis' life story was enough for anybody; indeed, too much for some of the more tenderhearted. To hear the whole life story caused total suspension of belief, as Nokomis had learned over the years to her cost. Thus she had developed a certain artistry and daintiness about the telling of it by now, which left her hearers sad rather than aghast. She invariably edited it so that the hearer was left in the state to which she mentally called "on my side." If the listener's attention had not been wrung by the mode of telling, they might have paused to think that the story as told by Nokomis did seem to be one-sided.

Assuming that the whole story had been told, Mr. Hetty settled down to a pleasant evening, saying he would take her "home" before returning to his own home in his carriage; since they were not far from Westminster they would have an interesting walk along the stricken riverside from stairs to stairs. At which Nokomis became remarkably silent, and finally Mr. Hetty asked if anything were wrong.

Yes, something was wrong, very wrong. Nokomis had to tell him that the house she was at present living in belonged to a wealthy relative in the East India Company. It was due shortly to be demolished, but her relative had left all his furniture and effects in the house until such time as he had made arrangements to be stored. And Nokomis was in residence in the role of caretaker for the present.

"But the house is haunted," she said, pausing with her glass halfway to her mouth, as though suddenly reminded of this last horror. "If you can believe it," she added.

"A ghost!" cried Mr. Hetty.

"A . . . a. . . ." for the moment Nokomis had forgotten the word she had heard used. "A kind of spirit, which one does not see, but it makes frightening *sounds.*"

"A poltergeist!" Mr. Hetty was delighted. "I have never had the experience of a poltergeist, but I believe we have one in our own family. Yes, indeed! They say it came over from France with us when we fled from the

Revolution, and no wonder; our mansion in Paris was no place, even for a poltergeist. They are quite harmless, of course."

Harmless? But why argue, he would see for himself.

"But sir, I beg you, they are by no means harmless! This one throws things about, breaks mirrors, vases, tosses the crockery in the kitchen all over, hurls heavy copper pans—! It is only fortunate that I have not yet stood in the path of a missile. But what is worst of all is what I experienced yesterday; the whole house shudders . . . it goes like this": And holding up her hands she made them both shiver realistically ". . . until you think the house must fall."

Mr. Hetty let his monacle drop from his eye as he started seriously to consider. "But, my dear, they say it is not the house itself but the person who is in the house who causes this . . . this strange manifestation."

"What is a manifestation, sir, please?"

"It is a, now let me put it simply, it is a showing plainly something to the eye, or to the mind, indeed. *Proving something* might be a simpler explanation to you."

"But proving what?"

"Anything."

"I do not understand."

"Nor does anyone." Mr. Hetty quietly considered. "Supernatural!" And as Nokomis waited for elucidation he said: "The house might be showing its disapproval of you. *Not*, I hasten to say, because you have in any way erred but because . . . well, I can only repeat *disapproves*. But I am in no way knowledgeable or in the very slightest bit clever. I grope . . . I grope."

"Mr. Hetty. . . ." Nokomis' face had lighted up and her great popping eyes shone like beacon lights. "Mr. Hetty, would you go into the house without me and see what happens?"

Mr. Hetty attacked his second chop vigorously, hoping to appear that his mind was filled with the task of eating only and not the prospect of danger in any way. He masticated his mouthful energetically, swilled it down with beer, then said bravely and firmly: "Certainly, my dear, certainly. And I shall report the result, if any, to a good friend of mine who is a member of a small amateur society or club for the research of psychical phenomena."

Under these unusual circumstances Mr. Hetty rethought about walking back with Nokomis to Westminster but sent the potboy to tell his coachman to come for him at Sam's Chop House in the Strand.

Later, when the meal was over and Nokomis was sitting beside Mr. Hetty in his stuffy carriage with the footman so close to the tiny rear window that he seemed to be peering into their ears, Nokomis guided them down Whitehall and into the awful building confusion.

The coachman reined his horses and jumped down for further instructions. Nokomis pointed. "There are the roofs of the part-street in which I live, just visible amongst the new scaffolding. Perhaps it would be better if we were to get down and walk, Mr. Hetty, sir. There are so many wagons to obstruct. . . ."

Mr. Hetty would have preferred to have the coachman's support upon this foray, but he also greatly cared for horses and particularly their feet. He decided to leave the coach in a spot which he pointed out to the coachman, close to the Abbey; he beckoned to the footman to follow him and he and Nokomis made their way on foot. The surface was terrible, and it would have been almost impassable if it had been raining, but mercifully it was quite dry and within five minutes they had picked their way to Nokomis' abode.

She stood at the bottom of the steps and gave Mr. Hetty the key.

"I shall stay here and you may prop open the front door, sir, so that I may not be cut off from you. Shall I give you five minutes? I can tell you, you will not have long to wait if there is to be, as you call it, a manifestation."

"Adieu, fair maid," Mr. Hetty said flippantly, as though waving a fond farewell, he ascended the steps, unlocked the door, and Nokomis could see him walking across the hall. She waited with her hand on the black iron knob of the bottom rail, glancing back to see the footman at attention some twenty yards away.

She waited. Not a sound.

She waited.

It was very quiet because the building operations were over for the day, it being near ten o'clock on a light evening approaching midsummer. After about seven minutes she called. "Mr. Hetty, sir."

No reply.

She called louder, then swore: *"Satan!"* She picked up her skirt and ran up the steps, through the hall and up the first flight to where the door of her bedroom stood wide open and she could see through the windows across the river pink-surfaced in the light of the setting sun.

"Mr. Hetty!" she screamed and brought the roof round her ears, or seemed to do so. She stood anguished with her hands over her ears. The ghastly indescribable sound faded away as the house started to shudder.

Mr. Hetty's footsteps were heard on the oilcloth as he clattered down from the two top floors. "Who did that?" he shouted and Nokomis could barely see his twisted face standing in the doorway.

The house was shuddering and everything in it was shuddering. It would stop, she had experienced it before, and she knew it ended in a few minutes.

But Mr. Hetty was sick with fright. He was not going to

202

allow a few minutes to pass, nor even seconds, he fled for his life and rushing to the front windows overlooking the street Nokomis saw him being helped by the footman, stumbling and staggering back the way they had come and toward his carriage, a sorry sight.

"I shall never see him again, and it is all your fault!" she screamed to the devil within.

Before Mr. Gritley and Mr. Killarney had time to "get in touch" again with the family in Buck's Walk, Thomas sustained yet another stinging blow. He had considered that he had struggled out from under the weight of worry that had held him in thrall for the last three months and that a fair future with the new library lay ahead. But alas, there came a harmless-looking letter with the mildest possible postmark: Lyme Regis. Can any bad thing come out of Lyme Regis? he thought as he slid the point of his paper knife into the corner of the envelope and slit it neatly open.

It was from good Albert Niton whom, he now remembered, had taken his sick wife for a fortnight's holiday to that salubrious and sheltered Devonshire resort.

My dear Thomas,

By Gad! You poor soul; as some unfortunate walks through Billingsgate and stands on a stinking fish, carrying a piece away with him in his shoe he is constantly reminded of its presence and though he may take steps to rid himself of it, it remains with him wherever he goes.

That poisonous and damnable jingle about:
Thomas Dyce
He was not nice

that some drunken half wit made up in the good ship Berenice as she made her way home, has followed you even into the holy of holies. I am trying to be funny because if I did not I might as well be writing your obit. In plain English it was brought up by, I will not tell you who, in the Committee Room of the F.E. Club on its third meeting since you became a member and the Chairman has decreed that this must not be hushed up or concealed in any way. He has declared that he is proud to have the son of Dyce of Scinde as a member and has every faith in your integrity. In short, he wishes to have discreet inquiries made as to who, amongst the army people, was present on that voyage.

Thomas, my Catherine has been here only three days but has benefited greatly already. Our youngest daughter Trix is about to join us and I will take the opportunity of returning to town and staying for a few days at the club and playing the detective. I shall somehow get to see the passenger list of that voyage in 38-39 and go on from there. Do not write to me, it will distress you; but leave it to your old chum

> Albert Niton
> alias Elbow. (*Measure for Measure*)

Seeing Miss Amelia Nateby-Dyce sitting out on the grass after dinner reading, Mr. Daniel Ramble-Smith came out on to the grassy bank leading down to South End and squatted beside her: "Hallo, Miss Amelia!"

"Just the person we need," Amelia hissed, "you are always away these days!"

"It is, or I should say, it was, my old, old aunt who was occupying me. She has now died but not such a sad death, because she was indeed very aged, as you know."

"So you will leave your cottage in Buck's Walk! Madame Mirabelle says you will move into your aunt's great house in Cavendish Square."

He laughed. "Pure guesswork! I shall have to find, first, a wife who will consent to live in such a barracks. I am afraid you are a little too young for me, Amelia!"

"How I hate it when people say *too young*! Papa has forbidden me to go with Roddy, my friend, you know, and find Nokomis."

"Why do you wish to find her?"

"She is supposed to be living *here*, in Buck's Walk. Two gentlemen have come from America—no, *one*, the other lives here. The American one is a lawyer and has come to take her back to New York."

"Why?"

Amelia looked both important and mysterious, as though charged with dynamic information with which she had no intention of parting. She said, "Nokomis has not slept one night in our house since she came. My parents think that she would have what they call a bad influence upon me. I suppose they are right. But my papa does not want to tell the gentleman from America that this is why he has failed in the mission." She chuckled. "I heard Madame Mirabelle tell Miss Blockley that Miss Pennyform was, to the Nateby-Dyces, 'like a bull in a china shop.' "

"Amelia, I wish to talk to your papa. And I do not wish you to overhear. Is he at home now? Yes? Well, I will wait upon him. Now, you stay here and I shall watch you from your parlor window, and if you come in I shall leave, because I know that you are not so much an eavesdropper, but let us say that everything that is said in your home you consider to be your business, is not that so?"

"... she asked me to meet her in Piccadilly on Saturday afternoon, and though I did not tell her *yes* I had every intention of doing so. It was my great-great-aunt's death that prevented it. And now. . . ?"

Thomas said, "And I assure you, young man, that I have no idea at all where Nokomis is living. Though I did not challenge the American lawyer with it, I feel sure that they did not give me Nokomis' correct age; she was said to be eighteen, but my wife would not be surprised to hear she was anything between twenty-five and thirty. One can see that the lawyers would consider themselves entitled not to give the correct age. To take in a grown woman of the world is a different matter from giving house room to an unfledged girl. And if I may say so, I would consider carefully before taking her on yourself. May I ask how old you are?"

"Twenty-six. But I have no doubt that she may even be a little older than myself. Were I to ask her to marry me, I would be under no illusions regarding her. You see, sir, I have been petted and made much of all my life, by this crowd of aunts and great-aunts; there are no males on the horizon in my family and I am fully aware, thanks to the forthright speech of my tutor at Oxford, that I am what he called, a mother's darling. Do you agree?"

Thomas stroked his chin thoughtfully; he could have smiled broadly but refrained from doing so. "I see what your tutor meant. . . ."

"Well, if I am to deal successfully with all this property that is being heaped upon my unwilling shoulders, I must be wed to a woman with character and ability, a woman who does not sit all day making sovereign purses in the parlor."

"I see."

"I admit the quiet kittenish girl has an attraction for me."

"So you feel the need to be organized?"

He nodded.

Thomas shuddered. "It is as well we do not all have the same tastes."

"Since you think I have some reason for wishing to see Nokomis again, will you, then, assist me to trace her? Yes, I am well aware she may be lying in the arms of another, but if I find her whereabouts I can discuss with her the proposition of our marriage and I would, of course, make it clear that I should expect moral behavior; I should assure her that our marriage would be the end of her 'wild oat' period."

"I declare to you that I am willing to assist you in finding the girl. I admire the way in which you have thought out your affairs, but I confess that I have no ideas as to where she is or what she is doing. I have been visited by the solicitors with whom I have had dealings regarding my mother's affairs and the associate firm in America, who are expecting me to assist them in exactly the same manner. I feel totally bewildered by this girl Nokomis; I have no knowledge at all as to her interests, ambitions, preferences, pastimes . . ." Demonstrating the great void in his mind regarding her, he opened his arms wide to show just how empty of plans for her reclamation he was. "To be perfectly honest with you I should wish nothing more than that someone would tell me she had already left for her return to America. I know this sounds bitterly selfish, and I apologize but it is the truth."

"I understand perfectly, sir. It is Amelia's safety that worries you, and you will feel great relief if Nokomis has already gone, because you will feel Amelia is safely out of her . . . clutches shall I call it? If I may say so I think your worries about Amelia will never cease but if she were my child, my delight in her would never cease, either. She tells me you have absolutely forbidden her to join in any search for Nokomis but perhaps, sir, you would not forbid her to do some thinking about it? It is rare to find a girl of Amelia's age who does any thinking at all; it is not fashionable."

"I cannot stop her thinking."

And even as her father was speaking Amelia was no longer sitting upon the grass within sight and calling distance, she was speeding down the hill to South End, to the dairy and general baker's where she often went to buy cream for the household.

The owner, a stout, noisy woman, did not herself serve but was constantly in and out of the back premises and had known Amelia since she was a baby. She listened with attention. "Bless you, love, I cannot remember every customer that comes into the shop."

"But I was with her, do you really not remember? Once she wore this long trailing scarf made of feathers?"

The woman roared with laughter. "No, never, I never see'd a long feather scarf, no not me!"

"Well, I think you will."

"What makes you fink that?"

"She is in love."

"O . . . o . . . h!" The woman made a comic face.

"You may not see her in that feather scarf again, but she's the kind you have to look at twice. Long black hair scraped back so that you can't see any hair. And sometimes she don't wear a bonnet and she, kind of, wriggles, like this. You *know*!"

"Well, love, wot if I see her?"

"Tell her, please, Amelia wants to see her."

"Amelia wants to see her. . . ."

"You see . . . she may be here soon . . . because the person she is in love with lives near here. I just know she will come. And she will be hungry and need some buns or whatever you have ready . . . she eats a lot."

The woman made the comic face again and she looked down at this urgent, rather small girl. "How shall I remember, now?"

"Write it down on a piece of paper . . . 'tell Amelia.' "

"Then what?"

"I will call in on my way home from school and see if she has been."

And as she scrambled back up the hill Amelia thought: She will not be able to keep away because she will want to know what I want! And she chuckled, a wicked sound.

Thomas had a feeling of hopeless ineptitude regarding Mr. Melbury and Mr. Gritley. He knew that from the start, when in his office Mr. Melbury had announced Nokomis' imminent arrival, he had not entered into the spirit of the thing as Mr. Melbury might have expected of anyone receiving the glad news regarding his mother's legacy. He was aware that Mr. Melbury on the way back to town was saying something like: *I don't understand Nateby-Dyce at all. It is as though from the very day I reported his good fortune to him, he has behaved almost as though he were being unwillingly awakened from a long sleep. He has never taken to Nokomis and is glad that she has absconded (if that is the right word).*

So, in an attempt to banish this idea from their minds, he sent a note inviting them to the Far East Club for dinner. He would not keep away from that establishment in view of the letter he had from Albert; indeed, it seemed more important now to make an appearance.

XV

NOKOMIS had tied one staylace to the bedpost and, clutching the other she was pulling with the energy employed by the cheesemonger cutting Double Gloucester cheeses with a wire cutter. She was ten inches from her goal of an eighteen-inch waist which an eighteen-year-old girl should achieve. Thus she had no breath left with which to scream when the second console mirror between the windows "cracked from side to side" and then the glass came tumbling down and left the frame standing naked. She let go of the staylace, releasing her breath, and flung herself upon the bed, abandoning herself yet again to hysterics in fine style, drowning any supernatural noise that might be occurring.

And while screaming and flinging herself about, she did manage to wonder why no passerby's attention was attracted to the house. But then, there were no ordinary passersby, only navvies with shovels over their shoulder; anyone who might have to go along the road avoided it in its present state.

She screamed for minutes, until she was weak and could consider. What was going to happen about the condition of the house? What was the owner going to make of it? Would he come home from India to inspect it? Would he simply instruct his lawyers to have the furniture and effects sent into storage when it reached the point when the demolition navvies wanted to start their work on the house?

But there was little that was breakable left unbroken. The Thursday man had really taken fright and had disappeared, apparently without payment for his cleaning efforts. He may or may not have accepted the phenomena, which he had certainly witnessed once, and felt that to disappear would be the better part of valor.

Was Nokomis going to have to give a demonstration of what occurred when she was in the house to the solicitors? The thought of having to do this gave her agonizing pain, which made her moan and roll about on the bed. How shaming, how disgraceful, how unbearably weird and devilish to have to leave the lawyer upon the doorstep while she walked inside, leaving the front door open so that he could see and hear what occurred. How entirely bereft of all dignity she would be. To be able to arouse the powers of darkness merely by her presence was a long way from anything ladylike. Some witches were relegated to limbo.

She pulled out the jewel case from beneath her pillow and, taking out the Inguta jewel, she stared at it for a long time. Of course, she had not entirely invented Mrs. Dyce's remarks regarding the jewel, but she had greatly exaggerated them in order to cause the Nateby-Dyces to take against it and give it to her; a feeble and childish ploy, she now realized.

But nevertheless there was something unnatural about it; even to hold it in her hand filled her with an indescribable excited mental state, and she was more aware of this emotion now that one great diamond had been wrenched away.

It was not a question of being wise or unwise to have

the diamond torn out; it was a matter of expediency; she had no money upon which to live in the manner she had planned or, indeed, any other money without going begging to Mr. Melbury, which would be shaming and distasteful after that first visit. This and this only stood between herself and destitution; the life of a woman of the streets, which awful fate had been shaken before her eyes by old Mr. Pennyform's fist since she reached puberty.

"On the streets!" she would repeat to herself, and real streets so few and far between and many of them so muddy and filthy that one would have to wear pattens. And how could one walk with any kind of grace and trailing skirts in *pattens*?

And now what?

Her numerous possessions, the dresses, the new things she had bought in New York, the raccoon great coat . . . everything lay about the room, either underneath or on top of quantities of broken china and mirror glass. She longed to start afresh, going first to the Melburys where she could have gracefully accepted the first installment of her tiny, but real, allowance. Then taking a cab to Buck's Walk and making herself invaluable to the Dyces and the Lady Mirabelle. A little thought, a little care and she could easily have refrained from her immoderate behavior with "Dandylion" Ramble-Smith. She could have him on his knees before her if she had only stopped to think.

As she thought these things she held the Inguta jewel in her hand and stared at it and it seemed to be staring at her. She could go to the Mansion House and offer it to the Lord Mayor of London to wear for great occasions; but no doubt he had a similar one and questions might be asked as to how she came by it, and if these answers were acceptable they would suggest she keep it for her own use lest the Lord Mayor be accused of accepting bribes.

She could return it to the Nateby-Dyces. Yes, this seemed by far the best idea. But then how was she going to live?

Married to the Dandylion. That seemed, finally, the only easy answer.

In fact, the only answer.

But she could not do that without bringing him at least once to her dwelling. She would have to open the door and enter the house and then what? If he were not going to be quite the coward that old Mr. Hetty was, he was certainly not going to like what would happen. He would try to get away quickly but with some dignity. To get away from something evil was the reaction of everybody.

The trouble was the laziness inherent in Nokomis. She was capable of great energy in pursuit of her own well-being but not an unlimited amount. She had not, for instance, the power to pick up all her belongings, shake them free of broken glass and china and pack them all away. Or to tidy up all the mess as best she could and go to the house owner's lawyer and beg him to come to the house and see for himself. Nor could she open the front door and enter, telling him to stay where he was, letting him go inside like Mr. Hetty to view the horrors the house released at her presence.

Had she done all this, "the King of Terrors might no longer be Terrible," as Carlyle, a mile away, once wrote to his mother.

Spurred on by sheer wickedness, she had the power to sit down and spell out a couple of dozen poisonous accusations regarding Thomas Dyce who had never in any way hurt her, address and stamp and post them, but she could not bring herself to write a decent letter to Daniel Ramble-Smith; she was no letter writer, she constantly told herself. What she had to say to him was negligible in comparison with what her hands could do and her lips. If only she could find him he would soon be hers, to have and to hold and for very much richer.

Wearily she got up from the bed and put her pattens on to protect her feet from the broken glass. She clattered downstairs to the basement where there was a tin jug, and took the milk out of the dark larder. She had a long refreshing drink and went upstairs again, this time with the broom which she used to clear a pathway, indeed several pathways, between the breakages so that she could walk about her room. She dressed carefully and tossed her feather boa over her shoulders, then peevishly tore it off and threw it upon the disordered bed; it was too hot even for that. Finally she took her parasol and her reticule, leaving behind under her pillow, ninety-eight sovereigns and the damaged jewel in its case. She regretted now her action over the jewel. If she had no luck with her Dandylion she would bravely face Mr. Melbury in Red Lion Square and ask humbly for her tiny allowance. It was foolish to spend a diamond out of the jewel, on oysters and porter and penny buns with cream.

At the White Horse in Piccadilly a stage was waiting to start for Highgate and she climbed on it.

Emma was never one for emotional scenes; as a rule she wept in privacy, but there were times when her unspoken thoughts overwhelmed her and she could not refrain from tears. One of these times was when Thomas prepared himself for a dinner in town at his club with Mr. Melbury and the American gentleman. He came to kiss her good bye and though she had lifted her face happily to be kissed, she at once buried it in her hands and wept. Thomas drew her hands away from her face. "Tell me." She shook her head. "You must tell me."

"Oh, Thomas. You are so brave."

"Brave?"

"You are so gentle and quiet and yet you are such a strong man. You never show the agony you suffer. Tonight, for instance, you are taking two gentlemen to dinner at your club and yet you know the place has been seething with vile and silly gossip about you. Bless you, my darling, you stand and face your troubles as you would stand and face a firing squad." She had stopped crying and was screwing her handkerchief about.

So that she could not see his face Thomas stooped over his foot, adjusting the strap that went below his shoe and had become twisted. He straightened up and took his shiny hat off the hook, putting it on, then adjusting it to a slightly sloping angle. "We will overcome," he said and they smiled at one another. He looked at his watch. "I shall just catch the stage. Where is Amelia?"

"They are outside on the green playing shuttlecock, I think."

"Say good night to her for me; I shall be home after she is asleep."

That evening there was an excellent curry on the menu and his guests had no hesitation in their choice. The meal passed pleasantly with light conversation about India and Indian cooking, and it was only when they had reached the cheese that Thomas was amazed to see a neighbor from Hampstead hurrying, flustered-looking, through the dining room evidently searching for him.

He stood up, still holding his starched table napkin. "Sir, are you looking for *me?*"

"Indeed I am, Major Dyce, our children have disappeared."

Thomas gasped.

"And, sir, it is with great regret that I have to say that if there be a scapegoat, it will be found to be your Amelia. My Roderick is constantly coming home with flamboyant talk which he picks up from your young lady. I very much regret it but I have no hesitation in saying that they are now embarking upon an escapade entirely suggested and led by Amelia."

All eyes were upon them now and through Thomas' mind there whisked the thought: God send me the firing squad *now*!

There was an entirely ghastly silence, everyone in the dining room stopped eating lest they should miss one syllable of what was being said, or indeed, shouted. But Thomas raised his voice too and cried that if there be an escapade promoted by his daughter it would be a well-planned one which was entirely successful. At which there was a gratifying sound of subdued laughter from the members and disciplined murmurs of "Hear hear!" and "Well said!" and "Up the Buffs," and somebody knocking their fork upon the tabletop.

"Roderick has taken with him my map of London," Roderick's father shouted in indignation. This was clearly about to develop into a lark. "One moment please. . . ." Thomas begged his guests to continue to eat their cheese, then to withdraw to the saloon for coffee. He gave orders accordingly to the waiter and left. If there were to be a vulgar wrangle, it would continue in the street.

But yes, it was worrying because neither of the children had been seen by Roddy's parents since they walked up from school together as usual. Outside in the square the two gentlemen conferred. Thomas' mild manner had put to shame Roderick's father's blustering. They were now two gentlemen in serious conference; Roderick's father wished to go to Scotland Yard at once, and Thomas pointed out, Scotland Yard had barely settled down from the uproar caused by the shooting at the Sovereign in Constitution Hill barely three weeks before.

216

However, after consideration it was decided that they should go together to that office in Great Scotland Yard, the headquarters of the Metropolitan Police, and now used for the examination of suspect persons.

Recently a periodical had appeared which had been widely read in regard to the account of the instructions given to uniformed policemen about to go on duty by their sergeant. It demonstrated plainly that everyone of Her Majesty's subjects about the metropolis upon their lawful *or unlawful* way was liable to scrutiny from an officer of the law.

> 1. Be sure to look sharp after flower-girls. Offering flowers for sale is a pretence. The girls are either beggars or thieves; but you must exercise great caution. You must not interfere with them unless you actually hear them asking charity, or see them trying pockets; or engaged in theft.

And:

> 2. Now, men, I must again beg of you to be very careful in your examination of empty houses. See the doors are fast; and if not, search for any persons unlawfully concealed therein ... thieves get into them from adjoining premises and then there's a burglary.

Thomas knew almost nothing about this new look for the peelers, and Roderick's father's unwelcomed arrival at the Far East Club now took on a useful light. The two gentlemen paced soberly down Whitehall and turned into the lane to Scotland Yard where they reported to the interested sergeant on duty the disappearance of their

217

two children and a detailed description of their aspect.

Had they not taken a cab northward home to Hampstead, they would have seen their children hurrying down Whitehall hand in hand toward Westminster Abbey where, being miserably lost, they decided first to pray and then to settle down for the night.

XVI

NEXT day . . .

The misery of the respective parents of Amelia and Roderick was in either case typical: noise on the part of Roderick's parents, and frozen, silent misery on the part of Amelia's parents. Roderick's mother had constant fainting fits, a choking sensation, an attack of the shivers, and his father stamped and ranted about the house, alloting blame first here, next there, issuing awful threats of what would happen when the "culprit," that is, he or she who was responsible for his son's disappearance, was discovered and returned.

After roll call every child in the school was interviewed in private by the headmaster with the Roderick's parent in attendance.

And all was fled save gall. . . .

Except that a note arrived by hand from Red Lion Square for Major Nateby-Dyce. His presence was urgently required by Mr. Melbury. And this gentleman had had the consideration to send the bearer of the note to Buck's Walk in his own chaise, and Major Nateby-Dyce was requested to return to Red Lion Square in it to save time.

219

He left Emma with every drawer in her bedroom turned upside down and the contents spread about the room so that she could carefully go over every inch of every garment in search of repairs required, thus occupying herself so that all her thoughts were not turned to her missing Amelia.

And as William Penn said in 1718: "No gall . . . no glory."

A gilt-framed canvas was propped up against the file shelves in the dark office of Mr. Melbury, and that solicitor had lighted the newly installed single central gas jet to show it up.

Mr. Gritley from America, who was much younger and less sober than his counterpart, sat with a smile barely concealed behind his hand and watched the face of Major Nateby-Dyce.

Mr. Melbury started by thanking Thomas for the dinner last night, so sadly interrupted; he hoped that very soon they would have good news of their Amelia. He said that they had planned to have a talk with Major Nateby-Dyce after they had dined, but as things had turned out, the talk had to be now. It would start with Mr. Gritley, and he turned to that gentleman who began to recount how and why he had come by the canvas.

As a result of the friendship between Mr. Brian Killarney and Mrs. Eleanor Dyce, Mr. Killarney had *some years ago* written to Christie, Manson & Woods, the London auctioneers, requesting that if a portrait should ever turn up in the auction room of the Lady Mary Dyce, daughter of the seventh Earl of Rivington who had recently died, they should buy it for clients of theirs. And as Mrs. Eleanor Dyce had, in fact, known that the eighth Earl had sold up the contents of the seventh Earl's London home, it was not long before the required portrait turned up, was bought by the auctioneers and sent to America. Mr. Gritley had brought it over with him on this visit to England because it was now the possession of Thomas Nateby-Dyce, inherited from his mother.

Mr. Melbury, who enjoyed small moments of drama in his quiet office, announced with barely concealed glee, "Your late wife, Major, and the mother of the present Maharaja of Inguta." (And all the angels fell about.)

The portrait of head and shoulders was by a refugee from France, Madame Vigée le Brun, who had painted a number of young girls of the aristocracy, avoiding the absurd high wiglike hairdo of the *fin de siècle* and creating a simpler youthful style, with young girls wearing their hair in small gentle wisps across their foreheads. This girl had a long neck and from huge eyes was glancing over her shoulder with an entrancing near smile and with one barely covered breast about to overflow out of the picture altogether. Unfortunately the value of the picture was considerably lowered since there was plainly a real gunshot wound right through the escaping breast.

Mr. Melbury said, "Christies were told that the legend went that the girl's father, upon hearing that as a married woman the wife of Thomas Dyce of the Bombay Grenadiers had given birth to a boy who was to become, at the age of fourteen, chosen heir to the Maharaja of Inguta, had taken his gun and shot at the picture, after which it had been stored for some time in an attic."

The Earl had more sons than any earl would be likely to need, and one daughter, Mary, who was his beloved. She had gone to India with her mother to stay for some time with her brothers, enjoying the gay society, and there had met Thomas Dyce and married him with a fine wedding in Bombay Cathedral and honeymoon in Naini Tal.

After her mother had returned to England Mary had

221

embarked upon this secret and iniquitous liaison upon which no decent woman would care to dwell. This beautiful half-English half-Indian boy was swept away from his mother at birth; and so jealous of this treasure was his father, the Maharaja of Inguta, that she was never allowed to see her boy, and the doors of the palace were cruelly closed to her forever.

Sitting in the lawyer's dusty office, Thomas, so far removed now from all these things, was both dumb and motionless. It ill became a late officer of Her Majesty's Indian Army to weep, but weep he would he if were not careful. Silent endurance had been his conduct with Mary from the moment she told him that she was prenant with Inguta's child. He had made no comment then or at any other time; the hurt he had sustained was a long way beyond endurance but endure it he did because he believed in his marriage vows, made before God.

One look at the beautiful nut-brown baby was enough to convince anyone in doubt.

There was such a long and deathly silence that Mr. Melbury could not bring himself to break it with any reference to what he had just said. He would have liked to chatter on about the new maharaja, now just fourteen who was at the present twenty-two miles away and a colleger at Eton, probably devouring pink cocoanut candy at this moment, with some nabob's son, and no doubt enjoying it.

Mr. Melbury and his son, nominally about their lawyer's business, had driven down to that school in the chaise, to interview the headmaster, who had pointed out the young maharaja to them as that youth scrambled ungainly with others across the quadrangle. To see him was all that was needed to be convinced of his existence; he stood out from the others like the prince he was, more black than white.

But good Melbury had the remedy for this frigidity on the part of his client in a tough well-used envelope now tied with pink string.

"And now, my good sir . . . your father's sister, your father's sister who lived in Hampstead Square and with whom you and your wife lived whilst you went house-hunting after your second marriage. Need hardly ask if you remember her."

"Indeed not, I loved her dearly."

"And she you, Thomas. But she also loved your wayward mother, her brother's wife Eleanor . . . you were considered too young to be told at first, and then . . . later . . . your two marriages . . . somehow or other . . . she could not bring herself to tell you, she thought you might be upset in some way . . . she thought better not."

"Tell me what?" Thomas asked patiently.

"Tell you how your mother fared after her madcap elopement with that stupid Pennyform. A man exceptionally good-looking and with a few good qualities, but weak, pitifully weak and religious in a doubting way. It was certainly his looks that attracted your mother, she admits that much here!" He tapped the envelope upon his desk.

"In letters from your mother, not frequent, perhaps two a year, she tells the whole story . . . how, after crossing the ocean with Pennyform and setting up together in a wooden frame house on the outskirts of expanding New York, she could not bring herself to marry him. He maddened her with his stupidity, she tells in these letters." He held them out for Thomas to take them and he did so. "You will have a few happy hours reading these, sir; I have taken the liberty to do so. Gritley advised me to read them, and I have had pleasure in doing so. She was, over and above her wild behavior in middle age, a good woman and one of whom you will be proud, when you have read all these.

"Naturally your aunt in Hampstead Square replied fully to these letters, telling your mother any news she had about you." Mr. Melbury looked meaningfully at Thomas with the message that she would have passed on any news she had about Thomas, which would include the death of Lady Mary at Oman and what followed. But these letters Eleanor Dyce had wisely destroyed after reading.

"When your aunt died, her letters were sent back to America and were about to be destroyed by your mother, but were captured from her and put in the safe by Mr. Brian Killarney, who said they should be kept for posterity."

"Mr. Brian Killarney constantly crops up," Thomas said, in spite of himself, irritably. "Finally we have this horror about his death. That Nokomis Pennyform was responsible for it seems to me beyond belief. What do you think, Mr. Gritley, seriously and in a few words? Do you really intend to take the girl back home and if so, what do you intend to do with her?"

"I have no doubt whatever what I intend to do," this gentleman answered vigorously. "She must be detained, and I mean kept in confinement. Not so long ago, in a less enlightened age, she would have been hanged, but now I and my partners and indeed the victim himself, old Mr. Killarney, have watched her grow up, and the girl is undoubtedly the pawn of heredity. Wild uncouth Indian blood runs through her veins; suddenly thwarted she will strike in retaliation and cannot stop herself. We think we have managed to save from the wreck of Mr. Pennyform's fortune, enough money to lodge her with someone who will understand her propensities, an exgaol master, experienced in dealing with the violent criminal."

". . . and we are given to understand," Mr. Melbury put in, "that most of the money Mr. Pennyform accrued from the bare land he bought finally was dissipated by fear; he thought he knew that he could buy himself to heaven; he gave liberally to any and every society."

Thomas leaned forward, his face now unstiffened, he looked more like himself: "But have you any proof that Nokomis pushed . . ." and he mouthed that foul word *pushed* with extreme distaste, "*pushed* old Mr. Killarney to his death?"

"Unfortunately, we have. Mrs. Eleanor Dyce had a blue chiffon scarf, as the ladies call it, of the finest quality. Nokomis was seen wearing it after the lady's death, as she was seen wearing other of her clothes; Mrs. Dyce dressed beautifully. Mr. Killarney was lying upon it, dead on the hall floor upon which he fell; it was firmly beneath him and he was clutching some of it in one of his stiff hands. He had torn it from Nokomis as he grabbed at something which would stop his fall."

And later, Thomas asked what would be done with the le Brun picture of Lady Mary.

Since the auctioneers had been able to buy it for very little, they agreed completely that it should be the property of the young maharaja, but Thomas begged that it should first be sent to the best picture restorer in London (at his own expense), who would make good the damage caused by the firing of a gun or pistol at it before it was sent to India with the young maharaja when he returned there.

Thomas walked back to Hampstead with the parcel of letters beneath his arm; these he would read in the long winter evenings; his mind was in too much of a tumultuous state to be able to look at them at present.

As he approached his home he saw Daniel Ramble-Smith pacing up and down the little path before the houses in Buck's Walk. He rushed to Thomas. "My dear sir," he wrung Thomas' hands and, indeed, wept emotionally. "Those two poor children," he cried. "But I have an idea. I believe they are with my Nokomis. I believe they are on some wild, some wild . . . they would call it an adventure. They have been looking for Nokomis and so have I since I failed to meet her on Saturday when I was still fully occupied by my great-great-aunt's death. She is a good-hearted girl where young people are concerned. Oh yes, she has been close friends with your Amelia, and everything your Amelia does, so does Roderick. I declare if we find one, we find the three."

"But where, my dear boy, *where?* What enterprise would they have embarked upon that would include all three?"

"She told the children she was living in Westminster, but she refused to tell them where, in what street or tenement or cluster of mean houses."

"I do not believe she is living in a tenement; I have to tell you, Daniel, my child Amelia," and Thomas fairly choked in the telling, "gave her an extremely valuable jewel I recently inherited from my mother. She had some foolish idea that it had brought us bad luck. Nokomis told her my mother had given it to her upon her deathbed but that the solicitors in New York refused to hand it over to her. That was just the sort of story that would arouse Amelia to action. No doubt at all she had good intentions . . . she is a great one for *rights* . . . one day she may fight for women's suffrage."

"Were you angry with her, sir?"

"Indeed I was."

226

Daniel Ramble-Smith shook his head sadly. "She cannot bear to be on bad terms with you. I believe she honestly meant well when she took the matter of giving the jewel to Nokomis in her own hands."

Thomas groaned. "Then if you are right and the children have gone to Westminster to get the jewel back from Nokomis and put right Amelia's mistake, it may be they have succeeded and on the way home they have been accosted by . . . what? . . . pickpockets? . . . or some wayfaring harpy?"

They stood in silence, thinking over the implications until Ramble-Smith said that in view of the recent happenings in his family he had been driven to think over the versatilities of Nokomis, "since she had certain qualities which, in my new status, I might find invaluable. For one thing, she has some energy, she might well be a helpmate. . . ."

Thomas was aghast and could not conceal it.

"You don't agree, sir?"

"This is no time to discuss your future!" he snapped and instantly regretted it. "Let us first find all three and then look calmly at your problem.

"I must tell you that you are not the only one searching for Nokomis. My own solicitor has American associates of which one of the principals has arrived in this country with the express purpose of taking Nokomis back with him."

"Indeed!" Daniel Ramble-Smith cried. "But what if I decide to ask her to be my wife?"

The Misses Eglington could not pull themselves away from the window even to have meals. They blamed the parents of those children, they told Miss Blockley, who were left to play alone, unattended, all evening upon the green and even allowed to run down to South End to buy

227

lollipops. "Who knows what horrors have befallen them?" they cried.

Miss Blockley was, in a mild way, in love with Thomas and disliked Emma because she, and not Miss Blockley, was married to Thomas. She joined in the Eglington excoriations. She bitterly tore strips off Emma, who had no right to be a mother at all, she declared.

But Madame Mirabelle was smitten to the dust; she withdrew from sight into her little house, told Craskie she could see nobody and went into purdah leaving her millinery establishment to fall to wrack and ruin, as she described it, if only for one day. She reminded herself of the deaths of her own beloveds upon the guillotine and did not even contemplate that Amelia and Roderick could still be alive.

And then, when Thomas entered his house and called for Emma, there was no answer and rushing upstairs he found her being violently sick into the basin upon her washstand in the closet.

"My darling!" he cried in great distress and took her in his arms to wipe the sweat from her brow.

"I'm not ill, Thomas, do not worry." They sat together for a few minutes and when she had recovered a little she said that it was so strange that it should happen just *now*, after all these years . . . and when Amelia was missing. "Oh Thomas, I do not know whether to cry . . . or laugh."

"Laugh!" Thomas exclaimed aghast. *"Laugh!"* He turned and looked at her for a long time. "You don't mean. . . ."

And she half laughed, nodding.

They had been on the green playing shuttlecock, and Nokomis had seen them as soon as she had positioned herself among the bushes at the edge of Willow Road, which ran down toward South End, but she was not going to let them see her. From where she stood she could see all five houses in Buck's Walk; she could also see the bun shop at the bottom of the hill and, hungry as always, she went to buy something to eat while she waited. The woman in the shop was serving her with buns when Amelia's fat friend carried in a fresh batch from the oven and stopped to stare at Nokomis. Finally she leaned forward over the counter and said, "That Miss Amelia has given me a message for you."

This was the turning point in Nokomis' fate. Without the message that Amelia wished to see her, she would have lost patience, she would have tired of watching for her Dandylion, she would have sickened at the thought of returning to Crockett's Oyster Bar for oysters and porter. She would have gone humbly to Mr. Melbury's office and asked for her small allowance. She would have redeemed the diamond and had it replaced in the Inguta jewel.

But she would also have been followed by someone from Mr. Melbury's office to her house by the river and later Mr. Gritley would have captured her and taken her by persuasion or by force, back to New York to become a prisoner for life.

But Amelia, quite unconsciously, saved her from a "fate worse than death."

XVII

EATING buns from a paper bag, Nokomis returned to the inconspicuous situation among the bushes and, by constant waving, attracted the attention of Amelia and of course Roddy, who sauntered casually in her direction.

"Nokomis, where have you been?"

"In my house in Westminster, child, where else?"

Amelia affectionately put her arms round her. "Nokomis, please, please . . ."

"Yes, what?"

"Papa is so grieved and angry. I have *stolen* the Indian jewel, that is what they think. I did terribly wrong to give it to you. I . . . I should not have done so. Please, please may I have it back to return to them?"

Nokomis was suddenly faced with a possible truth. Perhaps the Inguta jewel did bring bad luck; misfortune had certainly swamped her since she had it.

"Yes, Amelia . . . you may have it back. I shall give it to you when I have had it repaired."

"Repaired?"

"Yes, repaired. I had to use one of the diamonds . . . for living."

"What do you mean?"

"Never mind what I mean. Where is Mr. Ramble-Smith?"

"He does not live here anymore, all the time. He will soon sell his little house."

"Where does he live now?"

"In a big house his aunt lived in . . . she has died . . . he lives there partly anyhow, and now his manservant lives there too."

Roddy felt left out and put in helpfully, "He doesn't love her anymore."

"Oh, he *does*," Amelia cried kindly. "He comes here to see if she is here sometimes . . ."

Nokomis looked at both of them, asking sternly: "Is that true?"

Amelia said, "No."

Roddy said, "Yes." Roddy also said that he saw Mr. Ramble-Smith this evening; at least, he thought he did, at least he saw a horse tied to the post. "Silly boy," Nokomis snapped, "do not you know the difference between a horse and Mr. Ramble-Smith!"

"But it might be his horse . . . shall I go and see if he is there?"

And now good luck was, as always, to escape Nokomis, for when Roddy went back to Buck's Walk the horse had gone and the house seemed empty. Roddy rang the bell and there was no answer. He hurried down the green with the bad news. A few minutes later Daniel Ramble-Smith returned, having left his horse at the smithy in the village to be shod and returned by the back entrance.

Nokomis had hardened, she had started to believe in her bad luck; she turned away with a snort and said, "To hell with him!" And as she walked off up the hill quickly to prevent herself from crying, they heard her say, "To hell with you all!"

231

Amelia ran up the hill after her, "But the jewel, Nokomis. . . ?"

"To hell with it! Here, Amelia . . ." Nokomis fumbled among her petticoats and brought out the pawn ticket. "Give this to your father to buy the diamond back; it will cost him a hundred pounds and more!" She gave a croaking laugh as she hurried away with angrily swinging skirts.

"But the jewel, Nokomis," Amelia wailed loudly.

She turned round, flushed in the face, and from a distance cried, "When I have received my allowance from that damned solicitor, I will send you the jewel by post, and God rot you all!"

"Then we will never see you again . . ." Amelia shrieked.

Amelia, too, had a petticoat pocket and she put the ticket safely away before hissing, "Come on, Roddy, let's follow the old silly and see where she is living. Papa gave me my pocket money this morning. I have two shillings and some pennies."

She was swinging up Willow Road now and hurrying toward the village. Keeping their distance Amelia and Roddy scrambled after her. "She's going to the stage stop, I bet!"

There was a half-hour wait before the horses on the stage to Piccadilly came sweating down the High Street, and during the wait Roddy and Amelia concealed themselves not very well in a sweetshop, keeping their eyes upon their prey. And if Nokomis had not been so self-immersed, she could easily have seen them. And again, as she mounted and chose a seat, she could have seen them struggling aloft, for a half-seat outside, giggling. However, absorbed in her own thoughts and frowning as she picked at her fingernails, she was vaguely unaware of her surroundings and when she alighted in Piccadilly and hurried down through St. James' and across the Park toward Westminster, she looked straight ahead, seeing nothing in her frustrated anger.

She entered the street where she lived and lifted her skirts so that passersby could see her ankles painfully turning this way and that as she hastened over the shocking surface of the causeway.

Amelia and Roddy stopped now, sure that she would enter one of the houses and, indeed, she turned abruptly as she arrived at Number 14, leaped up the steps, thrust the key into the door, opened it, entered and slammed the door after her.

Triumphantly they pushed one another about, still giggling.

"It is Number fourteen," Roddy said, "but what's the name of the street? Half the houses are gone!"

"Never mind the namof the street, we can easily find it again. She's so upset I don't think it is a good time to ring the bell and ask for the jewel again *now*. Let's leave it, Roddy. Look, it's going dark. How on earth are we going to get back? Oh, Mama will be worried!"

Amelia knew there would not be another stage to Highgate at this hour. Papa would take a cab home when he returned late. And they had not enough money for a cab. Neither of them thought of taking a cab, nevertheless, and telling the jarvey that their parents would pay at the Hampstead end.

At ten to eight the following morning one of the vergers of Westminster Abbey found them asleep, lying full length feet to feet upon the coir pews in the chancel. He took them by the scruffs of their necks in great indignation to Scotland Yard, where they were kept without refreshment in the charge room. A note was taken to Roddy's parents at his home address, which Roddy gave because Amelia was reluctant to give her home address, and his mother came for them in a cab.

There was a rumpus, oh yes, there were hard words. Roddy fared worse than Amelia. He was beaten. And the hard words were spoken by Roddy's parents about Amelia, who was entirely blamed for the escapade even though Roddy was beaten for it. Amelia was a wicked, irresponsible tomboy, they said, and Roddy must have no more to do with her under pain *forte et dure*.

And as for Thomas and Emma, they were so delighted to have her restored to them that they could not bring themselves to scold her, which was just as well because Amelia felt she had embarked upon the adventure with the best intentions, that of benefiting others, in this case, Nokomis and Daniel. In fact, she felt herself to be a heroine.

Roddy's parents were caused to feel considerably chastened by their immoderate behavior because Roddy was the only other child from that particular part of Hampstead who went to the Downshire Hill school, and neither child could be allowed to walk to school alone. They were obliged to look foolish when Roddy started out alone next morning; they glared at him as he wrapped the strap of his satchel around him before leaving, but they could find no suitable speech to make.

Thomas was preparing for town, intending first to call upon Mr. Melbury and inform him that his young daughter, as an escapade, had followed Miss Pennyform to what appeared to be her lodging in Westminster and it could be arranged at his convenience that he, Thomas, could bring Amelia down to the office and lead them both to the house, she being unable to tell them the name of the street but only the number . . . 14.

As he was about to leave his front doorstep, he was startled by the sound of a horseman approaching very fast; indeed it was Albert Niton, and he drew up his horse with a spectacular triumph and a flurry of dust as he waved his whip and shouted something which Thomas failed to hear in the ferment. He dismounted and tied up the sweating mare.

"Thomas, Thomas, you lucky brute!" he cried and sent the Misses Eglington almost crashing out through the window in their excitement to get from the breakfast table in time to miss nothing.

Thomas just wished he would not shout but: "You are utterly vindicated!" Albert cried so that everybody in Buck's Walk heard except Mr. Ramble-Smith, who was not there.

"Dieu soit béni!" Madame Mirabelle whispered and she signed herself with the cross.

Thomas dragged him into the house, but he had already started telling, telling and telling.

That servant, Abdul Latif, the syce of Colonel Edgware, whom one saw so frequently in the entrance to the Far East Club guarding Edgware's mare. He who, before Thomas' time, would always run beside the Colonel's gray, but the Colonel stopped it because the syce was getting old. He had come to England in the autumn of 1838 on the good ship *Berenice* as a servant and syce to Brigadier White, who was on a long leave owing to ill health and who died within a year of arriving home.

Major and Lady Mary Dyce had been passengers upon this ship, and going through the Indian Ocean, Brigadier White's syce, Abdul Latif, had found for himself for use during the hours of darkness a comfortable resting place in one of the long boats. When darkness fell and most people were asleep, he would creep out from the servants' quarters, undo the tarpaulin cover of the long boat just enough to slide in and pass the hours of darkness alone in peace and quiet, not like his fellows, sharing a yard or so of sweltering, torrid endurance in the forward hold.

During the day the space on deck nearest to the long boat was occupied by the deck chairs of Major and Lady Mary Dyce in which they would often sit in the cool when night had fallen. Thus Abdul Latif had ample time to hear, if not to listen to the odd conversations they had from time to time. He remembered no exact words, but he concluded that they were both unhappy and not on good terms with one another. He could not help listening because it seemed somebody had stolen her baby and would not let her have it back or ever see it again. Abdul Latif had mused very much upon this sadness, but he observed that the gentleman was always kind.

At first the fact intrigued him immensely; he wondered why she could not have her baby. He pondered over this a great deal and during the day he would pass and repass them very often, staring at them, in fact, because he was intrigued; she was so beautiful and her husband was such a fine man; to him they were creatures who deserved the blessing of Allah.

And then one evening she stood there alone. She stood for a long, long time and he could see her in the dim lantern lights they left on all night in the saloons. He was watching, with the canvas cover raised just the inch required to allow him to see, when she drew up her skirts and climbed so quickly, he had no time to do anything . . . three, four seconds and she had gone (!) over the side and he heard a faint splash from far below.

He lay there shivering and the dawn came. And the Major came to look for his wife. And Allah's humble servant Abdul Latif did nothing and said nothing because he was afraid. And what could have been done?

From the first day he saw Major Dyce in London, Abdul recognized him and remembered him, but could

236

not remember when he had seen him. And it was the servants' gossip which he overheard at the Far East Club (that terrible verse!) that had finally made him come forward. And it was because he had seen Sahib Niton so often in the company of Sahib Dyce that he knew they were friends and that Sahib Niton was the man to whom he chose to tell his tale.

For several days the secretary was helping Abdul Latif tell the story to him in his own words and repeating what he had said so that the secretary could make sure he was not inventing but repeating the plain truth as he experienced the events. Being unable to write, he was dictating to the secretary, and since the events took place nearly fourteen years ago Abdul Latif stood no longer in any fear that he would be punished for spending his nights in that terrible heat in a place where he was not allowed to be.

It took the secretary another day to decide on the final draft of the announcement which he pinned to the notice board:

> Will any member who has heard a certain un-
> pleasant little ditty to the detriment of one of
> our members, going the rounds, please report
> to the secretary who is in possession of a
> testimony which proves it to be not only vulgar
> but totally fallacious.

He pinned this up without having consulted his committee, but he was right in guessing they would turn a blind eye to it.

". . . and greater loyalty than this man Thomas Nateby-Dyce to his dead, unfaithful wife no man hath!" a member remarked.

XVIII

EVENTS were crowding fast upon Thomas, it was as though the gods, rewarding him for loyalty, were hurrying to crown him with awards. He had no time to tell Emma about his mother's portrait as a young girl, and the gunshot wound; no time to speculate as to which of his dead wife's family had fired the gun; one of the brothers . . . or her father? No one would ever know.

At breakfast the morning after, the children were walking down to school, Roddy almost on tiptoe with ears burning scarlet; he fully expected to hear his father running after him to snatch him back from the wicked influence of Amelia and to cause them to walk separately with a hundred yards apart.

As it happened, they were pursued by a father, but it was Thomas who had a note asking him to come to the office quickly. A Mr. Ramble-Smith would like to see Mr. Melbury and an appointment had been made for midday, but Mr. Melbury must first see Thomas.

"You must come with me, Amelia, because only you and Roddy know where Nokomis lives, and Nokomis must be present in that office as soon as possible."

"And Roddy, Papa?"

"If Roddy does not turn up at school there will be

another fuss. You will have to go, boy, but please make my apologies to the principal. I shall write him a note in explanation if you are late."

Amelia was charmed. "Am I dressed well enough to go out with you, Papa? May I not return to put on my blue alpaca?"

But, yes, she would be asked to lead one of the solicitors to Nokomis' dwelling in Westminster.

"But Roddy should be with me to help."

"You will remember quite on your own, dear."

"But Roddy wants to see the Amphitheatre which was burned down not long ago and all the zebras were saved. It was burned *down*, Papa, at the foot of Westminster Bridge where the steps are. . . ."

"I will take both you and Roddy to see the ruin very shortly, I promise. And now you can run indoors and change from your school clothes."

"Oh, Papa, I forgot!"

"You forgot what?" Amelia was fumbling about in her petticoats and finally brought out triumphantly the pawn ticket. "Look Papa, Nokomis gave me this, the address of the pawnshop is written small, see?"

"For heaven's sake child, what is this? What are you asked to redeem in a pawnshop?"

"A diamond from the Inguta jewel. She said she had it wrenched from the circle of diamonds."

"Why?"

"She said . . ." Amelia faltered, "she said to buy things to *eat*."

"What is one to do, what can one do with her? Now, Amelia, make haste, we must be at the solicitors' before Mr. Ramble-Smith. . . ." And as she ran off Thomas stood looking around at the familiar scene in front of him, the city lying detached from the problems of mankind like a dozing cat.

239

In despair he covered his face with his hands, oblivious of the straining audience. A new baby on the way and here he was, potentially the happiest man on earth with a festering cormorant hung round his neck. No, not festering, that implied a dead cormorant, which would be harmless; this was alive and insatiably greedy.

Nokomis had arrived back at Number 14 with the sole object of packing her goods during the night and setting off in time to reach Mr. Melbury's office as it opened for business, so that she might see him at once and get the apology over before the business of the day commenced. She would then, having a small amount of money which Mr. Melbury would have to give her, set out to find a small room to rent somewhere in the run-down district toward Chelsea. She would then find a porter to wheel her baggage and, as she put it, *start again.* She would start again and this time she would be God's own saint and force herself to behave exactly as Grandpapa Pennyform would have wished. He had informed her so frequently that God did reward good behavior; she would at least give it a try, just this once.

If she felt herself about to lose her temper she would . . . yes, she would stick a pin into herself and she fixed quite a large pin into her fichu, in readiness.

"Slow," she said out loud, "I shall be slow; I am too quick, I make up my mind too quickly about everything. I must *slow down . . .*" she shouted to the house which might well be holding its breath listening, it was so still, so quiet.

It was deathly. Had the poltergeist run out of energy?

She started around three o'clock by candlelight to tidy up, but it was a hopeless task. She had let everything go on too long. She should have left the house at once after the first ghostly demonstration of the vase that first night and not set herself to endure. Now all the mistakes she had made, all the absurdities she had carried out, all the deficiencies of her own behavior crowded round her like begging, importunate relations, less welcome, even, than the raving of the poltergeist.

And now, in one gooseflesh-making flash of self-recognition, she realized that it was her own distinctive personal character which roused the noisy ghost to visible demonstrations.

A fish-colored dawn was developing as she sat upon the window seat and held the Inguta jewel loosely in her cold hands. Fishing boats lay haphazard upon the gray, deserted shore as the river was sucked seaward by the tide. She, too, felt sucked by the tide, no longer wanting anything.

Clearly Mr. Melbury was devoting his day to the Nateby-Dyce case; Mr. Gritley, though he was enjoying his visit to London, was honor bound to return to his business in New York at the earliest possible moment, since all the expenses of this trip were being paid by his firm. Nor was he looking forward to his trip home on a passenger boat with a captive maiden.

His imagination crumpled when he tried to picture this unwelcome voyage home complete with huge trunk, two gladstone bags, two carpetbags, a basket with a wide leather strap, a basket with a hard handle, an umbrella, a string bag and Miss Nokomis Pennyform.

A Miss Nokomis Pennyform, murderer and potential gangster, who would be expected to sit quietly beside him upon a deck chair. He had only that morning declared to

241

his brother at breakfast that he would procure a strong lead, such as one would use for a fierce bloodhound.

"Yes," his brother agreed, "but to what would you attach it?"

Gritley was clearly gasping with anxiety when the Nateby-Dyces, father and daughter, arrived. "It is absolutely essential that we find the girl. Nobody anticipated, when I set forth upon this mission, that we should be faced with these problems; I declare, I have found my whole task even mortifying. If I am to miss this sailing from Liverpool back home, I may have to wait weeks before I can get another booking for two, and I am beginning to wonder if it will be safe taking her at all, since she will have to be left on her own among the ladies on the ship a great deal. I am asking myself if we should ask for special accommodations for this . . . yes, this young criminal!"

"Peace, Gritley, peace! Things may turn out to be better than you anticipate. The girl is capable of consistent good behavior, that has been proved by her time with the milliner," Mr. Melbury said.

Later Mr. Gritley looked with dismay at the cool and polished appearance of the child Amelia. This chit was to lead them to the rampant murderess! He cast his eyes heavenward and prayed for strength. All along he had recommended that they ask for the assistance of the police. And all along Mr. Melbury had insisted that they carry out the whole operation in absolute privacy, as recommended by the firm of Killarney, Gritley & Co. with this particular member of the firm quietly confident of his ability to do so.

Mr. Melbury was becoming madly impatient to start out upon their mission when Mr. Daniel Ramble-Smith was shown in, and he begged him to make known his requirements as quickly as possible. Mr. Ramble-Smith did so, saying simply that he wished to pay his respects to Miss Nokomis Pennyform with a view to marriage, but that he could not do so without actually meeting her in person; he looked to the solicitors to produce the young lady, since no one else seemed able to do so, and he understood that she was their ward.

Mr. Melbury impatiently swept him out of sight to the waiting room, and when Thomas and Amelia arrived Mr. Melbury was ready to start out. That he was unused to the young was clear from the way he looked down upon Amelia, like a scientist examining some rare species through a magnifying glass.

"Are we to walk? Are we to follow this young, this young lady in a trail through the streets of London, looking for a house with the number fourteen and no further clue?"

"We are evidently going to do just that," Mr. Gritley exclaimed as Mr. Ramble-Smith rejoined them, and they set off down the steps into the Square. Four men and a smallish girl.

Mr. Melbury hailed a cab. "Westminster."

The gentlemen stood back waiting for Amelia to step in and the purple-faced jarvey leaned precariously out and screeched, "Whereabouts in Westminster, sirs?"

Amelia, holding herself at her best, turned to him and said: "To the steps."

"Which steps?"

"The Westminster steps . . . on to the sand . . . with the boats. . . ." And later she said, "We will have to get down here, Papa; the workmen . . . and it is very rough walking. Bricks and plaster falling about . . . you have to take care. There is no clear thoroughfare."

Silently the little procession followed.

Number 14 was marked out as soon as it came into view; two policemen were standing in conference upon the top step. The front door stood wide open so that anyone passing by could see some of the ruin inside. On a broken paving stone, fallen against the railings, lay an incredibly old, battered, galvanized bucket with a tarred brush beside it, and from the bucket was dripping diluted tar, the main part of which had poured itself from the bucket into the basement, leaving its long track against the retaining wall.

"We found the door open, sirs," the policemen said, "and we have sent to the Yard for help."

The other one simply pointed to the steps upon which was written in tar, one word to a step, and there were only three steps,

ENOUGH
IS
ENOUGH

Upon the top step stood the four men and the two policemen, and though they peered into the hall, no one wanted to enter; and as the crowd upon the doorstep speculated and waited for reinforcements from the Yard with whom to start investigations, Thomas took Amelia's arm gently and led her away.

Papa does not wish me to be here and to listen, Amelia thought, and her great eyes rolled around toward the specter of the burned Astley's Amphitheatre at the foot of Westminster Bridge where the fifty horses and two zebras were saved as it was burned out last week.

She reached for Thomas' hand. "Come Papa," she whispered.

". . . phenomenal happenings. . . ." They heard Mr. Melbury's raised voice, but Amelia gently pulled her father away. They walked in silence.

When they stood upon the Bridge and looked at the depressing blackened pile of the recent place of amusement for the crowd, Thomas' mind was still upon that doorstep. "What surprises me is that she could spell *enough* correctly!"

When Amelia had stared her fill at the ruin they turned and walked slowly back toward the steps, looking at the sluggish river below.

The tide had turned and a partially sunken, small fishing boat was drifting slowly upriver; at one end a weight was almost capsizing it.

Even in death Nokomis had to show off; the boat disappeared from sight below the Bridge and they crossed to see it emerge below, in an attempt to confirm what they thought they had seen. The weight that was pressing the boat to fill with water was Nokomis, and as the sinking craft appeared from below the Bridge, the half-submerged body slid around so that they could see her upper part entirely. Her face, no hair visible, her forehhite and bare, her clothes clinging to her neck and shoulders and floating free about the rest of her which was in the water, and upon the sodden material around her breast shone the Inguta diamonds. Beneath and und her arms, some large drowned animal seemed to be clutching her.

Neither Thomas nor Amelia recognized it, but what was pulling down as though dragging the alreay drowned from view, was the raccoon coat.

Was it for coziness she set out wearing it in a fishing boat upon a midsummer's evening? Or was it that she aimed for the deep water of the river's middle, wearing the garment which would pull her down when she climbed overboard, when she instinctively tried to save herself . . . prevented it?

And then, as Amelia screamed, Nokomis slid off the craft and disappeared below the dirty, littered surface.

A decomposing cat floated over the spot.